MW01078971

Praise for
The Cranberry Cove Mysteries

"Peg Cochran has a truly entertaining writing style that is filled with humor, mystery, fun, and intrigue. You cannot ask for a lot more in a super cozy!"

—Open Book Society

"A fun whodunnit with quirky characters and a satisfying mystery. This new series is as sweet and sharp as the heroine's cranberry salsa."

—Sofie Kelly, *New York Times* bestselling
author of the Magical Cats Mysteries

"Cozy fans and foodies rejoice—there's a place just for you and it's called Cranberry Cove."

—Ellery Adams, *New York Times* bestselling
author of the Supper Club Mysteries

"I can't wait for Monica's next tasty adventure—and I'm not just saying that because I covet her cranberry relish recipe."

—Victoria Abbott, national bestselling author
of the Book Collector Mysteries

Books by Peg Cochran

The Cranberry Cove Mysteries

Berried Secrets
Berry the Hatchet
Dead and Berried
Berried at Sea
Berried in the Past
Berried Motives
Berry the Evidence
Berried Grievances

The Lucille Mysteries

Confession Is Murder
Unholy Matrimony
Hit and Nun
A Room with a Pew
Cannoli to Die For

Farmer's Daughter Mysteries

No Farm, No Foul
Sowed to Death
Bought the Farm

The Gourmet De-Lite Mysteries

Allergic to Death
Steamed to Death
Iced to Death

More Books by Peg Cochran

Murder, She Reported Mysteries

Murder, She Reported
Murder, She Uncovered
Murder, She Encountered

Young Adult Books

Oh, Brother!
Truth or Dare

Writing as Meg London

Murder Unmentionable
Laced with Poison
A Fatal Slip

Open Book Mysteries

Murder in the Margins
A Fatal Footnote
Peril on the Page
A Deadly Dedication

Berried Grievances

A
CRANBERRY COVE
Mystery

Peg Cochran

BEYOND THE PAGE
PUBLISHING

Berried Grievances
Peg Cochran
Beyond the Page Books
are published by
Beyond the Page Publishing
www.beyondthepagepub.com

Copyright © 2023 by Peg Cochran
Cover design and illustration by Dar Albert, Wicked Smart Designs

ISBN: 978-1-960511-23-2

All rights reserved under International and Pan-American Copyright Conventions. By payment of required fees, you have been granted the non-exclusive, non-transferable right to access and read the text of this book. No part of this text may be reproduced, transmitted, downloaded, decompiled, reverse engineered, or stored in or introduced into any information storage and retrieval system, in any form or by any means, whether electronic or mechanical, now known or hereinafter invented without the express written permission of both the copyright holder and the publisher.

This is a work of fiction. Names, characters, places, and incidents either are the product of the author's imagination or are used fictitiously, and any resemblance to actual persons, living or dead, business establishments, events or locales is entirely coincidental. The publisher does not have any control over and does not assume any responsibility for author or third-party websites or their content.

The scanning, uploading, and distribution of this book via the Internet or via any other means without the permission of the publisher is illegal and punishable by law. Your support of the author's rights is appreciated.

Chapter 1

Monica Albertson buzzed down the window of her husband Greg's Volvo station wagon—which was nearly old enough to be considered vintage—and breathed deeply as cool, fresh air blew in and ruffled her hair. They were approaching downtown Cranberry Cove and dusk was hovering on the horizon. Greg flicked on his headlights.

The sun was hanging low over Lake Michigan and the shadows were deepening.

The breeze whipped the waves rolling in on the lake and created tiny bubbles that floated like foam on top of the water.

Cranberry Cove had gone all out for the Fourth of July. Flags hung from every building, bunting was stretched across Beach Hollow Road from one side to the other, and red and white geraniums bloomed in the baskets hanging from the streetlamps.

The road was dotted with colorful bits of confetti flung here and there during the parade that morning when children scrambled for the candy thrown by Miss Cranberry Cove Fourth of July and her attendants as they rode past in a bright white convertible.

Monica and Greg passed the traveling carnival that had come to town and had been set up in an empty field. The shouts of the barkers and the tinny music from the carousel drifted on the air. Monica sniffed. She smelled something frying—funnel cakes most likely. She used to beg for those when her parents took her to county fairs, although for a long time—after she'd eaten too many and had been sick—she had shied away from them.

They were headed to the Cranberry Cove Inn, set on a bluff above the lake, to join Monica's college roommate, Kelly Cargill, who was staying there with her family. She'd invited Monica and Greg to join them on the terrace for drinks and the Fourth of July fireworks show.

The parking lot was nearly full when they arrived. Greg squeezed into a space between a Ford Explorer and a Toyota. Two cars down from theirs was a bright blue sports car.

Greg walked over to it and whistled appreciatively. "Look at this baby. Isn't she a beauty?"

Monica wondered why, like with boats, all cars were assumed to be female?

1

"What kind of car is it?" Monica said. Her knowledge of cars was limited to the ones that were easily recognizable, like VW Beetles and MINI Coopers.

"You don't usually see these around here—in Beverly Hills maybe but not Cranberry Cove. "It's a Lamborghini," Greg said, his eyes round with awe.

"Yes." A man came up behind them, startling Monica. "It's a Lamborghini Aventador. Max speed of three hundred fifty-five kilometers per hour."

"She's a real beauty," Greg said as he took Monica's arm and began to lead her to the entrance to the inn.

The lobby was bustling with groups of people scattered around the huge stone fireplace, chatting, drinks in hand. The occasional peal of laughter mingling with the tinkling of ice against glasses echoed off the high beamed ceiling.

Monica waved to Dawn Dykema, who was manning the front desk. Her husband Bart owned Bart's Butcher Shop in town, which he'd taken over from his father and was a Cranberry Cove fixture.

Greg put a hand on the small of Monica's back and guided her gently across the room toward the door to the terrace.

She was nearly waddling, Monica thought as they made their way through the crowd—now that the baby was only a few weeks off. She hadn't put on a lot of weight but what she had gained was all out in front, which Janice, her new helper at the farm kitchen, had insisted meant she was carrying a boy.

She felt as lumbering as an elephant, although Greg had assured her that wasn't the case. The baby protested, giving Monica a sharp jab in the ribs, and she had to stop for a moment to catch her breath.

"Are you okay? Is it time?" Greg asked anxiously, his brows raised in alarm. "It's still a bit early, isn't it?"

He had been asking her that for the past two weeks and Monica tried to remain patient as she reassured him that she would let him know the minute her labor started.

Kelly was waiting for them outside. The flagstone terrace sat up high and offered an unobstructed view of Lake Michigan a short distance beyond. Several barges were anchored offshore as the fireworks crew waited for the sun to go down to begin the show.

Numerous round tables were arranged around the terrace, their bright blue umbrellas closed now like morning glories at the end of the day. A waiter circulated among them with a tray laden with various drinks.

Kelly jumped up from her seat when she saw Monica and Greg approach, her hands extended.

"Monica!" she exclaimed, taking Monica's hands in hers. "And this must be Greg." She motioned toward the empty chairs around the table. "The rest of the family should be along any minute now." She turned to Monica. "Do you remember my aunt Violet Cargill? She visited me at school once during our freshman year."

"Vaguely," Monica said, trying to conjure up an image of Kelly's aunt.

Kelly jumped up from her seat again. "Here she is now."

Monica turned toward the door. An elderly, frail-looking woman was making her way toward their table. She was leaning on the arm of another woman who looked to be slightly younger although well past middle age. Violet had silver hair shaped into a twist and piercing blue eyes that Monica couldn't help but noticing even at this distance.

She was wearing flowing linen pants and a tunic-length top in the same fabric, which Monica recognized as being from a designer whose clothes had a particularly high price tag. A heavy gold chain with a diamond and carnelian pendant hanging from it was around her neck.

Unbidden, a waiter bustled over with a padded chaise longue that he pulled up close to the table. Violet's companion helped her onto it and tucked her in with the light blanket she'd been carrying over her arm.

Kelly introduced the woman as Edith Evans, a longtime friend of her aunt who served as her companion. Unlike Violet, Edith was the sort who went unnoticed in a group—hair halfway between blond and brown, hazel eyes and a pale complexion.

"My aunt suffers from diabetes and a heart condition," Kelly whispered to Monica and Greg as Violet got settled and Edith sat down beside her watching over her protectively.

"We're here," a voice called as the door to the terrace opened.

A young man hurried over to Violet, bent and kissed her on the cheek. It was the fellow they'd met in the parking lot who owned the Lamborghini.

3

"My grandson, Aston Cargill." Violet beamed, taking hold of Aston's hand.

"Hey." He looked at Monica and Greg and nodded in recognition.

He was good-looking and Monica suspected he knew it. He was tall, had blond hair streaked white from the sun and a deep tan. He'd popped the collar on his navy blue polo shirt, which was tucked into distressed white jeans.

Monica almost didn't notice the woman who had followed behind him and had silently joined their table. She was in her forties but obviously trying to look younger. Her hair was dyed red, her eyelashes were false and her forehead was so smooth, Monica strongly suspected she'd had work done. The huge emerald-cut diamond on her finger was blinding and extended nearly to her knuckle.

"Oh, and this is Sherry Cargill," Kelly said. She smiled apologetically at Sherry. "Sorry, I didn't see you there for a minute." She turned back to Monica. "She's my uncle Ray's wife." She leaned closer to Monica and whispered, "Second wife."

"Late to the party as always," Violet said as another woman took a seat on the other side of her. "My sister Beatrice." She waved a languid hand weighed down by heavy gold rings toward the woman.

Beatrice had the same patrician features as her sister but her slumped posture made the effect less impressive. She nodded at everyone with a pained smile.

"Here's Uncle Ray," Kelly said, motioning toward a man headed in their direction.

He grunted a greeting as he pulled out an empty chair and collapsed into it.

His hairline was receding, leaving an expanse of shiny scalp visible and his chin was sagging over the collar of his shirt, but it was still possible to see that he'd been quite handsome in his youth. He was wearing khaki trousers, a brown polo shirt and a well-worn pair of boat shoes.

"Uncle Ray owns Cargill Newspapers," Kelly said to Monica and Greg. "They publish papers all over the country — even your *Cranberry Cove Chronicle*.

"He must do quite well," Greg whispered to Monica. "Did you notice his wife's engagement ring?"

Monica widened her eyes. "You can't miss it."

Ray snapped his fingers for the waiter, who sprinted to their table, his empty tray tucked under his arm.

They ordered drinks all around—a vodka on the rocks for Ray, a white Russian for Sherry, beers for Aston and Greg and flavored seltzer for the rest.

The waiter left and Ray turned to Aston. "All set for the race tomorrow? Who's crewing for you?"

Aston tipped his chair onto its back legs. "Ned Stevens. You don't know him."

"Is he good? Do you trust him?"

"Yeah." Aston let his chair fall back into place. "He's a good guy."

Violet reached for Aston's hand again. "I'm sure you're going to take home the trophy or whatever it is you get when you win a regatta."

Aston patted Violet's hand before pulling his own away.

The waiter appeared with their drinks and passed them around. Ray immediately took a large gulp of his vodka like a man dying of thirst. Edith fussed around setting Violet's seltzer on the table where she could reach it.

"What did you get up to this afternoon?" Violet looked at Sherry. "Shopping, I presume."

Sherry's hand tightened around her drink, whitening her knuckles. Her gaze briefly flickered to Ray but then she lowered her eyes and stared into her drink.

"I was lying down. I had one of my headaches." She massaged her temples.

"Don't you have something for that?" Violet said. "I seem to recall you went to some pricey specialist who prescribed something."

"I'm out of it. I thought I had another vial but it was empty." Sherry's voice trailed off.

Ray had already finished his drink and was signaling to the waiter for another. He fiddled with his cocktail napkin, slowly peeling off strips and crumpling them between his fingers. He jumped when the waiter put his fresh drink on the table.

The beach in front of the inn was slowly filling up with people spreading out their blankets or anchoring their lawn chairs in the sand. The sun had finally disappeared below the horizon and a pale moon hung in the blue-black sky.

A murmur rippled through the crowd and everyone turned their attention toward the lake.

The first firework was modest—a spray of red sparkles against the night sky. They increased in intensity until the finale, when the sky lit up with red, white and blue bursts. The sound nearly shook the ground and a chorus of oohs and aahs rose from the crowd.

The lights on the terrace, which had been turned off during the show, were now raised and chatter burst out among the guests.

Aston yawned and as he stretched, the sleeve on his polo shirt rose up revealing a tattoo of a sailboat. "I've got an early start tomorrow," he said as he pushed back his chair. "See you all in the morning."

The others began to rise from their seats as well.

"Time to get you to bed," Edith said to Violet as she pulled her cardigan sweater around her shoulders. She turned to the others. "Looks like the poor dear has fallen asleep."

"Mother," Ray said sharply. "It's time to go."

By now the waiter was swooping down on the quickly emptying tables, piling the used glasses and crumpled napkins on his tray.

"Mother," Ray said again more loudly. "Give her a shake," he said to Edith.

Edith gently rocked Violet's shoulder. "Oh, dear," she said. "I hate to wake her. Violet," she said in a soft voice.

"Oh, for heaven's sake." Ray exhaled loudly. "Mother, get up." He grabbed Violet's shoulder and shook it briskly.

Violet's head lolled limply to one side.

Ray's breath caught in his throat. "Mother, are you okay?" He glanced accusingly at Edith. "Did she have her insulin shot before dinner?"

Edith's chin quivered. "Yes, of course. Right on schedule."

Beatrice was white-faced. "Feel for a pulse."

Ray leaned over the chaise and put his fingers on Violet's neck. His face sagged. "There's no pulse."

He turned toward the rest of the group. "I'm afraid she's dead."

Chapter 2

The words were barely out of Ray's mouth before Beatrice collapsed into a chair, weeping and moaning.

Edith hovered uncertainly over Violet's body. "Should we perform CPR?" She knitted her hands together. "I'm afraid I don't know how." She looked at the others.

Ray cleared his throat. "I fear it's too late for that."

A waiter came rushing over to them, his face white and his expression grave.

"We've called nine-one-one. The ambulance should be here any minute." He looked at Violet and began to back away. "Is she dead?"

"Yes, I'm afraid she is," Ray said in somber tones.

"Oh." The waiter looked nervous. He gestured over his shoulder. "I'd best be getting back. Lots to do," he mumbled as he moved toward the door.

"Do we have to stay?" Sherry said, sitting down again. She rubbed her temples.

Ray shot her a look. "You could at least pretend to care about Mother. You'll be happy enough when the money comes through."

Sherry crossed her arms over her chest and stared into the darkness beyond the terrace.

Greg nudged Monica. "Maybe we should say good night?"

But before Monica could reply, they heard a siren in the distance.

"I'm so glad you're here," Kelly whispered to Monica. "This is just terrible." She sniffed loudly. "Poor Aunt Violet."

"We'll stay as long as you need us." Monica squeezed Kelly's arm. She looked at Greg.

"Yes, of course. Anything we can do to help . . ."

Moments later they heard the clack of a gurney's wheels on the stone floor of the lobby. Edith had pulled a handkerchief from her pocket and was winding it between her fingers. Beatrice was still sagged in her chair, her arms clasped over her chest, rocking back and forth as if to comfort herself.

There was a soft thud as the EMT crew maneuvered the gurney down the step from the lobby to the terrace. They bustled with efficiency, their moves smooth and practiced.

The taller of the two, who in Monica's opinion looked too young to be a trained EMT, leaned over Violet's body. Monica squeezed Greg's hand.

"I'm sorry for your loss." The EMT turned around to face the group. "We'll be taking her to the emergency room, where a doctor can pronounce death and order an autopsy."

"An autopsy?" Beatrice cried, clutching her hands to her chest. "Whatever for?"

"Protocol," the EMT said. "It's standard operating procedure when an unexpected death occurs outside of a hospital."

"But surely at her age . . ." Ray gestured toward Violet's inert form.

The EMT shrugged. "It's not up to me, I'm afraid."

"Oh, my poor sister." Beatrice put her hands over her face. "Being cut open like that."

The EMTs got busy transferring Violet's body to the waiting gurney. They pulled the sheet up over her face.

"I want to go with you," Beatrice declared. "I don't want my sister to be alone."

The two EMTs glanced at each other. "It's normally not allowed," one said. "You're welcome to follow in your own vehicle."

"Please?" Beatrice clasped her hands together.

The EMTs exchanged another glance. The taller one shrugged.

"I suppose this once . . ."

"Aunt Beatrice," Ray said. "You don't want to do that. It will only upset you." He glanced at Sherry. "Let us take you to your room."

Beatrice's face was set in stubborn lines. "Thank you, Ray, that's very kind of you, but I insist on accompanying Violet. It's the least I can do for her."

• • •

As soon as Monica and Greg pulled into their driveway, they heard excited barking coming from inside the house. Hercule was at the door waiting to greet them, his tail wagging so fast it was a blur.

"Okay, boy," Greg said, bending down to get his face licked.

Mittens appeared from the living room and wound in and out between Monica's legs, meowing with pleasure when Monica scratched her under the chin.

"Care for some tea?" Greg said, reaching for the kettle on the stove. "Decaf, of course." He smiled at Monica.

"Sure," Monica said as she bent down to pet Hercule.

They carried their cups of tea into the living room. Monica collapsed on the sofa feeling a bit like an overinflated balloon. She was going to need Greg's help to get up from the enveloping cushions.

"That was interesting tonight," Greg said, pulling the ottoman closer and putting his feet up.

"Kelly did warn me that her family was a bit . . . eccentric is how I think she put it."

"That wasn't quite the word that came to mind." Greg took a sip of his tea. "Dysfunctional is more like it. It was obvious that Ray and Sherry's marriage was hanging by a thread."

"Sherry certainly seemed awfully unhappy. Ray wasn't terribly nice to her."

"One thing was obvious." Greg shifted in his seat. "Aston was the golden boy, at least as far as his aunt was concerned." He shook his head. "Such a shock finding she'd died so suddenly."

"I wonder if the others resented her favoritism?"

"You're not thinking what I think you're thinking, are you?" Greg said, an eyebrow raised.

"What?" Monica feigned innocence.

"Not all sudden deaths are murders, you know." His tone was light.

"But it did seem a bit sudden, don't you think?" Monica held her hands out, palms up. "And silent," she added. "Of course, with the noise of the fireworks it's no surprise we didn't hear anything."

"I'm quite sure the autopsy will reveal that her death was due to perfectly natural causes." Greg looked at Monica and raised his eyebrows. "Bedtime? You look tired."

"I am a bit." Monica struggled to the edge of the seat.

She held out a hand and Greg pulled her to her feet.

Monica paused at the top of the stairs to peek into the nursery. She flipped on the light and admired the pale green paint they'd chosen. Both Monica's mother and stepmother had complained that the paint color gave nothing away and Monica had explained to them that was the point. They wanted to keep the baby's gender to themselves until the birth.

Greg had spent a Sunday afternoon putting together the crib and Nancy, her mother, had sewed a set of bumpers in a charming fabric with a pattern of nursey rhyme figures. Monica felt a stirring of impatience. She couldn't wait till a little one was sleeping peacefully in that crib. It wasn't long now but the last few weeks had felt like an eternity.

• • •

It was cool when Monica headed out to the farm kitchen the next morning. The sun was still low in the sky and a soft breeze rustled the leaves on the trees. The climbing roses on Monica's trellis were in bloom, filling the air with their musky fragrance.

The cranberry bogs were in flower as well, the delicate pale pink and white blooms fluttering in the air. One of Jeff's workers was making his way down the row, plucking out weeds as he went.

Jeff was standing at the edge of the bog and waved when he saw Monica. He began to walk in her direction.

"Hey, sis," he yelled as he got closer.

"Looks like you're busy," Monica said, motioning toward the bog.

Jeff gave a wry smile. "Yeah, people think cranberries grow like magic and all we have to do is harvest them in the fall. In reality, it's a year-round operation."

A truck came rumbling down the dirt road, its wheels kicking up dust.

"That must be the bees," Jeff said. "It's time to pollinate the flowers." He made a face. "Honey bees aren't attracted to cranberry flowers so we have to have more brought in." He hooked a thumb through the belt loop in his jeans. "Maurizio is just about done with the weeding. Fortunately, we don't have to worry about the weeds that won't hurt the crops."

He glanced at the bog where the hives were being unloaded from the truck and jerked a thumb in that direction. "I'd better go check on things. See you later, sis." He took off at a trot.

Monica watched as Jeff made his way back to the bog. She was pleased to see her half brother so happy. He'd come home from Afghanistan bitter and with an injured arm. Sassamanash Farm had given him a new lease on life and his fiancée, Lauren, had made the transformation complete.

A new employee was starting at the farm kitchen. The work would be too much for Nancy, and Janice, her other employee, now that Kit was running Monica's Café in Book 'Em, Greg's bookshop. Monica was slowing down and she planned to take some time off after the baby arrived.

Her new employee was the nephew of Gus Amentas, who ran the Cranberry Cove Diner in town. He was newly arrived from Greece, clutching his government-issued work permit, and anxious to get a job.

"Good morning," Monica called out as she pushed open the door to the farm kitchen.

"Michalis," Monica said, as she approached the counter, "welcome to Sassamanash Farm."

"Please, call me Mick," he said with a smile.

He had dark hair and dark eyes with incredibly long lashes, and his teeth were a brilliant white against his tanned skin. Monica had been startled when she first met with him. She hadn't expected him to be so swooningly handsome. She could tell by Nancy and Janice's reactions that they had also fallen under his spell, and even now they kept stealing glances at him from under lowered eyelids.

His sleeves were rolled up, revealing the tattoos on his strong forearms as he kneaded a lump of dough studded with cranberries, slowly turning it smooth and silken.

Monica began to work on the batter for some cranberry muffins. They were always popular with the crowd that came to the farm store for a quick cup of coffee.

She tired easily now and had to pause for a moment to catch her breath. She rubbed her tummy, feeling the kicks of tiny feet against her hand. Suddenly, she felt Janice's gaze on her.

"What?" Monica said. She felt her shoulders tensing. Janice had turned into a model employee but she was highly opinionated, especially when it came to Monica's pregnancy.

"You don't want to go rubbing your stomach too much. You'll end up spoiling the baby."

Mick ducked his head to hide a grin and Nancy swallowed a snort.

Monica took a deep breath. "Thank you, Janice. I didn't know that."

She'd quickly learned that it was useless to argue with Janice or to point out that these myths were just that—myths. It was easier simply to grin and bear it.

The morning went by quickly as they whipped up various cranberry goodies for the farm store and Monica's Café.

Monica was taking a break when her cell phone rang. She pulled it from the pocket of her apron and answered.

"Monica, it's Kelly."

Monica frowned. Kelly sounded panicky and that wasn't like her.

"Is everything okay?"

"Yes. I mean, no."

"What's happened?" Monica stretched out her legs and propped them on the chair opposite her.

Kelly's voice was hushed. "I'd rather not say on the telephone. Could we meet for a cup of coffee? At the diner?"

"Sure. I could use a break anyway. I'll be there in twenty minutes."

"Great." Kelly's sigh of relief came down the line.

Monica wondered what Kelly had to tell her. Did it have to do with Violet's death or was it something else entirely?

Whatever it was, it sounded serious.

Chapter 3

It was the beginning of the lunch hour and the diner was crowded. There was a line waiting for takeout and all the seats at the counter were filled. Monica craned her neck but the booths appeared to be full as well and Kelly obviously hadn't arrived yet.

A couple got up from one of the booths in the back. The man tossed some bills onto the table and followed his companion to the door. The waitress immediately swooped down and filled her tray with the dirty dishes. She returned with a wet rag, swabbed the table and put the salt and pepper shakers back in their place.

Several people were waiting so Monica was surprised when the waitress came up to her. She glanced at Monica's stomach and smiled.

"I have a booth for you in the back," she whispered to Monica. "Follow me."

She led Monica to the table she had just cleaned. Monica slid into the seat, her stomach nearly grazing the edge of the table.

She ordered a decaf iced tea and the waitress had barely left before Kelly slid into the seat opposite.

"Thanks so much for meeting me," she said.

Her face was pale and Monica thought she looked strained.

The waitress reappeared, took her order for a Vernors and departed for the kitchen.

"What's going on?" Monica peeled the wrapper off her straw. "You sounded upset."

Kelly ran a hand through her hair. "I am upset. It's awful. The police came by the inn this morning with the results of Aunt Violet's autopsy. It seems they think there might have been foul play."

"But how could that be? We were all right there."

Kelly pulled a tissue from her purse and blew her nose. "It seems they found some drug in her system—suma . . . sumatriptan. People inject it for relief from migraines."

"How do they know your aunt didn't take it herself?"

"She's never complained of migraines and her doctor confirmed that he had never prescribed it for her."

"But if it's given for migraines, surely it's not a dangerous drug."

"Not normally, no. But it can cause a heart attack in someone with a heart condition and that's apparently what killed Aunt Violet. She's had diabetes and a weak heart for years. The fact that she lived as long as she did was a miracle."

"You said the police came to see you. Was it detective Tammy Stevens?"

Kelly looked slightly startled. "Yes. How did you know?"

Monica paused. "I've made her acquaintance on several occasions." She twirled her straw around in her glass. "She's always been fair. Don't worry. I'm sure she'll get to the bottom of this. There must be some explanation." She put her hand over Kelly's.

Kelly shook her head. "I hope you're right. Otherwise, it means that one of us must have killed Aunt Violet."

Monica said goodbye to Kelly and headed next door to Book 'Em. She paused to look in the window, where Greg had created a display of books from the Golden Age of Mysteries—Ngaio Marsh, Agatha Christie, Josephine Tey and his prized first edition of a Dorothy Sayers.

He was shelving books when Monica walked into the shop. He gave her a quick kiss.

"To what do I owe this honor?" he said with a smile.

"I was next door at the diner with Kelly Cargill."

"Oh?" Greg's eyebrows rose. "Holding a postmortem of yesterday's events?"

"Sort of. Detective Stevens paid the family a visit this morning."

"Oh," Greg said again, his eyebrows rising even higher this time.

"They've completed the autopsy on Violet Cargill and it seems she was injected with a drug used to cure migraines—sumatriptan. In someone with a heart condition like Violet, it can trigger a heart attack."

"You don't mean . . ."

"Yes. It's possible she was murdered. Stevens is investigating."

"There certainly seemed to be enough tension among the members of that family. And I gather a sizeable amount of money is involved."

A young girl made her way toward them and stood very close to Greg.

"Monica, this is Wilma Butkus, my new assistant." Greg turned to Wilma. "Wilma, this is my wife, Monica."

Monica thought she saw a shadow cross Wilma's face briefly before she smiled and said hello. She wasn't very tall and had dark unruly hair trying to escape from a scrunchie. She was wearing blue and white tie-dyed leggings and a long maroon-and-white-striped T-shirt. Her gaze was riveted on Greg.

"I thought I'd check and see how the café is doing," Monica said.

"Let's go check." Greg waved her toward the spiral staircase to the second floor.

Monica noticed that Wilma was right on Greg's heels as she followed him up the stairs. She smiled to herself. It looked like Greg had an admirer. She just hoped it wouldn't become a problem for him.

Monica paused at the top of the steps to catch her breath. She looked around.

Even though she'd seen it before, she still felt a thrill when she saw the sign with *Monica's Café* written on it. She'd had to close her little café in Chicago when a chain coffee shop had moved in nearby, but now Greg had recreated it for her right here in Cranberry Cove.

All the tables were filled with patrons happily sipping tea or coffee and munching on slices of cranberry cake or cookies. Monica couldn't have wished for anything more.

Kit was beaming as he came out from behind the counter to say hello.

"It looks like you've got a full house," Monica said.

Kit nodded. "Business has been good since the day we opened. I think people enjoy having a quiet refuge where they can relax and decompress."

A bell jingled as the door to the shop was opened.

"You'd better go see if they need any help," Greg said to Wilma.

"Sure."

They watched as Wilma trotted down the stairs to the main floor.

"I think she has a crush on you," Monica said. She reached out and straightened Greg's collar.

Greg rolled his eyes. "I know. But I suppose I can live with it as long as it doesn't interfere with her work."

"She seems very eager to please. I think you made a good choice."

"You're not jealous?" Greg teased.

"Not a bit."

Greg made a sad face and snapped his fingers. "Darn."

• • •

Bart's Butcher shop was right next door to Book 'Em so Monica decided to stop in and pick up something for dinner. Bart was behind the counter wearing a blood-stained apron when she walked in. He was cutting a pork loin into individual chops.

"Well, there she is." He put down his knife and smiled at Monica. "I'm betting you'll be having that baby any day now. My wife nearly had our second in the car on the way to the hospital." He chuckled. "I told her I wasn't ready to deliver a baby and she'd better hold on until we got there." He shook a finger at Monica. "Now, the first baby, that's a whole different kettle of fish. She really made us wait. I began to think Dawn would never have the baby."

Monica smiled wanly. She didn't really want to think about it. She and Greg had been to prenatal classes and at least knew what to expect, but it would still be like walking into the unknown.

"Now, I don't suppose you came in here to hear me talk. What can I get for you? Red meat is good for the blood cells, they tell me."

Monica looked at the array of meat arranged in the case. It all looked tempting. She was starving all the time now.

"Maybe some lamb chops?" She tapped the glass with her finger.

"Coming right up. Will two do you or are you planning on company?"

"Two would be fine."

Bart pulled a length of butcher paper from the roll and selected two of the choicest chops. He quickly wrapped them and tied the bundle securely with twine.

"Quite a to-do over at the inn last night. My wife Dawn is working at the front desk part-time. With the son going off to college in a year, we're going to need all the savings we can get." Bart moved to the cash register and rang up the lamb chops. "Did I tell you that Dawn is Violet Cargill's niece?"

"Oh?"

Bart nodded. "Yup. I would be lying if I said we aren't hoping there will be a little bit of money in the will for us." Bart leaned forward and rested his forearms on the counter. "But that's the problem, see? The police got hold of the fact that she's related to the deceased and they showed up to interview her this morning. She was so upset she had to go lie down afterward." Bart handed Monica the package. "It seems they're not convinced that Violet's death was completely natural."

"I don't think they've come to any conclusions yet," Monica said. "I imagine they're interviewing everyone who was around that evening to get a sense of what happened," she said in what she hoped was a soothing voice.

"I suppose you're right." Bart looked down at his hands. "I don't suppose you could do a little investigating? Ask around a bit." He glanced at Monica, his eyes wide open. "Nothing dangerous, of course. But you have a way of getting people to open up."

Monica thought Bart was exaggerating her abilities. Sure, she'd figured out who the culprit was a couple of times but the police had been right behind her. She was pretty sure they hadn't really needed her help.

Still, she'd promised him she'd do what she could. But she would talk to Dawn first.

• • •

It was a pleasant walk along Beach Hallow Road to the Cranberry Cove Inn. A breeze was blowing in off the lake, tossing Monica's hair across her face. She tucked it behind her ears and stopped for a moment to admire the view. The waves were tipped with white and colorful umbrellas dotted the beach, giving the scene a festive air. Gulls squawked raucously and swooped down low, skimming the water as they flew.

When she got to the inn, Monica was surprised to find the lobby empty. Dawn was behind the reception desk, her elbows on the counter, her round purple glasses slipping down her nose.

"It's awfully quiet," Monica said as she approached.

Dawn smiled and closed the magazine she was looking at. "Everyone is out enjoying the nice weather and getting ready for the regatta. There's probably quite a crowd at the Cranberry Cove Yacht Club."

"When does it start?" Monica glanced at the clock on the wall.

"Tonight is the sunset regatta at six o'clock. Of course, the sun won't be going down by then given that Cranberry Cove is in the most western part of the eastern time zone. Tomorrow the races will start bright and early."

Monica cleared her throat. She wasn't sure how to broach the topic she'd come to talk to Dawn about. Perhaps the best way was simply to plunge in like a swimmer diving into cold water.

"I understand you're Violet Cargill's niece," Monica said. "I'm sorry for your loss."

Dawn ducked her head briefly. "Thanks. I didn't know Violet very well. My father — her brother — was estranged from the family."

Monica raised an eyebrow.

"He never talked about it." Dawn tucked the magazine she'd been reading under the counter. "He died when I was only fifteen years old. You know how kids are at that age — all wrapped up in themselves. It never occurred to me to ask him about it. Now it's too late."

The telephone rang and Dawn held up a finger. "Wrong number," she said as she put the receiver down moments later. "The Cargills came here to Cranberry Cove every summer and in the winter during the holidays. As a matter of fact, we used to all skate on that pond behind the house you and Greg are building. My mother believed in letting bygones be bygones so she made peace with them and we were frequently invited to their house on the lake. Of course, that soon ended when Aunt Violet and my uncle sold the place."

"Why did they sell?" Monica's feet were beginning to hurt and she leaned on the counter for support.

Dawn shrugged. "They wanted to travel and I guess they didn't want the responsibility anymore."

"I just came from Bart's shop," Monica said. "He seems concerned — concerned that the police might think you're a suspect in Violet Cargill's death."

Dawn's face turned red. "Bart is being silly. Just because Aunt Violet might leave us a bit of money doesn't mean I'd stoop to murder to get it. Besides, that detective said that since the death was unexpected, they're only following up a few loose ends. It didn't mean anything."

Monica put her hand over Dawn's. "You might want to reassure Bart."

Dawn's face relaxed into a smile. "Bart's an old dear but he does worry about everything."

"He seemed to think that the visit from the detective had upset you to the point where you had to lie down."

Dawn rolled her eyes. "I told him that I had a headache, the old fool," she said fondly. "I'll talk to him, don't worry."

• • •

"We're certainly having a whirlwind social life all of a sudden," Greg said as he and Monica drove into town that evening. "I hope it's not wearing you out." He glanced at her, his eyebrows raised.

"I'm enjoying it. Kelly and I haven't seen each other in ages. I think she's anxious to make use of our time together."

They were on their way to the Cranberry Cove Yacht Club, where Aston Cargill was taking part in the regatta. The sunset race would be later in the day and Kelly had invited them to join her.

Monica looked out the window as they passed the carnival, which would move on at the end of the week. There was a line for the Ferris wheel, she noticed — a rickety-looking thing with peeling paint. She wouldn't let her children go on something like that. It couldn't be safe. She put a hand on her belly. She realized that thought would never have occurred to her before she became pregnant but now, she already felt protective of her child, even though it hadn't arrived yet.

The parking lot of the yacht club was almost full.

"Here we are." Greg pointed to a spot between a Range Rover and a sleek black Lexus.

The yacht club boasted a wide wraparound porch that overlooked the harbor and was the perfect viewing spot for the regatta. Today, it was decorated with pennants in red, white and blue and bunting in the same colors was strung along the railing.

Eager guests were gathered on the porch, many with binoculars hanging around their necks, the men in white pants, polo shirts and boat shoes and many of the women in colorful sundresses. The atmosphere was festive as waiters circulated with trays of glasses sweating with condensation.

Kelly had managed to secure a table and several chairs. Monica was surprised to see Edith and Sherry were seated with her.

Kelly jumped up to greet them. She gave each of them a hug as Edith and Sherry smiled and said hello.

"It might seem insensitive coming out for the regatta so soon after Aunt Violet's death," Kelly said as she sat down. "But we wanted to support Aston in his race. He couldn't pull out on such short notice and let his teammates down, so Uncle Ray decided he should go ahead with it."

Edith was wearing black capris and a black linen blouse and had a cardigan around her shoulders. She looked terribly somber in contrast to all the colors around them.

She pulled a handkerchief from her pocket and dabbed at her eyes.

Kelly put a hand on her arm. "Are you okay? Do you want to leave?"

"No, no, I'm fine." Edith fiddled with the handkerchief. "I just can't believe Violet is gone, the poor thing. She was always so good to me. I don't know what I would have done . . ." She made a brave attempt at a smile. "But I'm sure the race will cheer me up. You're right—we have to be here for Aston."

"Is Ray coming?" Greg said.

Edith sniffed. "He said he'd be along later. He didn't want to have to sit here listening to us chatter while we waited. But he'd better hurry up if he doesn't want to miss the beginning of the race."

Monica looked out at the harbor, where colorful sails billowed in the wind and the boats bobbed up and down in the choppy water.

"Which one is Aston's?" She leaned closer to Kelly. "Can you tell from here?"

"Yes. The one with the blue-and-white-striped sail." She pointed into the distance.

A waiter stopped at their table. "Anything to drink?" he said. "The Club makes excellent lemonade and the signature alcoholic drink tonight is the Sea Breeze—vodka, grapefruit juice and cranberry juice."

They ordered a round of lemonades and the waiter scurried away to fill their order.

People began shifting in their seats and several looked at their watches.

"I think the race is about to start," Kelly said.

They angled their chairs so that they could see the water. The boats were rising and falling on the waves as if impatient to get going.

A chair scraped against the porch floor as Ray pulled it out. He glanced at the water. "Hasn't started yet, I see." He flagged a passing waiter. "I'll have a Sea Breeze."

He drummed his fingers on the table and Monica noticed that his right leg was jiggling. Was he anxious about the race? she wondered.

The waiter had just put Ray's drink on the table when people began craning their necks in anticipation.

"What's going on?" Monica said.

"They'll be starting soon," Kelly said, leaning forward eagerly. She pointed toward the water. "The starting line is between that buoy over there" — she gestured toward it — "and the flag on that boat over there. It's the racing committee boat. They will be overseeing the race."

A horn blared and Monica jumped.

"That's the warning flag," Ray said, pointing toward the water. "That means it's five minutes to start time."

There was another horn blast. "Four minutes now," Kelly said. "They've put up the preparatory flag."

Monica noticed that a flag with a large *P* on it was now flying from the racing committee boat.

There was a long horn blast and Edith jumped.

"Preparatory flag's down. One minute to start," Ray said.

"Those horns are quite annoying," Edith said, fidgeting with the handle of her purse.

Monica found herself leaning forward in her chair in anticipation and that time she was the one who jumped when the starting horn finally sounded.

"Off they go," Ray said. He leaned back in his chair and took another sip of his drink.

Monica watched as the colorful sails filled with wind and the boats shot forward. Suddenly one boat began to head back toward the starting line.

Ray laughed when he saw the puzzled look on Monica's and Greg's faces.

"Their boat must have been over the course line before the start. They have to go back to the non-course side of the starting line and begin all over again. It's going to cost them some time."

The waiter brought another round of lemonades and a fresh Sea Breeze for Ray. The sun was getting lower in the sky and a cool breeze was blowing off the water, sending the tendrils of hair around

Monica's face swirling. She noticed that Edith had put on the cardigan that had been around her shoulders.

Ray suddenly leaned forward, nearly knocking over his drink. "Aston and his team have pulled out in front." He pointed toward the boat with the blue-and-white sail that was slightly ahead of the others.

Monica found her eyes beginning to droop. Greg put his hand over hers.

"Tired?"

Monica squeezed his hand. "I'm fine. Just relaxed."

Suddenly, Ray jumped up from his chair. "He's won. Aston's team has won." He beamed at the others.

Before long sailors from the earlier races began to trickle onto the porch, their damp hair brushed back from their foreheads, their faces red from the sun and wind.

A fellow plopped into a chair at the next table and let out a loud sigh. He ran a hand through his blond hair leaving it in runnels. The skin on his nose was peeling and there were crinkles under his eyes.

An older gentleman at the table said something and the fellow scowled.

"We would have won if Aston hadn't cheated," he said loud enough for Monica to hear.

She inched her chair closer.

"Come on," the older man chided. "How do you know Aston cheated? Surely the judges would have picked up on any illegal maneuvers." He leaned back and took a sip of his cocktail.

The blond fellow shook his head vigorously. "Not like that. If Nate hadn't gotten sick — we had to replace him on the crew with Ben — I'm sure we would have won." He frowned. "Ben isn't nearly as seasoned and it lost us time."

The older man chuckled. "How on earth could Aston be responsible for Nate getting sick." He pointed a finger at the blond fellow. "You're clutching at straws. Aston's team won fair and square as far as I can tell."

"Then how come we've beat Aston's team every other time we've competed with them?"

His companion shrugged. "There's always a first time for everything."

The blond fellow narrowed his eyes. "Nate was fine until he had drinks with Aston. He got sick right afterward. I don't think that's a coincidence."

"He might have been coming down with something," the older man said. "I think you're trying to make something out of nothing."

The blond fellow lowered his eyebrows and glowered at his companion.

"I don't think so," he said, throwing himself back in his chair, a mutinous look on his face.

Chapter 4

"And here's the winner," Ray said as Aston approached them. "Good going, son." He grabbed an empty chair and pulled it up to the table.

Aston had changed into a pair of slacks embroidered with anchors and a fresh polo shirt.

He clapped his father on the shoulder and dropped into his seat.

"Congratulations," they all chorused.

"Thanks." Aston stretched out his legs and crossed them at the ankle.

Ray looked around for a waiter. "How about a drink?"

"Sure." Aston groaned as he stretched his arms over his head.

"I don't know about you," Kelly said, "but I could do with a bite to eat." She looked at Monica and Greg. "Anybody?"

"You go on ahead," Edith said. "I think I'll go back to the inn and check on Beatrice. The poor thing has been quite distraught."

"Good idea," Kelly said. "I imagine the restaurant here is full. We'll probably have better luck at the inn anyway."

Fortunately, the restaurant at the inn was able to accommodate them. They had barely sat down when Monica realized she needed to use the restroom—something that had been plaguing her the entire pregnancy. She excused herself and headed out to the lobby.

On her way back to the restaurant, she noticed a woman sitting in one of the armchairs and realized it was Beatrice. She had a ball of yarn in her lap and was knitting something.

Monica stopped to say hello.

Beatrice looked up from her knitting.

"How are you doing?" Monica said. "This must all be so hard for you."

Beatrice pulled a tissue from her pocket and dabbed at her eyes.

"The police won't let us leave, can you believe it? Something to do with an investigation. What is there to investigate? My poor sister's heart finally gave out. It hadn't ever been that strong."

"I can imagine how you feel," Monica said, perching on the edge of the armchair opposite Beatrice. "Edith seems to be taking it quite hard as well."

Beatrice's head shot up and her eyes widened. "Edith?"

"Yes. I gather she was quite close to Violet."

Beatrice snorted. "Hardly. Violet treated Edith horribly. The poor woman was run off her feet day in and day out. Bring me my shawl. Get me a cup of tea. I'm cold, close the window." Beatrice shook her head. "It was never-ending."

"Why did Edith put up with it?"

Beatrice shrugged. "I don't know."

Monica heard footsteps behind her.

"Here you are. I was worried." Greg took her hand.

Monica smiled. "I didn't mean to worry you. I stopped to say hello to Beatrice."

As Monica and Greg walked back to the restaurant Monica thought about what Beatrice had said. If Violet had been so horrible to Edith, why did she stay? There had to have been a reason.

• • •

Mick was already hard at work when Monica opened the door to the farm kitchen the next morning. He gave her a big smile that showed off his gleaming white teeth, so startling against his tanned skin.

Nancy was at the table sipping a cup of coffee and tying decorative ribbons around jars of Monica's cranberry chutney. Janice was dropping tablespoons of dough studded with cranberries and chocolate chips onto a cookie sheet.

Janice nodded at Monica. "Good morning." She paused with her hands on her hips. "Should you be working so close to your due date?" She pointed at Monica's belly.

"The doctor said it's perfectly okay as long as I don't get over-tired." Monica tried to keep the irritation out of her voice—Janice asked her that same question nearly every morning.

Janice pointed toward the ceiling. "It's a full moon tomorrow night. You know what that means."

Monica sighed. "No, I don't know what that means."

"Full moons bring on births. You're likely to be starting your labor any minute now." She shook a finger at Monica. "Rest while you can because you won't get any rest after the little one arrives."

"I promise I'll put my feet up this afternoon," Monica said, hoping that would satisfy Janice.

Janice didn't look completely convinced but she didn't say anything and went back to her cookie dough.

Monica's phone buzzed and she pulled it from her pocket. It was Kit.

"Darling, do you have any muffins ready? It's been such a morning, you wouldn't believe it. The oven is being a bit dodgy and we're waiting for the repairman." Kit groaned. "He can't get here till this afternoon. Just pray it doesn't need one of those proverbial parts that have to be imported from somewhere overseas."

Monica put her hand over the phone and motioned to Mick. "Do we have any muffins ready? Kit needs some for the café."

Mick gave her his most winning smile. "We do. Do you want me to package them up for you?"

Within minutes, Monica was on her way back to her cottage and her car with a batch of warm cranberry muffins. She put the package on the passenger seat and the enticing aroma drifted around her as she headed toward Beach Hollow Road.

She was grateful to find a parking spot right in front of Book 'Em. She pulled into the space, grabbed the box of muffins and crossed the sidewalk toward the entrance.

Greg must have seen her coming because he pushed open the door for her and took the box out of her hands.

He inhaled deeply. "These smell delicious."

Monica clucked her tongue. "No touching. They're for the café."

They were heading up the stairs when Wilma, Greg's new assistant, suddenly appeared. She followed them up to the second floor.

Monica took the box of muffins to Kit, and when she got back to Greg, she noticed Wilma was standing nearly on top of him. Poor Greg, she thought. Wilma was attached to him like Velcro. At the moment he found it amusing, but how long before it became annoying? She felt sorry for Wilma—she should be crushing on boys her own age.

Monica was a little out of breath after coming down the spiral staircase so she paused for a moment to survey Greg's shelf of new mysteries.

A woman stood next to her, flipping through the latest by Harlan Coben. Monica glanced at her and realized it was Edith. She reached out and touched Edith's arm.

Edith startled and put a hand to her mouth. "Oh." She blinked at Monica. "I didn't see you there. I'm afraid I was engrossed in looking through this book." She held it up so Monica could see the cover. "I finished the novel I brought with me to read and I thought getting something new might take my mind off of things."

"Violet's death, you mean?"

"A detective came to see me this morning." The book trembled in her hands. "They asked so many questions."

"I think they're questioning everyone. It's normal and nothing to be worried about."

Monica looked at Edith as she thought back to her conversation with Beatrice. According to Beatrice, Edith had every reason to want Violet dead. But she was so tiny and frail. She looked as if she would snap in two like a spindly branch caught in a storm. And so . . . ordinary-looking. Monica found it hard to picture her as a cunning murderer. But then, she'd been surprised before when the least likely looking suspect had turned out to be the killer.

"It was most distressing," Edith said. She touched her hair. "They asked all sorts of questions—did I always give Violet her insulin, how long had I been her companion, what did I do before that. And on and on until I thought it would never end."

Edith's face had blanched white and her lips were clamped shut into a thin, colorless line.

"I'm sorry," Monica said, patting Edith's arm. "But I can assure you, it's perfectly normal."

Edith stiffened. "But they took some of Violet's things. They took the syringe I used for her insulin as well as the bottle of insulin. What can they be thinking?" She looked at Monica with frightened eyes.

"Since you had nothing to do with Violet's death, you have nothing to worry about."

"True." Edith lifted her chin. She tucked the book she'd been holding under her arm and shifted her tote bag from one hand to the other. "I do believe I'll get the Coben. I always enjoy his books. And I feel so much better now that I've talked to you. Thank you, dear." She went up to the counter.

Monica waited until Greg had finished ringing up Edith's purchase, then wandered over to the counter where he had started arranging a stack of books.

"Is that for a display?" Monica said, leaning against the counter and scanning the titles.

Greg nodded. "Yes. Only a book is missing." He scratched his head. "I swear it was here before we went upstairs."

"Oh?"

"It was that first edition Margery Allingham I picked up at that estate sale last week. I can't imagine where it's gone to." He shrugged. "Oh, well. No doubt I'll find it misfiled somewhere — tucked in with the new books perhaps. At least I hope so — it was quite an expensive purchase."

"I was talking to Edith Evans," Monica said. "She said a detective — I assume it was Stevens — wanted Violet's syringe and insulin bottle for testing. She seemed shaken up about it but I assured her it was standard procedure."

Greg raised an eyebrow. "You're not getting involved in this investigation, are you?"

"No," Monica said, leaning across the counter to kiss him. "Sealed with a kiss," she said as she waved goodbye.

• • •

Monica wasn't surprised that the police had confiscated Violet's insulin and syringe. They were obviously trying to trace the source of the migraine medication found in Violet's body during the autopsy and that seemed a likely place to look. She supposed they were going to check to see if the insulin bottle had been tampered with.

At the Fourth of July celebration, Sherry Cargill had mentioned that she got headaches. Were they migraines? Monica wondered. And had someone stolen her medication and used it to kill Violet?

Monica was about to head back to Sassamanash Farm when she changed her mind. She pulled into the parking lot of the Pepper Pot, turned around and headed back the way she had come to the Cranberry Cove Inn. She crossed her fingers that Sherry would be in.

The scent of suntan lotion lingered in the air of the lobby and Monica noticed several patrons with towels tucked under their arms heading toward the beach. It was a beautiful day—warm and sunny but with a slight breeze—and when she peered out the large lobby window, she saw that the stretch of sand leading down to the lake was dotted with colorful umbrellas.

Dawn wasn't behind the desk—a young man tapping on a computer was in her place. He looked up and smiled when Monica approached.

"Can I help you?"

He gave Monica Sherry's room number and pointed toward the house phone sitting on a small table near the desk. Monica let it ring numerous times but still there was no answer. She'd have to come back another time.

She was heading toward the door when Beatrice walked in. She waved to Monica and began to walk toward her. She had several packages in her arms, including one from Cranberry Cove's fancy boutique Danielle's.

"I'm furious," Beatrice said without bothering to say hello. She dumped her packages on a nearby sofa. "The police refuse to let us leave while they investigate Violet's death. Can you imagine? None of us had anything to do with it. And here we are—stuck."

"Hopefully it won't be much longer," Monica said.

Beatrice frowned. "I certainly hope not. There's nothing to do and frankly, I'm sick to death of the food here at the inn."

"There's also the diner and the Pepper Pot . . ." Monica began.

Beatrice waved a hand as if to chase Monica's words away.

"Dreadful places. Not what I'm used to at all."

Monica felt her face color and she opened her mouth to defend Cranberry Cove and its features but then closed it again. Nothing would be gained by arguing with Beatrice.

"I'm sure it's terribly distressing for you," she said. "Especially since you and Violet were so close."

Beatrice swiped a finger under her eyes. "Most distressing, indeed. Just thinking about it is giving me a headache." She pinched the bridge of her nose.

"Speaking of headaches," Monica said in what she hoped was an innocent voice. "Sherry suffers from headaches, doesn't she?"

Beatrice rolled her eyes. "Sherry is something of a hypochondriac, I'm afraid. She does it to get attention."

"Could they be migraines?" Monica said.

"Oh, no, nothing like that. Simply ordinary garden-variety headaches like we all get from time to time. Leave it to Sherry to turn it into a big drama." Beatrice glanced at her watch. "Must run. Good to see you." She gathered up her packages.

Monica walked back to her car. She was positive she remembered someone saying that the doctor had given Sherry medication for her headaches. Could it have been the same substance that killed Violet? If so, someone had to have switched the medications. Could it have been Edith? According to Beatrice, Violet had treated her badly. Perhaps she'd reached her limit and had snapped? But Edith was so meek and timid, Monica couldn't seriously imagine her killing anyone.

If Sherry was the source of the medication, it wouldn't be that difficult for her to switch the vials. Sherry obviously had expensive taste, and if she and Ray were in Violet's will, that might have been the incentive she needed to hasten Violet's death.

Now, more than ever, she needed to talk to Sherry.

Chapter 5

Monica was starting her car when her cell phone rang. She turned off the engine and rummaged in her purse for her phone.

It was Gina, her stepmother, asking if Monica could stop by her store — she had something to give her.

Monica had to admit her curiosity was piqued, although it was most likely something for the baby. Gina had already given her some bibs, a cute sweater in a neutral beige and several stuffed toys.

Monica found a parking space on Beach Hollow Road a few doors down from Gina's aromatherapy shop, Making Scents. The door to the Cranberry Cove Diner was open and tantalizing aromas drifted down the street. Monica looked at her watch and was surprised to see it was nearly lunchtime.

The smell of lavender essential oil hit her as soon as she walked through the door of Gina's shop. According to Gina, lavender was meant to be calming, so Monica took a deep breath and tried to feel whether she was more relaxed or not. Frankly, she couldn't tell.

Gina was at the counter wrestling with the seal on a carton while brandishing a rather wicked-looking utility knife with reckless abandon.

"Careful with that thing," Monica said as she approached the counter.

Gina blew a lock of hair off her forehead and gave it one more try. This time the knife sliced through the packing tape and she ripped the top open.

"Scented candles," she said to Monica as she removed a smaller box and placed it on the counter. "I saw them at that trade show I went to in Chicago and decided they were just what Making Scents needed." She swept an arm around the shop. "I'm thinking of expanding my inventory."

"Oh? With what?"

"Bath oils, some pretty diffuser lockets and charms — you put a few drops of the essential oil of your choice on the felt pad."

"That all sounds good," Monica said. She leaned her elbows on the counter — she had a cramp in her back.

"Before I forget." Gina reached under the counter and pulled out a small bottle. She showed it to Monica. "This is clary sage essential oil.

It's used to induce labor and to increase contractions."

Monica frowned. "I don't know. I'd rather let nature take its course."

Gina put the bottle on the counter and pushed it toward Monica.

"Take it in case you change your mind. I know I got quite impatient those last few days waiting for Jeff to arrive. I wish I'd known about clary sage back then."

Monica reluctantly took the bottle and tucked it into her purse.

"How is the decorating coming along?" Gina and her boyfriend, Mickey, had recently purchased a new house.

Gina clasped her hands together. "Wonderfully. Mickey gave me carte blanche. I've ordered a white leather sofa and some chairs covered in leopard print for the living room and I'm having one wall painted black."

Monica tried not to look surprised. She really shouldn't be, she thought as she glanced at Gina in her zebra-print leggings, black tunic top and earrings that were large black and white discs. It was obvious Gina wasn't going to go for something traditional like mid-century modern.

"Everything should be arriving soon and I can't wait to show it off. I want to hold a baby shower for you."

A sense of panic washed over Monica. Her mother had already told her she was going to hold the baby shower and she wasn't going to take kindly to Gina stepping on her toes. And she'd known Gina long enough by now to know she didn't like being told no.

This was a disaster in the making.

• • •

As Monica left Gina's shop, she realized she was starving. The smells from the diner were enticing — their chili was delicious, but that meant a certain case of heartburn. The thought of fries and a burger made her mouth water, but she'd been determined to eat healthy meals. She had all the salad fixings she needed at home — grilled chicken, lettuce and tomatoes nearly bursting with ripeness from the farm stand and an avocado for some healthy fat and a good dose of vitamins.

Clouds were blowing in swiftly across the lake and the sky was getting darker and darker as Monica drove home. Fat raindrops began to splatter against her windshield as she turned onto the road leading to Sassamanash Farm and she flicked on her windshield wipers.

Hercule was nearly delirious with joy when she opened the door to her cottage. He ran around and around her, his tail going like a metronome. Finally, he began to calm down and Monica was able to pet him.

Mittens peeked around the door to the kitchen and stared at Monica for a minute before slowly approaching her. She allowed Monica to scratch under her chin before dashing off again.

Monica hummed as she fixed her salad and mixed up some ranch dressing. She carried her plate to the kitchen table and sank gratefully into the chair.

Her mind was still occupied with thoughts about Violet's death. She wondered about Edith. Why did she put up with Violet's abuse? Or had Beatrice been exaggerating the severity of the situation?

She thought about searching for information about Edith on the computer, but Evans was such a common last name. Edith wasn't, though, so perhaps it was worth a try.

She finished her salad, cleaned up her dishes, fetched her computer and set it up on the kitchen table.

She was momentarily distracted by an advertisement for mobiles for the baby's room but finally she brought up her favorite search engine. She typed in "Edith Evans" without much hope of finding anything significant.

The first few entries were disappointing. An Edith Evans had died in Oklahoma in 1889 and another Edith Evans had passed away in North Dakota at the age of ninety-four. She kept scrolling and the entries became less targeted, several referencing Queen Edith of the Netherlands and others advertising Edith mints. She was about to give up when she hit upon an interesting entry.

An Edith Evans had been arrested for shoplifting at a store in Grand Rapids, Michigan. The article was from twenty years ago and the age of the Edith in question fit the age of Violet's companion.

Apparently, this Edith Evans had attempted to steal an expensive suede coat but had been caught by security shortly after leaving the store.

According to a neighbor interviewed for the article, there had been extenuating circumstances but the paper didn't elaborate on what those were.

Monica wondered what those circumstances had been. She told herself she wasn't investigating as she jotted down the name of Edith's neighbor and checked the address online. What she was doing was simply research. Yes, that's it, she decided. Research.

There was no guarantee that Edith's neighbor—a woman by the name of Jennifer Ashland—still lived at the address listed, but there was one way to find out. Her address was in a small town not far from Cranberry Cove and it wouldn't take Monica more than half an hour to drive there. But first she had to check in with Mick and the crew at the farm kitchen.

• • •

When Monica arrived at the farm kitchen, Mick was leaning against the counter and Nancy was listening to him with rapt attention. Monica didn't have to hear what he was saying—it was obvious by his gestures and the look in his eyes that he was flirting with Nancy.

Not again, Monica thought. Nancy had recently had her heart broken by a younger man. Was it about to happen again?

Janice was kneading dough—flinging it down on the counter as if she was mad at it—and occasionally glowering at Mick and Nancy.

Was she annoyed because they weren't working or was she jealous of the attention Mick was paying to Nancy?

Monica was beginning to wonder if she'd made a mistake hiring Mick but the baking was under control, he was always on time, didn't complain and produced delicious products, and she was grateful for that.

It was the perfect time to take an inventory of their supplies. Monica grabbed a clipboard off her desk, clipped a piece of paper to it and headed into the stockroom. She heard the door open while she was emailing the last order and wondered who it could be.

She was surprised to see Lauren, Jeff's fiancé. She'd been a huge help in planning a marketing campaign for the farm and its products.

She was wearing a floral sundress and had her long blond hair pulled back in a ponytail.

Mick gave her an appraising look and then, obviously liking what he saw, smiled broadly. Lauren stopped in her tracks when she saw him behind the counter, a white apron tied around his waist and flour on his hands.

Monica noticed her cheeks had turned a becoming pink and her hands were fluttering around her face as if she was nervous. Or entranced. Was she falling under Mick's spell as well?

"Oh, Monica, I didn't see you there." Lauren's face turned even pinker. "I have Instagram posts I want you to see." She put her tote bag on the table and pulled out her laptop.

"What do you think?" she said as Monica scrolled through the posts.

Lauren had taken some stunning pictures of the farm as well as charming photos of the farm store and several close-ups of their products.

"They're splendid."

"I'll be posting one a day," Lauren said, closing the lid on her laptop. "That should up our social media game."

"I should say so," Monica said.

"I'll be off then. I have an appointment in half an hour."

She put her laptop in her tote bag and slung the bag over her shoulder. She turned to go but not before giving Mick a last, lingering look.

Worrying wasn't good for the baby, Monica knew, but she couldn't help it. She plugged Jennifer Ashland's address into her phone's navigation app and started the car. But she couldn't avoid the troublesome thoughts about Lauren and Jeff that invaded her subconscious. She was probably being silly — they were a solid couple and Lauren had merely been appreciating Mick's good looks. She had to admit that she had done the same herself.

She managed to put the thoughts out of her mind as she followed the winding country roads that led out of Cranberry Cove. Fields on either side of her were green with tall stalks of corn waiting to be harvested.

The road was still wet from the rain but a brisk wind was blowing the clouds away, revealing patches of blue sky. The air coming in her open window smelled of damp earth and felt cool on her bare shoulders. She found herself relaxing the further she got from home.

The monotony of the passing scenery was soothing.

It wasn't long before she reached the center of the town where Jennifer Ashland lived. The buildings were old but well-maintained, with flags stuck in planters fluttering in the breeze and Fourth of July bunting still hanging from the lampposts.

Shortly after passing through town, Monica found Jennifer's house and pulled into her driveway. The development looked as if it dated from the nineteen-fifties. The homes had obviously been cookie-cutter at the time they were built but over the years, owners had added their own touches to distinguish them.

Jennifer's house was a fairly modest split-level with a large picture window and two-car garage. Monica walked up to the front door and rang the bell.

"Oh," Jennifer said when she opened the door. "Can I help you?"

She was middle-aged, had short blond hair and was wearing white Bermuda shorts and a navy-and-white-striped T-shirt.

Monica suddenly felt awkward but Jennifer was very gracious when she explained the purpose of her visit and invited her in.

Two sets of stairs faced the entryway—one leading up and the other down. Jennifer led Monica up the steps to a living room with traditional furniture and an upright piano against one wall.

"You're probably wondering why I'm asking about Edith," Monica said when they sat down.

A variety of emotions chased themselves across Jennifer's face. She cocked her head to one side.

"Edith was a companion to a woman named Violet Cargill. Violet died under mysterious circumstances and Edith is concerned that she might be a suspect. I told her I would do some investigating on my own. Edith seems like a nice woman but I'm afraid I don't really know anything about her." Monica felt the pulse beating in her neck but tried to sound cool and collected. "You were quoted in a newspaper article about a shoplifting incident involving her."

Jennifer nodded briskly. "Yes, I remember that. The poor woman."

"There were extenuating circumstances . . . ?" Monica let the sentence dangle in the air.

"Yes. I think the whole situation did something to her mind. She was such a nice lady. It was totally out of character. I felt so sorry for her." She fiddled with the hoop in her ear. "It was because her husband died, you see. That alone was enough to send anyone into a tailspin, but then she discovered they were completely broke."

"Broke?" Monica raised her eyebrows.

"Yes. It seems Mr. Evans had gambling problems that Edith didn't know about. He lost all their money. The house was mortgaged to the hilt and Edith couldn't afford to keep it." Jennifer smoothed a lock of hair behind her ear. "Up until then, Edith had lived a comfortable life." She waved her hand around the living room. "None of us are exactly rich, but we have what we need."

Monica tried to remember what the houses on either side of Jennifer's had looked like. She hadn't really noticed them but they were probably as unremarkable as Jennifer's—comfortable but certainly not mansions.

"Edith was desperate for money. She was a nurse but had been retired for quite some time. She didn't think she could stand being on her feet every day working in a hospital, so she was thrilled when she saw that advertisement for a companion to an elderly woman. She thought it was the answer to her prayers."

"I suppose her nursing background made her the ideal candidate."

"I think it gave her an edge, but I don't think it was really necessary. We met for coffee once after she'd started the job—she'd sold her house by then and moved in with her employer—and by all accounts, the woman was relatively healthy."

"Did Edith seem to be enjoying the job?"

"Oh, yes. She spoke very highly of the woman—Violet, you said it was? Violet was terribly kind to her and treated her more like a friend than an employee. Edith was thrilled. She had a lovely room in a gracious home with meals prepared by a cook." She gave a rueful laugh. "There are days when I could go for that myself."

"It does seem out of character that she would shoplift something."

"Right?" Jennifer said. "I'm sure it was because of what she was going through after her husband died. Fortunately, the judge agreed and let her off with a warning."

"I wonder what's going to happen to her now that Violet is dead. I suppose she's out of a job."

"She told me she wasn't worried about that. Violet had assured her that she would be taken care of."

As Monica drove home, she wondered what Violet had meant when she had said she would take care of Edith. Did she mean she was leaving her money? Even though Edith had insisted otherwise, according to Beatrice, Violet had treated Edith very poorly. Had Edith decided she wanted that money sooner rather than later?

Chapter 6

Janice called as Monica was on her way back to Cranberry Cove. The Cranberry Cove Inn had phoned to say they were out of Sassamanash Farm's cranberry salsa. Janice said there was a batch ready to go if Monica wouldn't mind picking it up.

Within twenty minutes, Monica was pulling into the parking lot of the inn with a carton of salsa destined for the kitchen. She drove around back to the service entrance, where one of the staff came out to her car and unloaded the carton.

She was about to head back to the farm when she changed her mind. Perhaps Sherry would be in now — she might as well check while she was already at the inn.

She parked her car and walked into the lobby. Dawn was behind the reception desk and waved when she saw Monica. Monica used the house phone to call Sherry's room but once again her call went unanswered. She was about to leave when she decided she would check the cocktail lounge first.

The room was reminiscent of an old-fashioned library with wood-paneled walls, bottle-green leather club chairs and small round cocktail tables. The bartender was wiping down the bar and a waitress was serving a tray of drinks to the four men sitting at one of the tables.

Sherry was by herself at a table tucked into the corner. She had a glass in front of her and was shredding the cocktail napkin underneath it. She was wearing white capri pants and a sleeveless purple blouse. Her pale skin was studded with freckles and her red hair was loosely piled on top of her head.

"Do you mind if I join you?" Monica said when she reached her table.

"I don't suppose you're here for a cocktail," Sherry said, nodding at Monica's stomach. She signaled for the waitress. "Would you like some iced tea or a lemonade?"

"A lemonade," Monica said when the waitress reached their table.

Sherry stirred her drink with her finger then put her finger in her mouth and licked it.

"When are you due?" She nodded at Monica's stomach again.

"Any day now," Monica said. "But first babies are often late so . . ."

Sherry peered into her glass. "Ray and I tried for a baby. I did the whole thing—the hormones, the procedures . . . the tears." She sniffed. "Nothing ever came of it, I'm afraid. The worst part was I don't think he minded half as much as I did. He already had a son, after all."

The waitress plunked a cocktail napkin down and slid Monica's lemonade in front of her.

Sherry frowned and massaged her temples. "Ray would have a fit if he knew I was having a drink so early but I needed one. My nerves are on edge from the stress of this whole thing with Violet."

"Are you okay?"

Sherry nodded. "I feel a headache coming on, I'm afraid."

"I'm sorry," Monica said. "Do you get migraines?"

"Yes." Sherry's face had become even paler. "The doctor prescribed medication for them but I seem to have forgotten it." She rubbed her forehead. "I could have sworn I remembered taking it out of the my makeup bag and putting it in the bedside table drawer but when I looked, the vial was gone. Ray said I must have forgotten it but I know I didn't." She held her hands out, palms up. "I wouldn't."

"Maybe someone took it?"

"Why would someone do that?" Sherry's face blanched even whiter. "You don't think . . . I mean, they found some sort of migraine medication when they did Violet's autopsy, didn't they? That's what Beatrice said." She looked at Monica, her eyes wide. "Do you really think someone might have taken it?"

"I don't know. Did you let anyone into your room?"

"No. Just me and Ray."

"No one else has been in your room?"

Sherry's gaze slid away from Monica's and she began fussing with the top button of her blouse. "No, no one at all." She pushed back her chair so abruptly it scraped against the floor. "I'm sorry. I have to go lie down."

Monica watched her leave. She'd been lying about not letting anyone into her room. Why? Did she know something she wasn't willing to reveal? Was she protecting someone?"

• • •

Monica opened the door to the cottage with a sigh of relief. She was tired and her back ached. All she wanted to do was collapse on the sofa with her feet up.

Hercule greeted her with his usual wild enthusiasm. He'd been like that ever since the day he'd wandered into Greg's bookstore, hungry and disheveled. Mittens was slowly adapting to his presence and she joined him in greeting Monica.

Greg was in the kitchen tossing a salad. He smiled when he saw Monica.

"I've made us some dinner—salmon, corn on the cob and a salad. How does that sound?"

"That sounds heavenly," Monica said, sitting down and easing her shoes off. "I'm starved all the time now." She rubbed the arches of her feet. "Do you need any help?"

"Nope, it's all under control."

"How's Wilma?" Monica said in a teasing tone.

Greg groaned. "Every time I turn around, she's right there. But she's a hard worker and the customers like her so I shouldn't complain. I'm lucky to have found her."

"By the way, did you ever find that missing book—the Margery Allingham?" Monica pulled out another kitchen chair and put her feet up.

Greg turned around with a spatula in his hand. "No. It hasn't turned up yet."

"Maybe you should ask Wilma if she can find it. That ought to keep her busy for a while."

Greg laughed. "And away from me. That's a good idea. I'm going to do that."

Greg served up dinner, and after they ate and cleaned up the kitchen, they settled in the living room. Greg switched on the television and Monica picked up the newspaper that was sitting on the coffee table.

She flipped through the pages, pausing occasionally to read an article. Her eyes were beginning to close and she was contemplating an early night when a particular headline caught her eye. *Is the Daily Paper Extinct?* She and Greg had discussed canceling their daily paper and reading the news online but had decided against it. They both enjoyed taking a break from their devices and they often did the crossword puzzle together.

There were a lot of dire predictions and statistics in the article. Monica wasn't surprised. Circulation of the *Cranberry Cove Chronicle* had been going down little by little. She was surprised, though, to see a quote from Ray Cargill. *All papers need an online presence to survive in this day and age,* he was quoted as saying.

That was interesting, Monica thought. Suddenly, she was wide awake. She grabbed her laptop and searched for Cargill Papers. There were numerous entries but none of them led to an online newspaper. She wondered why. Ray clearly felt it was necessary for a paper's success.

Perhaps it was in the works? Or maybe Cargill Papers wasn't doing as well as Ray liked people to think?

• • •

Monica spent a restless night, tossing and turning, as her brain churned out a series of strange and vivid dreams. Sherry, Ray, Edith and Violet were all characters cast in some of the bizarre nightmares that plagued her.

She woke with a start to find Hercule staring at her, his nose inches from hers.

"Is it time to get up, boy?"

Monica reluctantly threw back the covers and toddled into the bathroom. She felt slightly more awake after washing her face and brushing her teeth. She grabbed a pair of shorts and a T-shirt from the dresser and quickly put them on.

The aroma of coffee brewing was already drifting up the stairs. Monica knew Greg had made a decaf blend for her but even without the caffeine, she found the coffee had an energizing effect on her. She knew she had to be imagining it, but she was just glad it worked.

Greg was filling two mugs as Monica walked into the kitchen, Hercule at her heels.

"Hercule's been out," he said. "Don't let him fool you. And Mittens has fresh bowls of food and water." He handed Monica a mug.

She took it gratefully and sniffed the fragrant steam rising from the top.

She warmed some cranberry scones and put them and the butter dish on the table.

"You had a restless night," Greg said as he sat down. "Bad dreams?"

"Sort of. I dreamt that Ray Cargill killed Violet by hitting her over the head with a rolled-up newspaper and that Sherry and Edith got into a fight and Sherry stabbed Edith with an eyeliner pencil."

"That sounds more like a comedy than a nightmare," Greg said, buttering his scone. "You're not still thinking about Violet's death, are you?"

"I can't help it," Monica admitted. "Sherry takes medication for her migraines. It's possible it's the same medication that caused Violet's heart attack. She claims it was missing but that no one else had access to her room."

"Someone must have taken it." Greg reached for another scone.

"Of course, I haven't ruled out Ray. It's his room as well and it would be easy enough to grab the vial when Sherry wasn't there."

Greg crossed his arms over his chest. "It sounds suspiciously like you're investigating again."

"No, just trying to fit some of the pieces together." Monica took a sip of her coffee. "So, if it wasn't Ray, then someone else went into Sherry's room and stole that vial of sumatriptan. Who could that be?"

"The maid?" Greg carried his dish over to the sink and rinsed it, and put it in the dishwasher. "The maids have keys to all the rooms, although I can't think of what sort of motive they would have."

"I can't either. But maybe one of the maids saw something. It's worth a try."

Greg lowered his eyebrows. "Be careful. Please."

• • •

The morning breeze was cool when Monica headed toward the farm kitchen, but the clear blue skies and climbing sun promised warmer weather later in the day. Nancy arrived shortly after she did, bustling in with a folder tucked under her arm.

"You have to see these pictures." She tossed the folder on the table. "They've given me so many ideas for your baby shower."

Monica thought of her conversation with Gina and felt a sinking sensation in the pit of her stomach. Maybe she could persuade Nancy or Gina to hold a party for the baby's first birthday instead? Somehow, she doubted that would fly.

"Sit." Her mother patted the table. "I want to show you these."

Mick wandered over, drying his hands on a towel. "What is a baby shower? It rains babies?" he said with a laugh. "We don't have those in Greece."

Monica was glad when Nancy jumped in to explain it.

"Friends gather for a party and bring gifts for the baby. Sometimes it's only women friends of the expectant mother but sometimes fathers are invited as well."

Mick nodded his head. "When a mother gives birth in Greece, she does not leave the house for forty days. During that time friends and family visit and bring gifts. Some gifts are meant to ward off the evil eye. No gifts are given until the baby is born. It is bad luck."

By now, Janice had wandered over to see what was going on. She nudged Nancy.

"See? I told you. No gifts until after the birth or there will be bad luck."

Nancy sighed and opened the folder. She fanned out a number of pictures cut from magazines and pointed at one of them.

"This doughnut wall is adorable, isn't it?"

Before Monica could answer, she'd selected another photo.

"And this *Great Gatsby*–themed shower is very unique."

All the decorations were in black and gold and the cake was in the shape of a top hat.

Had her mother lost her mind? Monica wondered. She really needed to tell her about Gina's offer to throw the shower at her new home but she couldn't bear to burst her bubble. At least not at the moment.

Nancy continued to flip through the pictures she'd collected. "I know," she said so suddenly Monica jumped.

"What?" What could be worse than a *Great Gatsby*–themed shower? Monica wondered.

Nancy smiled triumphantly. "How about a Winter Wonderland theme?"

"But Mother! It's the middle of July."

"All right then, but what about this French countryside theme then? We could set up tables by the cranberry bogs. And Mick can do a cake for us." She smiled at Mick. "Would you mind?"

"I would be honored."

Nancy gathered the pictures together and put them back in the folder.

"What do you think?" She looked at Monica expectantly.

Monica had to clear her throat three times before finding her voice.

"Why don't you surprise me?" she said weakly. "I love surprises."

Chapter 7

"The baby's doing fine," Monica's doctor said as she slid off the table. "It should be here any day now, but first babies are often late, so don't be disappointed if you sail past your due date and nothing happens."

Monica mumbled something in reply. She wasn't really paying attention. Her mind was occupied with thoughts of Violet Cargill's murder. She really wanted to find out if any of the maids at the inn had seen someone sneak into Sherry's room.

She decided she would stop at the inn on her way back to the farm. She finished dressing, waved goodbye to the receptionist and headed to her car. Her fingers were crossed that Dawn would be behind the reception desk.

• • •

The rattle of dishes and cutlery drifted from the open dining room door along with various aromas as Monica entered the lobby. Monica peeked in. Almost all the tables were full.

She breathed a sigh of relief when she saw Dawn was manning the front desk. Her face looked pinched and Monica hoped she wasn't still worrying about having been interviewed by the police.

"Hey," Dawn said as Monica approached.

"Good morning." Monica glanced at her watch. "I guess I should say good afternoon."

"How are you feeling?"

"Fine. Enormous and clumsy though."

"It'll soon be over," Dawn said. "And then you'll feel tired all the time with middle-of-the-night feedings. Be sure to nap when the baby naps."

"I'll keep that in mind," Monica said. She felt a twinge of worry. How was she going to balance taking care of a baby and overseeing the bakery and farm store?

"I don't suppose you came by just to see me," Dawn said. "What can I do for you?"

"I'm wondering if I could speak to your maids?"

Dawn's eyebrows shot up. "I suppose so. Is this part of the investigation?"

"I'm not really investigating," Monica said, feeling her face flush. "I'm only gathering a few facts."

Dawn tapped some keys on her computer. "Macy should be doing the second floor."

Monica thanked Dawn and made her way to the elevator. The doors opened and she pushed the button for the second floor. The elevator stopped with a jolt and the doors opened. She glanced down the hall and saw that the maid's cart was parked outside a room at the end.

The maid was making up the bed when Monica knocked on the partially open door.

"Hello," she called and Macy jumped.

"Can I help you?" Her large blue eyes dominated her small face.

"I'm wondering if you can help me. Do you do room 202?"

"Yes," Macy said. She sounded hesitant and looked as if she wanted to run away. "I hope nothing is wrong."

Monica smiled reassuringly. "Not at all. I just wanted to ask you something. Do you remember seeing any strangers going in or out of that room on July second, third or fourth?"

"That's Mr. and Mrs. Cargill, right? The tall woman with the red hair and the huge diamond ring?" Macy blushed as if she'd given something away.

"Yes."

"I think it was on the Monday. That was the third, right? I saw a man leaving the room."

"Do you remember what he looked like? Could it have been her husband?"

Macy shook her head. "No. He was much younger and had blond hair. He had a small tattoo of a sailboat on his arm. Here." She pointed to her own arm.

Aston? Monica thought. He was young and blond and she thought she'd noticed some sort of tattoo on his arm when he'd reached for his drink and his sleeve had ridden up.

"Do you remember anything else?"

Macy frowned. "I do remember that I was waiting to do their room but the *Do Not Disturb* sign had been hanging on the door all morning." She made a face. "I had to do the third floor and then come back down here to finish up."

"You didn't see anyone going into the room? Not the young man with the tattoo?"

"No. He must have already been in the Cargills' room when I arrived." Her face brightened. "But you could check with LouAnn. She might have seen someone. She does the turndown service. I'm taking courses at the community college in the evenings so I only work part-time. I'm studying to be a paralegal." She blushed.

"Do you know what time LouAnn will be here?"

"She comes on at six o'clock."

Monica thanked Macy and walked down the hall toward the elevator. She would definitely check with LouAnn later. The odds were good that Sherry and Ray would have been out of their room at dinner, making it the perfect time for someone to sneak in and grab the vial of sumatriptan. Hopefully LouAnn saw them and could tell her who they were.

Meanwhile, she found it quite intriguing that Aston was seen leaving Sherry's room. Was the visit perfectly innocent? If so, then why hang up the *Do Not Disturb* sign? If they were having an affair, and Monica suspected they were, did it have anything to do with Violet's death?

• • •

Monica was about to start her car when she noticed a text pop up on her phone. It was from Greg suggesting she join him at the site of their new home. The framing was complete and the house was beginning to take shape.

It was hot in the car with the sun streaming through the windshield. Monica cranked up the air-conditioning and aimed the vents at her face.

The lot where they were building their house wasn't far—halfway between downtown Cranberry Cove and Greg's store and Sassamanash Farm. It was a good-sized piece of property with a stand of trees bordering it on one side and a small pond in back of it.

A number of cars were pulled up in front of the house along with a trailer and there was a porta-potty on what would eventually become the front lawn.

As Monica got out of her car, Hercule came running over to her, trailing his leash behind him with Greg trotting to try to catch up.

"He gets so excited when he sees you," he said, panting a bit. "I thought I'd bring him along to see his new house."

Monica glanced toward the trees and the open field in the distance.

"He's going to love it here. And I think we will, too."

Monica stood for a moment looking at the framework for their house. She felt a chill go down her spine. It was really happening. She adored her cottage at the farm—she and Greg and Hercule and Mittens were all very comfortable—but this felt like a fresh start, a new chapter. Together, she and Greg would make the house their own.

The house looked like a skeleton—its bones in place but minus its skin. She picked out the front door, the windows on the second floor, counting to the one that would be the baby's.

"Come on," Greg took her hand. "Let's take a look inside. I feel like I should carry you over the threshold," he said with a chuckle as they approached the entrance.

Monica laughed. "That would be some feat. I feel like I weigh a thousand pounds."

Hercule trailed after them, the leash slack in Greg's hand.

The interior smelled of freshly cut wood and sawdust motes danced in the air, made visible by the sunlight streaming in.

The foreman greeted them, his hard hat pushed back on his head and a red line running across his forehead.

"Come to take a look around?" He smiled, revealing a gap between his two front teeth. "Be careful," he said, looking at Monica. "Don't trip and hurt yourself," he called after them as they began to explore.

Greg stood in one of the rooms and spread his arms wide. "This will be the family room and over there"—he pointed behind him—"will be the kitchen."

Monica's breath caught in her throat. It was going to be magnificent to have so much space.

They walked through the rest of the first floor, pausing to imagine the finished product. A skeletal set of steps led to the upper level.

"Careful," Greg said. "There's no railing." He led her up them, his hand firmly on her elbow guiding her.

"This must be the master bedroom," Greg said, peering into one of the rooms.

"And this is the baby's room." Monica stepped inside. She pictured a crib, their baby sleeping peacefully inside. All of a sudden, she was impatient for their son or daughter to arrive. It felt as if it was taking forever.

They checked out the guest room and then carefully made their way back down the stairs.

Hercule began pulling Greg toward the door. "I think he wants to go out."

Monica followed them outside and around to the back of the house, where there was a small pond. The ground sloped down to the woods bordering the property.

Monica watched as a dragonfly landed on the surface of the pond, its wings iridescent in the sunlight.

Monica turned to Greg. "We should get some fish for the pond. Maybe some koi?"

The foreman had wandered over to join them. He had half a ham sandwich in his hand.

"If you're going to do that, you'll need a pump for the pond." He pointed his sandwich toward the edge of the pond. "See that algae? You need to get rid of it if you want to raise fish."

Greg frowned. "A pump? How do we do that?"

"I know a guy who can take care of that for you," the foreman said, swallowing a bite of his sandwich. "I'll give him a call and arrange it for you."

Hercule was becoming impatient. Monica shaded her eyes with her hand and watched as Hercule pulled Greg toward the woods in the distance. Hercule must have seen something—a squirrel or a rabbit. He pulled so hard Greg lost his grip on the leash and Hercule dashed into the woods.

Greg began to call for the dog as Monica headed in his direction.

Together, they wove their way through the trees.

"There he is," Monica said, pointing ahead of them. "He's digging. He must have found something."

"At least it's not a skunk like the last time he escaped," Greg said.

"What is it, boy? What have you found?" Monica said as she stood by the gully where Hercule was digging.

Hercule paid no attention to her but kept digging, sending clods of dirt and leaves behind him.

While Greg grabbed the end of Hercule's leash, Monica stepped closer and peered at his discovery.

And then she began to scream.

Chapter 8

"What is it?" Greg said immediately, his face gone a pasty white. "Are you okay?"

Monica nodded. She couldn't talk—she simply pointed at the spot where Hercule had been digging.

Greg got down on his knees. "They're bones," he said, his voice cracking slightly. "And while I'm no expert, these look like human bones to me."

Monica had finally found her voice but it came out thin and raspy. "We need to call the police."

Greg got to his feet and brushed the dirt from his trousers.

Having heard the scream, the foreman and several of his crew were rushing over to Monica and Greg.

"Whoa," the foreman said, stopping short when he saw what Hercule had uncovered. He took off his hard hat and tucked it under his arm.

His men stood in the background, forming a semicircle around him, gawping at the pile of bones. The foreman turned, gave them a look and they scattered like billiard balls, their hands stuffed in their pockets. One of them pulled out a pack of cigarettes and paused briefly to light one.

"I will get the police," Greg said, pulling out his cell phone. Moments later, he ended the call. "They're on their way." He glanced at the foreman, his brow furrowed. "Is there somewhere my wife can sit down and get out of the sun?"

"Sure. Come on." He gestured at Monica.

She followed him back toward the house. She was perfectly fine— she wanted to be at the scene when the police arrived—but when Greg got that determined look on his face, she knew it was useless to argue. She couldn't wait until after the baby was born when people would hopefully stop handling her with kid gloves.

"Mind your step," the foreman said as he led her through what would be the front door.

He flipped over an empty crate. "Have a seat. It's not very comfortable, but it's the best I can do."

"Thanks," Monica said as she brushed some dust off the crate and sat down. "My husband is sometimes a bit overprotective."

The foreman grinned. "I can't say I blame him. A lady in your condition needs to be taken care of."

Monica bit back a retort. She was hardly suffering from a condition. That made it sound as if she had a disease—like tuberculosis or leprosy. It was hardly the eighteen-hundreds.

Monica tapped her foot. She craned her neck to look between the studs. She didn't want to miss the police when they arrived.

As it turned out, the police heralded their arrival with wailing sirens and flashing red and blue lights.

Monica got up as two patrol cars skidded to a stop in front of the house. She began walking toward the woods as the officers got out of their cars and headed in the same direction.

For a moment they stood and stared at the collection of bones. The short one with the red face scratched the back of his neck and shook his head.

"Detective Stevens is on the way," he said, sounding like a drowning man who had just spotted the Coast Guard headed toward him.

They stood around, shifting from one foot to the other, until a car came down the road and pulled up in back of the patrol cars. Monica could almost hear them breathe a sigh of relief.

Stevens got out of her car and stood for a moment surveying the scene. She was wearing black cotton slacks and a blue short-sleeved blouse. Her blond hair, cut into a bob, was tucked behind her ears.

There was a sheen of perspiration on her forehead when she reached them.

She stared at the bones. "What's going on?" She looked from Monica to Greg and then back again.

Monica explained about Hercule digging up the bones.

Stevens squatted down and examined them. "How deeply were they buried?" she said over her shoulder.

"Not very deep," Monica said. "Hercule had only been scratching at the spot for a few minutes."

"I wonder why they've not been uncovered before," Stevens said as she stood up with a grunt. "You'd think someone would have disturbed them long before now." She looked around. "I guess there was no reason for anyone to be here. These woods are too shallow for hunting and don't lead anywhere. Nothing to interest hikers either."

She exhaled loudly. "Maybe forensics can provide us with some clues. Maybe those aren't even human bones. Fingers crossed." She held up her hand.

She cocked her head at the patrolmen. "Better get the scene taped off. I'll get forensics out as soon as possible."

She looked at Monica. "No need for you to stay. I know how much your feet can hurt at the end of pregnancy."

It was true. Monica's feet were beginning to throb.

Greg linked his arm through hers. "Come on. Let's get you home."

Monica was about to protest that she was fine, but in reality she was hot and her back ached and the thought of being somewhere cool, where she could put her feet up, was very tantalizing.

Wilma was waiting at the door of Book 'Em like an eager puppy when Monica and Greg returned.

"Come in and cool off," Greg said as he opened the door for Monica.

Wilma immediately began to give Greg a blow-by-blow description of all the customers that had been in the store in his absence. Monica smiled to herself when she noted the pained smile on Greg's face. Sometimes he was too kind for his own good.

"And I still haven't found that first edition of the Margery Allingham that's missing."

Greg looked extremely relieved when a customer approached the counter and Wilma scurried off to help.

"She is a model employee," Greg said with a wry smile.

"I'm going upstairs to see Kit," Monica said. "And to get a cold drink."

The café was buzzing with customers. A fellow with long hair and a beard sat at a table in the back alternately nibbling on a cranberry muffin and pecking on his laptop. Several people had books open in front of them and many were nursing cold drinks, condensation dribbling down the sides.

Kit looked slightly harried as he carried a tray of drinks to a group seated in the corner. Steam rose from the cups and wreathed his face.

Monica found an empty table and sat down. She sighed, slipped off her right shoe and began to rub the arch of her foot. She swore that before this pregnancy was over, her feet were going to be entirely flat.

Kit appeared at the table and dropped into the empty chair

opposite.

"What can I get you, dear? Something cold? You look like you're about to expire from this heat."

Monica could imagine. Her dark hair tended to curl wildly in the humidity and high temperatures always made her face look flushed.

Kit groaned and smacked his forehead with his palm. Monica looked at him in alarm.

"What's wrong?"

"I almost forgot. She's coming to visit this week. It's her birthday and I haven't gotten her a thing."

She? Her? Monica was confused. Kit and Sean were a couple so who was this mysterious she?

"Who is she?"

Kit widened his eyes. "She. She who must be obeyed in all things. Mrs. Tanner. My mother." He gulped. "And I don't even have a present for her yet and there's no time to shop." He waved a hand indicating the crowded café. "I can't leave Sunshine all by herself to cope," he said as the waitress breezed past with a tray of drinks.

"What sort of present do you want to buy for your mother?" Monica felt around for her shoe and slipped her foot into it.

"It doesn't have to be anything fancy. Mrs. Tanner does love those Droste chocolates they sell at Gumdrops."

"They do some lovely gift boxes," Monica said, easing out of her other shoe. "I could pick one up for you and drop it off."

"Would you?" Kit clasped his hands together in delight. "That would be splendid. Mrs. Tanner would really like that." He frowned. "If you don't mind. You have enough on your plate as it is." He patted Monica's hand.

"No problem at all."

Kit jumped to his feet. "Let me bring you a nice cold lemonade and a cranberry scone to sustain you."

• • •

Monica nearly gasped when she left Book 'Em and stepped out onto the sidewalk. The heat hit her like an anvil and she immediately felt perspiration running down her back. She passed the Cranberry Cove Diner and a blast of cold air carrying the scent of hot oil and sizzling meat followed a customer out the door.

Tempest was in the window of Twilight rearranging the display. She waved as Monica went by, the batwing sleeves of her purple cotton tunic flapping around her arms.

A bell jangled when Monica pushed open the door to Gumdrops. It was an old-fashioned candy store right down to the matching pink-and-white gingham shirtwaist dresses the identical twin VanVelsen sisters were wearing that looked as if they belonged in a nineteen-sixties time capsule.

One wall was lined with clear glass cannisters filled with an assortment of brightly colored candy — the kind that used to be known as penny candy before inflation raised the prices.

A gravity-defying tower of Droste pastilles in their angular tubes were stacked on the counter and boxes and tins of Edith Peppermints were proudly displayed on a table.

"Monica, dear, so lovely to see you." Gerda VanVelsen stepped out from behind the counter and took Monica's hands in hers. "How are you feeling?"

"Impatient."

Gerda, and Hennie, who had come out of the stockroom, both laughed.

"No doubt," Hennie said. "I'm sure you're anxious to hold your little one at long last." She eyed Monica's stomach. "Must be any day now?"

"Yes," Monica said. She hadn't told anyone her exact due date in case the baby was late and she was really glad she hadn't.

"Will your house be ready in time?" Gerda said, clasping her hands together.

Monica felt herself stiffen as the image of the bones Hercule had dug up flashed through her mind.

"Is everything okay, dear. Did something happen?"

Monica hesitated. Should she tell Hennie and Gerda what had happened?

"I can't say, I'm afraid. Not yet anyway."

"We wouldn't want to pry, dear." Gerda touched Monica's arm. Hennie shot a look at her, a frustrated expression on her face, but didn't say anything.

"No, of course not," Hennie said, her lips clamped into a thin line.

"The house is coming along," Monica said quickly, hoping to divert the sisters' attention. "It won't be ready in time for the baby, but we've fixed up the spare room at the cottage as a nursery."

"I'm glad that land is finally going to be used." Gerda fiddled with the top button on her dress. "It's been vacant too long."

Hennie nodded. "It originally belonged to old Mr. VanVliet. He had a small farm where he grew corn and garden vegetables like cucumbers, squash and sugar beets. When his wife died, he let it all go to weed."

"He eventually went into a nursing home," Gerda said. "Poor thing had a nasty fall and could no longer live on his own. He sold the land to a developer. They tore down the farmhouse. It wouldn't have sold — it needed too much work."

Hennie made a sour face. "We were afraid they were going to build some huge condo complex there. What an eyesore that would have been."

Gerda puckered her lips. "I can only imagine what Grandmother VanVelsen would have thought of that!"

"Fortunately, the developer went bankrupt and sold the land off."

"To your Greg." Gerda beamed. She got a dreamy look in her eye. "I remember we used to skate on that pond that's behind your new house. And Mother would have hot chocolate waiting for us when we got back."

"Our fingers and toes would be nearly frozen stiff," Hennie said with a shiver. Her face clouded over. "I remember reading in the paper that there was some sort of tragedy associated with that pond."

"Oh?" Hopefully the property wasn't cursed, Monica thought. Not that she believed in that sort of thing, although no doubt Janice did.

"I remember mother snatched the paper away from me — said I was too young to be reading about things like that."

"Do you remember anything at all about it?"

"I'm afraid not. Do you, Gerda?"

She shook her head. "I never saw the article. Mother must have disposed of the paper."

That was certainly curious, Monica thought as she left Gumdrops to brave the heat again, a box of Droste chocolates tucked under her arm. She'd have to see if she could find anything on it. She knew the library had copies of the *Chronicle* on microfiche. She just hoped the archive went back that far.

Chapter 9

It was Friday night and groups of people were passing through the lobby of the Cranberry Cove Inn, their voices creating a cacophony of sound. Some were headed to the cocktail lounge and some to the dining room. Noise spilled from the open door of the restaurant, snatches of conversation along with the usual rattling of cutlery as busboys dumped used plates into plastic tubs to be sent to the kitchen to be washed.

Greg had headed out to an estate sale—a family was selling their late mother's collection of golden age mystery novels and he hoped to find a gem or two worth purchasing. He frequently went to estate sales but often came home empty-handed, relatives having mistaken a collection of perfectly ordinary books—second and third editions at that—for something of value.

Monica glanced at her watch. Nearly six o'clock. Hopefully, LouAnn would be prompt and already on the job. She lingered in the lobby for a few minutes assuming LouAnn would have to first collect her supplies before heading to the rooms to turn down the beds. When the minute hand on her watch clicked over to ten past the hour, she took the elevator to the second floor.

It was quiet in the hall, the only sounds a few muffled voices coming from behind the closed doors. The maid's cart was outside a room at the end of the hall. The thick carpeting stifled the sound of her footsteps as Monica made her way toward it. She peeked in the open door. The maid was plumping the bed pillows and straightening the sheets. A stack of fresh white towels was piled on one of the slipper chairs ready to replace the wet ones heaped on the floor. Monica tapped on the doorjamb and the maid jumped and put a hand to her heart.

"I'm sorry. I didn't mean to scare you," Monica said.

The woman was wearing a cranberry-colored uniform that had *LouAnn Brown* embroidered above the pocket. She reminded Monica of an upside-down broom with her stick-thin body and short, frizzy blond hair.

"Can I help you? Do you need something?" LouAnn said as she caught her breath.

"I'm sorry to bother you," Monica said. "I'm a friend of the Cargills.

Violet Cargill died here on Tuesday night. I'm following up on some leads."

LouAnn threw her shoulders back and straightened the collar on her uniform.

"I've never been interviewed by the police before. I know they talked to Pat—she works down in the kitchen—and it's all she could talk about. As if she was someone important." She lifted her chin. "She won't be pleased to know she's not the only one. She'll find out she's not all that special after all."

Monica knew she should disabuse LouAnn of the notion that she was with the police, but it wasn't her fault LouAnn was jumping to the wrong conclusion. Besides, where was the harm in it? Any information she got she would immediately pass on to Stevens.

"Were you working on Tuesday night, the fourth?"

"Yes. I'm usually off on Thursday and Friday unless they need me to cover for someone. Some of these young people can't be counted on. Not like us old-timers."

Monica half expected LouAnn to pat herself on the back.

"So, you were here working on the fourth? When Violet Cargill became ill?"

LouAnn's mouth turned down and she shook her head. "Yes, and I missed the whole thing. Jack, he's one of the waiters, told me all about it. He said the ambulance came and everything. Just my luck I was stuck up here on the second floor."

Monica cleared her throat. "How about the day before, the third of July? Were you working then?"

"Sure. That was a Monday. I'm always here on Mondays promptly at six o'clock."

"Did you notice anything unusual here on the second floor? Mr. and Mrs. Cargill are in room 202, I believe?"

"Yes. I noticed them particularly because Mrs. Cargill asked that I leave them an extra towel. She said she needed it for her hair."

"Did you happen to see anyone go into Mrs. Cargill's room? Other than Mr. or Mrs. Cargill, that is."

LouAnn scowled and pressed a finger to her forehead. "I don't think so. But they could have while I was making up someone's room."

Monica was beginning to feel frustrated. Was she wasting her time when she should be getting ready for the baby? She still needed to buy newborn undershirts. Never mind that it was July and hot as the oven in the farm kitchen. According to her mother, the baby would need undershirts.

She decided to try a different tack. "Did you notice anything peculiar? Anything out of the ordinary?"

LouAnn's expression made it look as if thinking was actually painful. Her forehead was furrowed, her eyebrows lowered and her lips pursed.

"Now that you mention it, there was something peculiar." A door opened and she paused and looked down the hall. She lowered her voice and tilted her head toward Monica's.

"I had just parked my cart outside room 202 when the alarm on my watch went off." She held up her wrist so Monica could see. "It was time for me to take my pills." She pointed down the hall. "There's a sink in the utility closet at the end of the hall, so I went to get some water."

"Had you opened the door to room 202?"

"Yes. I had already put a stack of clean towels on the bed when my watch pinged. I knew if I didn't take my pill right then and there, I would forget. They're for my arthritis." LouAnn gave a deep sigh. "I know I shouldn't have, but I did leave the door cracked. I was only gone maybe a minute or so. It wouldn't have even been that long if the pill hadn't gotten stuck in my throat and I had to swallow the whole glass of water to get it down." LouAnn fiddled with the gold cross hanging from a chain around her neck. She looked slightly stricken. "I didn't think it would do any harm."

"Of course not," Monica said soothingly. "Did you notice anything that suggested someone might have been in the room? Anything out of order?"

"Let me think." LouAnn's face took on that same painful expression as she looked down at her feet. "There was something, but I didn't pay all that much attention to it. Matter of fact, I forgot all about it as soon as I finished doing up the room."

"Yes?"

"I think someone had been in the room."

Maybe this wasn't such a waste of time after all, Monica thought.

"What made you think someone had been in the Cargills' room?"

"My cart had been moved. I always park it in the same spot so that it's blocking the open door. It discourages people from peeking into the room. You wouldn't believe how nosy some of our guests can be. But when I came back after taking my pill, it had been shoved away from the door."

"Anything else?"

LouAnn closed her eyes as if picturing the scene. "The drawer in the nightstand was partially open. It wasn't like that when I went in with the clean towels."

"But you didn't see anyone?"

LouAnn pursed her lips. "I didn't exactly see anyone." She fiddled with her necklace again.

"Not exactly?"

"No. But the door to the stairs was closing. They put a door damper on it. That's what Jorge, he's the inn's maintenance man, told me it was called. It makes the door close real slow and keeps it from slamming. That wouldn't do at all. Most people take the stairs — too impatient to wait for the elevator. I have to admit, it is rather old and slow." LouAnn took a breath. "Anyway, we couldn't have the door slamming every time someone used the stairs. What a ruckus that would make."

It wasn't much, Monica thought. But it certainly sounded as if someone had gone into the room and was bolting down the stairs when LouAnn came back from taking her pill. Of course, there could be a perfectly innocent explanation — it could have been Sherry Cargill or her husband Ray. Or, it could have been the killer sneaking in to steal the vial of Sherry's migraine medication.

Which was it?

• • •

Monica was walking through the lobby when she noticed Ray Cargill sitting on one of the sofas. He was talking to a man Monica didn't recognize. She didn't think it was someone from Cranberry Cove. Most of the offices in Cranberry Cove had at least opted for business casual and he was dressed in an expensive-looking suit and was wearing a silk tie that even she could tell wasn't from Men's Warehouse but probably from some fancy store in Chicago.

Ray pulled a handkerchief from his pocket and swiped it across his forehead. What was making him sweat? Monica wondered. He appeared agitated—his movements were jerky, and despite his tan, his face had a pasty look to it.

There was a sofa table behind the couch with a large vase of flowers on it. Monica casually walked toward it. She looked around but no one seemed to be paying attention to her. Dawn wasn't behind the reception desk and the young man who was engrossed in doing something on the computer.

She looked around again and then ducked behind the floral arrangement. She was quite sure she wasn't visible thanks to the massive blossoms—orange garden lilies punctuated with white astilbe. In case someone wondered why she was lingering there, she pulled out her phone and pretended to scroll through her texts.

The lobby was now quiet. It was well past check-in time and the groups that had been gathered in the lobby earlier had dispersed to either the cocktail lounge or the restaurant, which made it possible for her to hear most of Ray's and his companion's conversation.

At one point her nose began to tickle and she was afraid she was going to sneeze and give away her position and she was relieved when the feeling passed.

A woman with three towheaded children walked into the lobby. They'd obviously been to the beach. The two boys and a girl were carrying brightly colored inner tubes and the woman had several damp towels thrown over her shoulder.

One of the boys began yelling that he was thirsty and the other two joined in. Monica felt a prickle of irritation. She was missing parts of Ray's conversation. The mother quickly shepherded them toward the elevator and luckily, she was able to hear again.

It sounded as if Ray was in some sort of financial trouble. She didn't understand most of what they were talking about but that part was clear enough—something about cryptocurrency and prices rising and falling. It sounded as if he owed the other man money and he was demanding to be paid. That would explain Ray's nervousness. As Ray was stuttering and making excuses, the sweat on his brow began to drip down the side of his face and under his collar.

Monica thought of Sherry and her expensive tastes. Her diamond engagement ring alone must have cost a fortune. Monica doubted she was the sort who would rise to the occasion and learn to scrimp and save. The vision of Sherry clipping coupons or hunting for bargains was laughable. Would she leave Ray if his money ran out?

For Ray's sake, it looked as if Violet's death had come at just the right time.

Chapter 10

"What's that delicious smell?" Monica asked when she got home. She glanced at the stove but there were no pots or pans bubbling away and the oven was off.

"Takeout." Greg held up a sizeable paper bag. "Compliments of Mickey and the Pepper Pot. I guess Gina told him she didn't think you were eating enough so he insisted I bring something home for dinner."

"What is it?" Monica realized she was starving.

Greg opened the bag and took out several containers. Hercule's nose began to twitch and he wagged his tail, obviously hoping for a treat.

Greg picked up one of the containers. A sticky note was attached to the lid that read *cedar-planked walleye*. He pried the lid off another container and held it out toward Monica. "Salad." He read the label on the final one. "Maple-glazed sweet potatoes."

"It all sounds heavenly," Monica said as she began to get plates and cutlery from the cupboards. "But Mickey really doesn't have to worry. I haven't been eating just for two—I swear I've been eating for a whole army."

After she'd set the table and they were sitting down to eat, Monica asked, "How did you make out at the estate sale?"

Greg wrinkled his nose. "It was a bit of a bust. A lot of dusty old paperbacks that practically disintegrated when I touched them, but I did score a box of Lee Child books so it wasn't a complete waste of time." Greg dabbed at his mouth with his napkin. "If you're up for it, I thought we might check out the carnival. I gather it's also part county fair with 4H exhibits so that should be fun."

"Sure. I just have to call Detective Stevens."

Greg raised his eyebrows. "Oh?"

Monica waved a hand in the air. "Nothing important but something she might want to know."

Monica dialed Stevens's number, but instead of getting an answer the call went to voicemail. She left a message asking Stevens to call her, helped Greg with the dishes, and after they'd given Hercule a quick walk, headed out.

The air coming in the car window was cooler than it had been earlier and Monica was glad she'd brought a sweatshirt with her for later in the evening. The tinny sound of canned music from the rides and the various bells and whistles from the games reached them even before the carnival came into view.

The Volvo's tires crunched over the gravel as Greg pulled into the parking lot and began to search for a spot. Someone was pulling out of the front row and he snagged the space with a sigh of satisfaction. Monica had to admit, she was glad they wouldn't have to walk too far.

The lights flashing from the rides and games of chance were dazzling and the Ferris wheel, as shabby as it was, looked majestic silhouetted against the dusky sky.

"What should we do first?" Greg said as he purchased two tickets.

"Churros," Monica announced decisively. "I can smell them and I have a terrible craving for them."

"I thought pregnant women were supposed to crave pickles and ice cream?"

"Ha! I'm sure Janice believes that."

Greg put his arm around Monica's shoulders. "Is she still spouting those old wives' tales at you?"

"I keep waiting for her to run out but she seems to have an endless supply."

As they passed the roller coaster, they heard the clank of the wheels against the tracks as the cars climbed up the hill and the subsequent screams of the riders as it made its stomach-dropping descent.

"Here we are," Greg said, stopping in front of the churro stand, where a round-faced woman was fishing the pastries from the vat of hot oil. Her face was bright red and the tendrils of hair alongside her face were damp.

She quickly dished up fresh churros onto a paper plate and gave them to Monica as Greg handed over the money.

Monica took a deep breath inhaling the heady scent of cinnamon, sugar and hot oil. Heaven, she thought as she took a first bite.

"Aren't you going to save me some?" Greg said with a teasing smile as Monica picked up the last churro and took a bite.

"Not a chance. Get your own," she said with a grin.

"I think I'd rather have some kettle corn," Greg said, motioning toward a booth next to the whip ride, which was spinning its occupants in dizzying circles.

By now, they were nearing the barns where the animals were being kept and the odor of hay and manure competed with the smell of sugar and frying food.

A loud squawking suddenly mingled with the reedy music and the shrieks of the children. Monica jumped when a chicken ran past her feet. It was followed by the sound of thudding as a young boy thundered past, his bare feet slapping against the ground and kicking up dust.

A wry smile played around Greg's mouth. "I guess that chicken was trying to make a break for it."

Monica watched as the chicken, followed in hot pursuit by the young boy, wended its way through the crowds.

"I don't know about you," Monica said, "but I'm rooting for the chicken."

"Me, too," Greg said as he nibbled on his kettle corn. He turned to Monica. "You're looking tired. Maybe it's time to call it quits for tonight and head home?"

"Let's. I am a bit tired and we've seen most of the carnival."

They were rounding the corner near the ring toss, where a woman stood grinning as she was handed a giant stuffed unicorn from the fellow manning the booth, when Monica caught sight of someone out of the corner of her eye.

It was the woman's red hair that had attracted her attention. It reminded her of Sherry Cargill's hair. She took another look and realized it *was* Sherry Cargill. She was talking to a man—it actually looked more like they were arguing. Sherry's face was flushed with irritation and the man's face was twisted into a grimace. He looked as if he might be one of the carnival workers—he had a smudge of grease on his cheek, his jeans were nearly worn through in the knees and the bill of his NY Yankees baseball cap was slightly bent out of shape. Sherry handed him something and he quickly pocketed it.

Who was he? Monica wondered. And what relation was he to Sherry? A relative or friend? She had assumed Sherry didn't know anyone in Cranberry Cove.

It was certainly curious. She would have to ask Kelly about it.

● ● ●

Monica arrived at the farm kitchen early the next morning. Greg had already left for work—Saturday was a busy day at Book 'Em, when locals mingled with tourists to find their next read.

The Cranberry Cove Inn had placed another order for cranberry salsa and by the time Nancy, Janice and Mick had arrived, Monica had already whipped up a batch and had the jars packed in a carton and ready to go.

"Do you want me to run those over to the inn?" Nancy said, whisking off her sunglasses.

"Thanks, but I think I'll take them myself. I've been on my feet for quite a while now and I could use a break."

Nancy gave her a worried look. "You're not overdoing it, are you?"

Monica smiled. "Don't worry. I'd tell you if I was."

"Let me carry that carton for you," Mick said.

"Thank you. I would appreciate that."

"At your service, ma'am." Mick flashed her a smile.

The sun had disappeared and the skies were overcast as they headed to Monica's car. Monica looked up at the sky. The clouds looked heavy with rain. Greg would be extra busy today if the weather got worse as disappointed beachgoers flooded Book 'Em looking for something to read.

"Are you settling into Cranberry Cove okay?" Monica said as she and Mick walked side by side down the path to her cottage.

"Yes, although I am a bit homesick. I miss my brothers and sisters. Uncle Gus has done his best to make me feel at home. He even made me my favorite pastitsio." He must have noticed the puzzled look on Monica's face. "It's like the Italian lasagna only with different spices, like cinnamon and cloves." He touched his fingers to his lips and blew a chef's kiss.

"That does sound wonderful." Monica felt her stomach growl. She hadn't been that hungry for breakfast and had settled on a piece of toast and a cup of tea. It felt as if the baby was compressing her stomach, making it uncomfortable for her to eat larger meals.

"Here we are," she said as they neared the driveway of her cottage. She opened the trunk and Mick put the carton inside.

"Thank you," she said, and he waved as he trotted back to the kitchen.

Traffic was snarled along Beach Hollow Road and she crawled past the Purple Grape and Bijoux. It appeared as if everyone was headed into town at once. She was relieved when she reached the inn.

She pulled into the parking lot and was about to head to the back and the service entrance when she noticed two sawhorses arranged in a line blocking the way. Even with her windows closed, the smell of hot asphalt filled the car. Two men holding rakes were standing next to a giant pothole that had formed in the macadam.

She was turning around when someone knocked on the driver's-side window.

Kelly smiled as Monica buzzed down her window.

"Do you have time for a quick breakfast?" she said.

Monica glanced at her watch. She really should get back to the kitchen, but then her stomach growled and she decided she could spare a bit of time.

Monica parked her car and joined Kelly at the front door of the inn.

"I've already had a little something to eat, but I'm still hungry. It will have to be quick though," she said as she followed Kelly to the dining room.

The hostess smiled broadly at them as she grabbed some menus and tucked them under her arm.

"Good morning, Miss Cargill," she said.

"They probably think we're moving in," Kelly whispered to Monica. "We've been here so long already. We're just lucky the rooms were available. I have a feeling some palms were greased to make it possible."

She opened her menu and Monica did the same, quickly scanning it as she noticed the waitress headed in their direction. She appeared at their table, her pencil poised above her order pad.

"I'll have the spinach omelet," Monica said, snapping her menu closed. The vitamin C in the spinach would be good for the baby.

Kelly placed her order, the waitress nodded and disappeared in the direction of the kitchen.

"Are the police keeping you up-to-date on the search for your aunt's killer?" Monica said, unfurling her napkin and placing it in her lap.

Kelly shrugged. "Not really. They fob us off with minor details and assurances that they're doing everything they can to solve the case." She rolled her eyes. "Every day they promise we can all return home soon but I've stopped believing them."

The waitress appeared with their order and swiftly handed out the plates and a cup of coffee for Kelly.

Kelly stirred sugar into her coffee and took a sip. "I've heard you've solved a few murder cases yourself." She raised an eyebrow at Monica. "Who do you think did it?"

Monica felt her face flush. "I'm afraid I have no idea. Sherry or Ray are the obvious suspects since they both had easy access to Sherry's vial of medication, however, someone else could have snuck into the room at some point." Monica decided against telling Kelly what she'd learned from LouAnn. It might mean nothing at all.

"It's all so distressing." Kelly twisted the napkin in her lap. "Poor Beatrice is beside herself."

"I gather she's also finding Cranberry Cove a bit stifling." Monica picked up her knife.

Kelly made a face. "She's not interested in going to the beach and that's the main attraction here. She can't seem to concentrate on much of anything. All she talks about is how much she misses Violet." Kelly sighed. "That's certainly understandable."

"Edith seemed terribly upset as well." Monica fiddled with her fork. "But Beatrice said that Violet treated Edith horribly."

Kelly's eyebrows shot up. "Really? I've never noticed. Certainly, Edith's never complained."

That was odd, Monica thought. Had Violet hidden her bad behavior toward Edith or had Beatrice been lying? And if she had been lying, why?

• • •

Monica was headed back to the farm when the car in front of her slowed. Up ahead she saw two patrol cars parked horizontally across the road, their flashers going. A patrolman was standing in front of them, in the middle of the road. What was going on? Monica craned her neck and saw an ambulance up ahead along with an overturned car on the shoulder of the road. Another car, pointed in the wrong direction, was in the southbound lane. An accident, obviously.

The patrolman motioned for Monica and the car in front of her to turn around. Monica waited for the other car then pulled onto the shoulder, reversed, then put the car in drive again and headed back in the direction she'd just come from.

She thought of her grandmother Albertson, who always said there was more than one way to skin a cat. Fortunately, Monica knew of an alternate route and turned down a street that took her past a small strip mall with a party store, laundromat, a fitness studio with a *Closed* sign in the window and the Cranberry Cove Motel, a rather seedy place advertising rooms for twenty dollars a night.

Monica nearly drove up onto the curb when she noticed a bright blue Lamborghini parked in the motel driveway outside of room seventeen. Could that be Aston's car? Monica had never seen a Lamborghini in Cranberry Cove before, let alone one in that distinctive color. It had to belong to Aston. A bookie wouldn't touch the odds of there being two blue Lamborghinis on the streets of Cranberry Cove with the proverbial ten-foot pole.

Without even thinking, Monica pulled into the motel parking lot. She parked as far away from Aston's car as she could get and settled down to wait. She would give it half an hour, and if no one emerged from the room by then, she'd give up and go back to the farm.

She didn't know what she expected to learn. Maybe Aston wanted to get away from the rest of the family and had decamped to the motel for some privacy. Or, he could be meeting someone who was staying in room seventeen, although Monica couldn't imagine who that might be. The whole place suggested something clandestine and possibly even illegal.

She was concentrating so hard she nearly jumped when the door to the room opened and someone walked out. She gasped when she realized it was Sherry Cargill. This was just about the last place on earth she expected to see Sherry, who was used to much finer things than this run-down place.

Sherry turned her head in both directions before stepping away from the door. Her movements were furtive as she headed toward one of the only other cars in the parking lot.

It wasn't possible that Aston and Sherry would be at this same motel at the same time and not be with each other, so she wasn't surprised when the door to room seventeen opened again as Sherry was pulling out of the parking lot and Aston stepped out.

So, her suspicions had been correct. They were having an affair. Why else would they be holed up together in this sleazy motel?

As Monica headed back toward the farm, she thought about how this new information slotted into everything she already knew about the rest of the case. What motive did Sherry or Aston have for murdering Violet? Unless Violet had found out about their affair and had threatened to tell Ray. Who knew what sort of prenup Sherry might have signed? She could have ended up without a cent if Ray divorced her.

But what about Aston? Did this impact him in any way? He was clearly the golden child as far as Violet was concerned. He depended on his father for cash, but if Violet had threatened to tell Ray about the affair, that money would most likely have dried up.

It seemed as if both of them had a perfectly good reason for wanting Violet dead.

Chapter 11

Everyone was working hard when Monica got back to the farm kitchen. Mick was pulling tins of muffins out of the oven and there were scones, drizzled with a sugar glaze, cooling on racks.

"Nora needs some muffins," Janice said as Monica shut the door.

"I've got a batch still hot from the oven," Mick said with a flourish. "And the scones are ready to go as well."

"I'll take them down to the shop."

"Are you sure?" Nancy knitted her brows. She glanced at Monica's stomach and raised an eyebrow. "You must be due any minute now."

Monica clenched her teeth. "Yes, but not *this* minute. I'm fine. The walk will do me good. The doctor did tell me to get some light exercise."

Nancy tightened her lips and looked away.

Mick helped Monica load the cart with all the newly baked goodies. The aroma was intoxicating as the scent of sugar, cinnamon and butter wafted toward her.

"These all smell so delicious," Monica said. "I had a perfectly good breakfast but lately I've been craving sweets."

Janice's posture perked up. "You know what they say about that."

Monica was fairly certain she didn't know what they said about that.

Janice crossed her arms over her chest. "It means you're having a girl." She gave a smug smile.

"Well, we'll find out, won't we?" Monica said with a sweet smile.

So much for Janice's old wives' tales, she thought as she wheeled the cart through the door and out to the path that led to the farm store. Janice had already told her, quite confidently, that her shape indicated she was having a boy. But now her craving for sweets indicated she was having a girl. One thing she knew for sure — she wasn't expecting twins.

• • •

She was glad to be back outside. The day was mild with a slight breeze and only scattered clouds floating across the blue sky. She felt her spirits rise and she was humming when she arrived at the store.

Nora gave her a brief wave and then went back to filling a customer's bag with slices of cranberry coffee cake and cranberry walnut chocolate chunk cookies. She rang the order up and handed the bag to the woman.

"Aha, replenishments," Nora said, eyeing Monica's cart. "Let's get these sorted out."

She handed Monica a piece of glassine and together they arranged the new stock in the baskets and on the platters in the display case.

Monica noticed Nora sneaking glances at her stomach. At least Nora wouldn't be spouting any pregnancy old wives' tales—she was much too down to earth for that.

They both stood back and admired the display they'd created. The baskets were threaded with red-and-white gingham check ribbon and the platters were antiques Monica had picked up in thrift stores.

"You must be due any day now," Nora said, eyeing Monica from the corner of her eye. "If I had to do it over again, I don't think I'd have kids." Seeing Monica's shocked face, she laughed. "I'm just kidding, but I have to admit the boys are quite a handful." She blew out a puff of air. "They've been complaining that they're bored ever since their game console broke. How can they be bored in the summer? There are so many things they could be doing outside." Nora slipped behind the counter again.

"The younger one broke his arm trying to climb a tree and his older brother refuses to have anything to do with him." She sighed. "It's a constant fight."

They both looked toward the door when they heard it open. It was Detective Stevens.

She said hello to Monica then ordered a coffee and a slice of cranberry coffee cake.

"I know it's rather hot for coffee," she said as she carried her tray over to one of the small round tables at the front of the store. "But I need a jolt of caffeine to wake me up. My son has one of those summer colds. I don't know why, but a summer cold always feels even more miserable than the ones you get in the winter."

Monica made a mental note to talk to Nora about carrying iced coffee in the summer. Just plain coffee—not any of those fancy drinks with impossible names they serve in some upscale coffee shops. The Sassamanash Farm store's customers were far from fancy.

Stevens touched Monica's arm. "I'm sorry I didn't return your call. What with the sick kid and some things going on at the station, I'm afraid I forgot. I hope it wasn't too important."

Monica took the seat opposite Stevens. She explained about the conversation she'd overheard and how Ray appeared to be in financial trouble.

Stevens nodded slowly. "That's interesting. I can see how Violet's death would have benefited her son if he needed money."

Monica brushed her hair off her face. "Has there been any other movement in the Cargill case?"

"Not much. At least not anything I can share at this time. I'm sure you understand." Stevens gave Monica a smile. "But I do have some information about those bones found at the site of your new house."

"Oh?"

Stevens gulped her coffee and made a face. "Hot," she said, fanning her face. "Bodies decompose at different rates—some more slowly than others. But given a couple of years, you wouldn't find much more than a skeleton no matter what."

She took a bite of her coffee cake and brushed the crumbs off her top.

"So, it's likely the bones are at least a few years old. Unfortunately, though, it's almost impossible to tell exactly how old." She took another gulp of her coffee. "There could be an innocent explanation for the bones being buried there, but it's hard to imagine what it could be. You can't just bury someone in your backyard. At least not without zoning approval and a permit from the Health Department."

"So, the person who had a house on that land originally had buried a relative there?"

"I've got someone looking through old records to see if a permit was ever issued. As you can imagine, not many people request approval to bury someone on their property. We're also looking into cold cases—someone who disappeared and was never found. Although that's like looking for a needle in a haystack."

Stevens finished her coffee and cake, said goodbye and left. Monica was preparing to take the empty cart back to the kitchen when the door opened again and Edith walked in.

She was wearing white capri pants and had a visor shading her eyes.

"I tried your salsa at the inn last night," she said when she saw Monica, "and I had to come and sample some more of your goodies. Dawn, at the front desk, said your cookies are heavenly."

Edith continued to chatter while Nora fetched two cookies from the display case and poured out a cup of coffee.

"Has there been any word from the police about poor Violet's death?" Edith said as she carried her tray to the same table Stevens had just vacated.

Monica leaned on the back of the opposite chair. "Nothing new, I'm afraid. At least nothing they're willing to tell us."

Monica wanted to leave to get back to the kitchen but Edith continued to talk until she finally pulled the chair out and sat down.

"I don't suppose the will can be probated while the case is still going on." Edith took a bite of the cranberry oatmeal cookie and sighed. "It's going to leave me in the lurch, I'm afraid. I do hope they'll let me stay in Violet's house in the meantime." She broke off bits of cookie and nibbled them like a squirrel. "Probate can take up to a year or more. I do have an elderly cousin out East but I wouldn't want to intrude. And I can hardly afford a house or apartment myself."

She blew on her coffee. "Violet wasn't stingy but she had trouble keeping up with the times and how much things cost. She never had to worry about money — her accountant took care of her bills and her financial advisor made sure her money didn't run out. She wouldn't know the cost of a loaf of bread if her life depended on it." She giggled. "Sorry. Unfortunate turn of phrase. I've been frugal and have put money aside, but I'm afraid it wouldn't last long. Not in this economy." She rolled her eyes.

Monica didn't know what to say. "Let's hope it doesn't take all that long."

A smug look came across Edith's face. "I'm expecting a tidy sum. Violet promised me that I would be quite well off. That will certainly be something new!"

Edith leaned closer to Monica. "I know Violet made some changes to her will before she died. Mr. Bishop, her lawyer, came to see her one day and they spent quite a bit of time closeted up in the library." She wet her finger and picked up the crumbs of her cookie. "And with the antics of those two, I wouldn't be surprised if Violet cut them out of her will." She sat back in her seat with a satisfied smile. "That means there will be more to go around."

"What do you mean — the antics of those two?"

"Violet was quite distraught when she found out. I hated to see her so upset, but I felt it was my duty to let her know." Edith put a hand over her heart. "It was only because I didn't want to see her taken advantage of."

Monica was ready to scream. What was Edith talking about? Or rather, who?

Edith leaned closer again. "I'm talking about Aston and Sherry."

Monica was beginning to think she knew where this was going.

"Aston and Sherry . . . ?"

"They were having an affair," Edith whispered. "Can you imagine? It would be improper under any circumstances, but Ray's son and his own wife! No wonder it upset Violet so."

"So, Violet knew Aston and Sherry were having an affair. And you think she cut them out of her will?"

Edith bobbed her head. "Yes. Well, Aston at least. I doubt Violet would have left Sherry a dime. Besides, Ray will get the bulk of the estate and no doubt Sherry will be running all over town spending the money as fast as she can."

Monica had felt that spending time talking to Edith would be a waste of time, but it had proved to be very informative indeed. She wondered if Aston knew he was being cut out of the will? Assuming Edith was right, of course. She could imagine how angry that would make him. And how desperate. And as for Sherry, if Ray found out about the affair, he'd most likely divorce her.

It reinforced the idea that each of them had a motive for murder.

It didn't occur to her until she was on her way back to the kitchen that cutting Aston out of the will might mean more money for Edith, and that gave her a motive as well.

Chapter 12

When she walked into the farm kitchen, Monica was surprised to see everyone standing around munching on cookies with various shades of delight on their faces. They looked slightly guilty when they saw Monica and Nancy quickly wiped some crumbs off the front of her apron.

"We thought you'd gone to the hospital," Janice said. "You must be overdue by now?" She raised her eyebrows. "What you need is a spoonful of castor oil. It brings on labor. And if that doesn't work, eating some spicy food usually does the trick."

Monica sighed in exasperation. She didn't have any castor oil — would downing a spoonful of hot sauce do the trick?

Mick gave Monica a triumphant smile and waved a cookie in her direction.

"Try one," he said.

Monica frowned. "What's this?" she said as he handed it to her.

Mick looked around at the others. "It's our newest creation."

"And it's delicious," Nancy said, mumbling slightly as she took another bite.

"What is it?" Monica repeated. She examined the cookie. It was a sandwich cookie, the top and bottom pieces studded with cranberries and held together with a faintly orange cream feeling.

"It's a cranberry oatmeal sandwich cookie with an orange-scented cream filling." Mick said. He watched intently as Monica took a bite.

"Mmmm," she said, taking another nibble. "Mmmm . . . these are delicious."

Mick bowed with a flourish, an arm bent in front and back of his waist. "Our newest creation," he said proudly.

"It's . . . absolutely delicious," Monica said, reaching toward the platter for another cookie.

"I'll have another one of those, too," Janice said, putting out a hand.

For a moment, they all munched in silence.

"What do you think?" Mick said, his eyebrows raised. "Should we put these on the menu?"

"Absolutely. But before we do that, can I have another one?" Monica grinned.

"Sure. I'll get started on another batch," Mick said with a look of triumph.

• • •

"I have an idea," Greg said when he got home from Book 'Em. He gave Monica a kiss. "How about we go out to dinner tonight? We won't have too many more opportunities." His eyes twinkled.

"That's a great idea. Let me freshen up a bit."

Monica hummed a tune under her breath as she climbed the stairs to the second floor. She was going to miss their little cottage, she thought, as she peered into the nursery. But the new house was going to be wonderful and she'd get used to it soon enough. Besides, it would be quite a few more months before it was finished.

Stevens had had the patrolmen cordon off the area where Hercule had dug up the bones, but fortunately it wasn't preventing work on the house from going forward. The foreman assured her they were still on schedule.

Monica took a quick shower—she'd begun to feel like a wilted flower needing to be restored—dabbed on a tiny bit of makeup and pulled her dark curls into a loose bun. She dove into her closet and surveyed the selection. She hadn't purchased that many maternity clothes—why spend the money when she'd only be wearing them for a few short months—but her mother had insisted on buying her one good outfit, as Nancy put it, for special occasions. Monica deemed this a special occasion since there didn't seem to be any others on the horizon.

She slipped on the gauzy white dress with its empire waist and fluttery sleeves. The material floated a couple of inches above her ankles and swirled in a circle when she did an experimental twirl. She fished around in her closet, pulled out a pair of strappy gold sandals and slipped them on.

Greg gave a long, low whistle when she descended the stairs. "You look magnificent," he said, his eyes glowing.

Monica felt her face turn pink as she picked up her purse, and they went out the door with Greg's arm around her waist.

• • •

The evening was still warm and Monica was relieved when they entered the air-conditioned atmosphere of the Pepper Pot. All the seats at the bar were taken and the bartender was hurrying from one end of the bar to the other, refilling drinks and making new ones. Several couples were seated on a padded bench against the wall in front of the hostess station. One gray-haired gentleman scowled and looked at his watch.

"We may have to wait," Greg said, nodding his head toward the people lined up on the bench.

"I don't mind. Gina said Mickey has put the grilled chicken satay on the menu for the summer and I'm dying for some."

"Sounds good. But let me know if you get too tired."

Greg was about to shepherd Monica to an empty spot on the bench when they noticed Kelly heading toward them.

"We have room at our table if you don't want to wait," she said.

Greg and Monica looked at each other and shrugged.

"Sure, why not," Monica said as they followed Kelly to a table for eight. Ray, Sherry, Beatrice and Edith were seated and four of the chairs were unoccupied.

Everyone stared rather pointedly at Monica's stomach. She was beginning to feel like a slacker for not having had the baby yet but you couldn't hurry Mother Nature.

Ray signaled for the waitress, who hurried over to their table. "What will you have?" he said to Monica and Greg.

They placed their orders and the waitress scurried away like an insect fleeing the light.

Ray took a long pull on his drink—a martini by the look of it. Monica noticed there was a green olive sandwiched between two ice cubes.

He put the glass down then immediately picked it up again and began shaking it so that the ice cubes rattled against the side of the glass. Monica wondered what was making him so nervous, although maybe it was normal under the circumstances.

The atmosphere of the Pepper Pot was comfortably casual and Ray was wearing a sport coat with an open-necked shirt and khaki trousers. Sherry, on the other hand, had opted for a more glamorous look in a white-and-gold-striped crochet dress that hugged her curves and had a low V-neckline and thin straps that offered a good view of her abundant cleavage. Diamond chandelier earrings that winked in the light dangled from her ears.

Beatrice was staring at Sherry with a look of disdain. She herself was dressed in a conservative navy blue dress with a white cardigan around her shoulders. The animosity between the two was almost palpable.

Their waitress had just taken their dinner order when Gina appeared at their table.

"Welcome to the Pepper Pot," she said, leaning on the back of the empty chair. "I'm grabbing a quick bite with Mickey." She jerked a thumb toward the back of the restaurant. "I'd ask you to join us but it's only a table for two."

"That's okay." Monica smiled and introduced her stepmother to the rest of the party.

"You look very glamorous tonight," Greg said, accepting a kiss on the cheek. "Like a movie star."

"Ha!" Gina snorted. "Have you seen what the stars wear these days? Ripped jeans, sports bras and sneakers. Unless they're going out for the evening, then it's a dress with barely enough material to make a scarf and sheer enough to see through." She shook her head. "That's too far even for me."

She eyed Sherry and Sherry eyed her back. Monica could tell the two women were assessing each other. Sherry was a good deal younger than Gina, although Gina did everything in her power to maintain her looks from Botox to hair extensions to juice cleanses.

Sherry seemed to recognize Gina as a somewhat kindred spirit. "Where's a good place to go shopping round here?" she said.

Gina rolled her eyes. "There's Danielle's Boutique and that's about it, I'm afraid. But they do have some nice things."

"I'll have to check it out." Sherry turned to Ray. "I'll need some money," she said.

"Money!" Ray exploded. "I've given you money. What have you done with it? For once I haven't seen you bringing in armloads of shopping bags, so where did it go? Did you flush it down the toilet?"

His face had turned a mottled red and his fists were clenched.

Sherry stared at him for a moment then pushed her chair back and ran from the table.

"Where is she going?" Ray demanded, the color in his face slowly receding. He scowled.

"Probably the ladies' room," Monica said. "I'll go check on her."

"I'll come with you." Kelly began to get up.

"I don't know what's gotten into Sherry," Kelly said as they wended their way between the tables. "She's been so nervous lately." She pushed open the door to the ladies' room. "I suppose Aunt Violet's murder could have put her on edge."

Sherry was leaning over the sink when they entered. She whirled around at the sound of the door opening. Her eyes were red and she had a scrunched-up tissue pressed to her mouth.

Kelly immediately went over to her. "What's the matter? What's got you so upset?"

"Nothing," Sherry insisted. "Everything." And she burst into tears.

Kelly put an arm around her and slowly Sherry's sobs subsided.

"Ray is being so mean," Sherry said. "I don't know what I'll do if he doesn't give me some more money."

"What do you need it for?" Kelly said. "Maybe whatever it is can wait until he's calmed down?"

Sherry shook her head vigorously. "It won't. It can't."

"What is it then?" Kelly said, slightly more firmly.

"I can't tell you. I can't tell anyone." Sherry yanked open the door. "I just can't."

• • •

On Sunday morning Monica stretched luxuriously and pulled the covers up to her chin. She wouldn't be working in the farm kitchen so she could stay in bed as long as she liked. She might have stayed in bed all morning if it hadn't been for the scent of frying bacon coming from the kitchen. She tried to ignore it but her stomach rumbled and she realized she was starving.

She dressed quickly and made her way downstairs. Greg had set the table and put out a platter of bacon and fried eggs. Thick slices of golden toast sat on another plate and opposite it was the Sunday paper.

"I thought you might be hungry," Greg said with a twinkle in his eye. He put his arms around Monica. "Can't forget you're eating for two."

"I know. But the doctor keeps reminding me it only takes an extra three hundred calories a day to nourish the baby. Anything over that goes on me and stays there."

Monica eased herself onto a chair. Hercule sat next to her, his tail swishing back and forth across the floor.

"I should give you a job sweeping the floor," Monica said as she pulled out her chair and sat down. Hercule stared at her with soulful eyes and Monica couldn't resist—she slipped him a tiny bit of bacon.

They divided up the newspaper—Greg handed Monica the first section and she offered him the sports page.

The headline above the fold on the right side of the front page caught her eye and she began to read. After several minutes she put down the paper and looked at Greg.

"*The Cranberry Cove Chronicle* is going online," she said, pointing to the article. "All of the Cargill Papers are."

"That's quite an undertaking, I should imagine," Greg said, peering over the top of the sports section. "Not to mention an expensive one."

If the conversation Monica had overheard between Ray and that other man was anything to go by, Ray was having financial trouble. Was this why he had borrowed money from that fellow? And had Violet's death been more than fortuitous?

"How about taking a walk on the beach?" Greg said when they'd finished clearing up the dishes. He glanced out the open window. "It's a beautiful day."

"Sure. Maybe a walk will get things going." Monica pointed to her stomach. "It's better than trying Janice's suggestion of castor oil."

Greg made a face. "I should think so."

Monica headed upstairs, conscious of the fact that she was moving slower and slower each day. How long before she caved in and tried one of Janice's remedies? She grabbed a tube of sunscreen from the bathroom and her straw hat from the closet before hurrying back to the kitchen.

Greg had Hercule leashed up when she got back downstairs. The dog was clearly raring to go. He loved the beach—chasing after seagulls and digging in the sand. Looking for buried treasure? Monica wondered. It reminded her of the bones found near their new house, and despite the warmth of the day, she shivered. She wondered if the police were any further along in identifying them. Was it possible they'd never know?

Hercule hung his head out the open car window, his pink tongue lolling, as they made their way down Beach Hollow Road to a small parking lot near a set of stairs leading to the beach. Greg let Hercule out of the car. He had to struggle to restrain him—he couldn't wait to start exploring.

Monica put on her hat. The sun was climbing higher in the sky and was glancing off the hood of the car in a starburst of light. She held the railing tightly as she made her way down the steps, which were covered in sand and had wet footprints here and there.

Colorful towels were spread out all over the beach. The umbrellas staked in the sand fluttered in the breeze and there was an occasional burst of music from someone's phone.

Greg held her hand as they walked down to the water's edge, Hercule dashing in and out of the waves rolling toward shore. Monica dug her toes into the warm sand. It felt heavenly and she found herself relaxing.

They were rounding the bend, where cliffs towered over the beach, when Monica spied a familiar-looking figure in the distance. As they drew closer, she realized it was Dawn. They stopped when they saw each other.

Hercule tugged Greg's arm and he stumbled in the sand. "I'd better let you chat while I go on with Hercule. He's getting impatient."

Dawn was wearing a navy blue baseball cap that shaded her face, a pair of capris and a loose top. Monica noticed her nose was beginning to turn red.

"Enjoying your day off?" Monica said.

Dawn looked like she was about to cry. She turned her head and looked out over the lake.

"Not really."

"What's wrong?"

"The police came to see me again." She sniffed. "I'm afraid they suspect me of . . . of killing Violet." She groaned. "It was that Detective Stevens. She asked all sorts of questions." She bit her lip. "I told her I never left my post behind the desk the night Violet was killed. She was nice enough but I could tell she didn't believe me." Dawn hung her head. "The problem is that isn't exactly true."

"Oh?"

Dawn didn't say anything. She toed the sand with the tip of her sneaker while Monica waited.

"I went upstairs to make a quick phone call. The people in room 204 had checked out so I ducked in there."

"You couldn't make the call in the break room?"

Dawn shook her head. "No. I didn't want anyone to hear. I made a huge mistake and I was trying to fix it."

"It can't be that bad." Monica couldn't imagine Dawn doing anything truly terrible.

"You know how we're saving money for Ryan's college tuition. I thought maybe I could help. I saw they were advertising for salespeople for this new product—some kind of vitamin that's supposed to help you lose weight. I realized too late it was one of those pyramid marketing schemes where the only people who make money are those at the very top."

Dawn grabbed at her cap, which the wind was threatening to send flying.

"I called them to tell them I'd changed my mind and that I wanted my money back but they said it was too late. They'd already shipped out the product. Bart is going to be so upset that I've lost that money."

"You didn't lose all of it, did you?"

"No, but we can't afford to lose any." Her mouth turned down. "Just my luck LouAnn caught sight of me as I was about to head back down the stairs and went and told the police."

"Can't you tell them the truth about the phone call?"

Dawn shook her head. "I can't take a chance on Bart hearing about it. I'm going to find a way to put the money back before he notices." She grabbed Monica's arm. "You've got to help me. You've got to find out who really killed Violet."

Chapter 13

Monica and Greg made another pass up and down the beach until Monica began to get tired. It was getting hotter and the breeze that had been stirring the waves had died to almost nothing. The lake had become calm, the placid water luring kids further in and even enticing parents and grandparents to join them.

Hercule appeared to have had enough as well—his tongue was lolling out the side of his mouth and his ears were drooping. As soon as they reached the car, Greg retrieved Hercule's bowl from the trunk and emptied a bottle of water into it. He handed a bottle to Monica and took one for himself.

They brushed the sand off their feet and Greg spread a towel on the seats, which were hot from the sun. They pulled out of the parking lot, Hercule now settled in the backseat, and turned onto Beach Hollow Road.

They were passing the carnival, and even with the air conditioner running, Monica smelled the heady aroma of funnel cakes, popcorn and frying corn dogs. She turned to Greg. "I could really go for a funnel cake right now. Can you smell them?" She took a deep breath.

Greg chuckled. "And who was it that said they thought pregnancy cravings were an old wives' tale?"

"Guilty as charged." Monica gave a small smile. "There were a lot of things I didn't believe before I got pregnant, but I still can't swallow Janice's superstitions."

"Those are a bit of a bridge too far," Greg said as he swung into the parking lot.

Hercule's nose was twitching with excitement even before they opened the door. He bounded out of the car and immediately stopped to sniff the air. Monica could swear he was actually salivating.

"We'll have to find Hercule some sort of treat while we're here. All these smells are too tantalizing for him."

"Aren't you going to share some of your funnel cakes with him?" Greg said in a teasing voice.

Monica pretended to be affronted. "Absolutely not." Then on a more serious note, "I don't think they'd be good for him."

By now they had reached the entrance to the carnival. Greg kept

Hercule on a tight leash and he was remarkably well-behaved considering everything that was going on around him, never mind the scent of all the carnival food.

They found the funnel cake stand and Greg ordered two servings.

"I can't eat all that," Monica said when he handed her the paper trays.

Greg just raised an eyebrow and watched as Monica devoured every last bite and even licked the powdered sugar off her fingers.

"I know the doctor said I should be careful not to gain too much weight," Monica said as she crumpled up her napkin and threw everything into a nearby trash can, "but I don't suppose it's going to make all that much difference now that I'm in the home stretch."

As they were walking, they passed a booth with a ring toss game.

"Land a ring on one of the pegs and win a stuffed animal," the barker called to them, motioning toward an entire zoo of toy animals hanging from the ceiling.

"Let's see if I can win one for the baby," Greg said, reaching into his back pocket for his wallet. "I'll go get some tickets."

He and Hercule went off at a trot while Monica settled on a nearby bench. She looked around at the crowd—children with sticky faces, tired or exasperated mothers, teenagers walking arm in arm. The sun was warm and she was nearly dozing by the time Greg returned with the tickets.

He grinned. "Let's see what I can do."

The fellow took Greg's ticket and handed him a stack of rings.

Monica held Hercule's leash while Greg tossed the first ring. It was wide of the mark.

He glanced over his shoulder at Monica. "I'll get this one, don't worry."

Once again, the ring failed to land over the peg. Within a few minutes, Greg had exhausted all his chances.

"Want to give it a try?" he said to Monica as he pulled another ticket from his pocket.

"Sure." Monica handed him Hercule's leash and took the brightly colored rings.

She had no luck with the first few and soon had only one left. She blew on it. "For good luck," she joked.

She squinted at the pegs, pretended to loosen up her arm and then finally tossed the ring. It flew through the air and landed right over one of the pegs.

"Brava." Greg clapped.

The fellow behind the booth, whose bored expression hadn't changed during the entire exchange, jerked his head toward the hanging stuffed animals.

"Whaddya want?" he said, collecting the discarded rings and putting them over his arm.

Monica surveyed the choices and finally settled on the three-foot-tall giraffe. He handed it to her and she tucked it under her arm.

The man smiled for the first time. "Is that for the baby?"

Greg put his arm around her shoulders and squeezed. "Yes. I can't wait to tell him or her that their mother won it for them." He turned to Monica. "Want to try another game?"

Monica looked down at her feet, which were beginning to swell in the heat.

"I think that's enough."

"Good luck," the fellow called after them as they turned to leave.

They made their way to the exit. "Why don't you wait here," Greg motioned toward a wooden bench, "and I'll go get the car."

Monica glanced at her feet again. "I'm not going to say no."

She watched as Greg wended his way through the parked cars toward their Volvo.

As she waited, a couple approached the gate. The man leaned against the fence and the woman faced him. Monica did a double take. It was Sherry and the man Monica had seen her meeting with before. He was wearing the same beat-up baseball cap and worn jeans.

They didn't say much, but Sherry pulled an envelope from her purse and handed it to him. The man glanced inside, riffled through the contents, smiled and tucked it into his pocket.

What was it? Monica couldn't tell for sure, but it looked like the envelope was filled with cash.

Who was this man and why on earth would Sherry be giving him money?

Did she owe him? Or was it blackmail?

• • •

Monica was reading with her feet up and a glass of iced tea by her side when someone knocked on the back door. She swung her feet off the ottoman and made her way to the kitchen. It must be Gina or Jeff, she thought. Anyone else would have gone around to the front.

Hercule was already by the door, wagging his tail furiously, although that didn't indicate anything. He greeted friend and foe the same way.

Monica pushed aside the curtain, peered through the window then opened the door.

"Jeff!" she said, but then when she saw his face, "what's wrong?" She motioned for him to come in.

Jeff immediately slumped into a kitchen chair. His mouth was turned down and his whole face appeared to sag. He swiped a hand across his forehead, which was glistening with sweat.

"Would you like some iced tea?" Monica said, one hand on the refrigerator door.

"Sure. Maybe it will perk me up."

"I'm afraid it's decaf so I doubt it."

Jeff's tone was lugubrious. Had someone died? Monica wondered.

"Never mind. It's not going to solve my problem anyway."

Monica got out the pitcher of iced tea, took a glass from the cupboard and filled it. She handed it to Jeff.

He grunted, reached for it and took a big gulp.

Monica pulled out a chair and sat down. "Are you going to tell me what's wrong?"

Jeff grunted again and Monica momentarily wondered if he'd lost the power of speech.

"It's Mick," Jeff finally said.

Monica felt her heart thump against her ribs. Was Mick quitting? Had something happened to him? How would she manage without his help?

"Is Mick okay?" Her heart was still beating hard and she sounded slightly breathless.

"He's fine. That's the problem."

Monica raised her eyebrows. "What's the problem then?"

"I think Lauren's in love with him," Jeff said so softly Monica could hardly hear him.

Monica frowned. "What makes you think that?"

Jeff shrugged. "She talks about him all the time—how good-looking he is. It's obvious she's attracted to him. I'm worried."

Monica rolled her eyes. "We all find him attractive because he is. But that doesn't mean I'm going to leave Greg and run off with him or Nancy is going to take leave of her senses and go after him herself."

She couldn't even imagine Janice doing such a thing. The very thought made her laugh.

Jeff grunted.

"There's something else, isn't there?" Monica said.

Jeff's shoulders slumped. "Why would Lauren want to marry a man with only one good arm while Mick has two functioning ones?" He pounded his fist on the table. "There's so much I can't do. It's frustrating for me and I imagine it's frustrating to her too."

"It didn't stop Lauren from falling in love with you in the first place."

"Yeah, but that was before. Before Mick came along with his two strong arms and killer smile."

"This may come as a surprise to you," Monica said. A smile hovered around her lips. "But women enjoy looking at attractive men just like men enjoy looking at attractive women. You can admire a beautiful painting or sculpture but it doesn't mean you want to possess it."

Jeff's head jerked up. "You don't think it means anything?"

"I don't," Monica said as firmly as possible.

Jeff's face brightened a bit and he sat up straighter.

"Do you have a date for the wedding?" Monica said to change the subject.

"We know we want to hold it in September when it's cooler and the cranberries are growing. We plan to set up a tent by the bogs—nothing too fancy, more of a casual vibe. Maybe some long wooden tables with greenery running down the center instead of vases stuffed with flowers." He scowled. "I was at this wedding once where the floral arrangements were so huge, I couldn't see the person across the table from me."

Jeff ran a finger down the rivulets of condensation on his glass. "We want to get married in the morning and have a late-morning reception. I guess you'd call it a brunch."

"It all sounds as if it will be lovely. Let me know if there's anything I can do."

Jeff smiled for the first time. "We'll need plenty of cranberry goodies to serve."

"Consider it done."

Jeff's face fell again. "Of course, that's all assuming Lauren doesn't run off with Mick in the meantime."

"Lauren wouldn't do that and I don't think Mick would either."

Jeff scratched his head. "I don't know. I was talking to Mauricio—you remember Mauricio, don't you? He helps with the farm sometimes."

Monica nodded.

"He's become friends with Mick and he told me that Mick really wants to be granted citizenship. And you know one way to do that, don't you?"

"No."

"Marry an American citizen. And Lauren is an American citizen. Besides, she seems to be attracted to him so that's half the battle, right?"

"Wrong," Monica said with strong emphasis on the word. "I think you're worrying for no reason."

Jeff hung his head while Monica drummed her fingers on the table. Finally, he looked up.

"You really think that? That I'm worrying for nothing?"

"I do."

• • •

Monica overslept on Monday morning.

"Why didn't you wake me?" she said to Greg when she'd dressed and gone downstairs to the kitchen.

"You need your rest." Greg cupped Monica's cheek. "Besides, I called Nancy and she said everything was under control as far as the baking was concerned."

"I *was* tired," Monica admitted as she grabbed a bowl, a packet of instant oatmeal and a handful of dried cranberries.

By the time she'd finished her cereal, Greg had left for Book 'Em.

Monica checked the animals' water bowls. Mittens's bowl wasn't completely full so she carried it to the sink and turned on the tap. The cat wove in and out between her legs meowing loudly. Monica couldn't tell if she was protesting the fact that the level in her water bowl had been allowed to get below the halfway mark or whether she was meowing in thanks.

Greg had already walked Hercule so Monica spent a minute or two scratching his stomach—something he thoroughly enjoyed—before saying goodbye.

Storm clouds were gathering on the horizon as she walked to the farm kitchen and the first fat drops of rain spattered on the path in front of her as she reached the door. She ducked inside quickly, glad to have made it before the skies opened.

Nancy pounced as soon as Monica walked in.

"We have to set a date for your baby shower or you will be having it after the baby is born. Do you want to do a gender reveal at the same time? I saw the cleverest thing on the internet—you fill a pinata with either blue or pink gumballs and let each guest have a swing at it. What do you think?"

Monica opened her mouth but she was speechless. It took her a minute to find her voice.

"But Greg and I chose not to know the gender before the birth so that's impossible."

Nancy looked crestfallen but then she perked up. "So, the decorations will have to be gender-neutral. I can work with that." She looked at Monica and tilted her head. "What's a good day for you?"

Monica felt panic squeezing her like a vise. "I don't know. I'll have to ask Greg . . ."

She pulled on her apron and got busy mixing dough. All along a mantra was playing in her head—*what was she going to tell Gina, what was she going to tell Gina?*

She was going to have to break the news to Gina at some point and the sooner the better. Heaven knows, she might have already ordered the party decorations. Perhaps she'd run into town at lunchtime and talk to her.

The morning went by quickly. Mick whistled under his breath as he baked sheet after sheet of oatmeal cookies for his new invention—the cranberry oatmeal sandwich cookie.

"I think these are going to be a hit," he announced as he pulled the last baking sheet from the oven.

His sleeves were rolled up, revealing his powerful forearms. It reminded Monica of her conversation with Jeff. She could understand why it had made him conscious of his own limitations.

"I think so, too," Monica said. "We'll give them a trial run this afternoon. Nora is excited about it."

By lunchtime, Monica's energy was beginning to flag. Nancy had noticed it, too.

"Why don't you take some time off," she said. "Go home and put your feet up for a bit."

"I think I might do just that," Monica said, untying her apron and hanging it on the hook.

No need to tell her mother that she was heading into town instead.

Chapter 14

Monica was lost in thought as she drove into town and almost didn't notice a car stranded on the side of the road. A woman was standing next to it, large sunglasses obscuring most of her face, but Monica recognized her as Sherry Cargill. She was obviously having some sort of car trouble.

Monica pulled over just ahead of Sherry's disabled car and got out. The sun was intense and she felt the heat of it through the fabric of her dress. It wouldn't take too long to get sunburned on a day like this.

She made her way over to where Sherry was leaning against her car, holding her cell phone in her hand and giving it a venomous look.

"Is everything okay?" Monica said.

"Obviously not," Sherry snapped. "I've got a flat tire." She pointed toward the rear left wheel. It was completely deflated and looked like a blob of rubber puddled on the macadam. "And my cell phone is dead, would you believe it? Of all the luck. I wanted to call Ray to come get me and to deal with the car." She kicked the nearest wheel. "I told him I needed a new set of tires but he was too busy to do anything about it."

She pulled off her sunglasses and wiped a finger under her eyes and down the side of her nose. Her face was already glistening with perspiration, threatening to ruin her artfully applied makeup.

The sun was right in her face and Monica noticed for the first time that she had one brown eye and one green eye. She'd had a classmate in high school with eyes like that. She'd rather proudly announced that it was called heterochromia.

Monica began to reach into her purse. "I can call a towing service for you."

Sherry scowled. "If you wouldn't mind."

"Not at all." Monica dialed the local towing company. She'd had enough trouble with her ancient Focus that she knew the number by heart.

She spoke briefly and then hung up. "They'll be here in half an hour."

Sherry's look turned sullen. "You mean I have to wait here for thirty minutes? What am I supposed to do in the meantime?"

"I can keep you company if you like."

"Would you? My nerves are on edge and I don't want to be alone. We can wait in my car." She looked up at the sky. "I've just had a facial and I need to stay out of the sun."

Monica went around to the passenger side and opened the door. Sherry's low-slung sports car made it difficult for her to maneuver into the seat. She finally managed it but it left her breathless for a moment.

Sherry slipped behind the wheel and flipped the rearview mirror so she could see herself.

"That esthetician was too rough and now my face is all red. I hope it goes back to normal by tonight or Ray will be upset. He's entertaining some business associates and wants me to look my best, but I'm going to claim a headache and have dinner in my room. I'm too upset to listen to all that talk right now. I don't understand the half of it but Ray expects me to look interested anyway."

"What's upsetting you?" Monica said. She'd thought Sherry looked distressed and it wasn't just because of her flat tire.

"I can't let Ray find out." A tear slid down Sherry's cheek and she brushed it away impatiently. "He'd divorce me in a heartbeat. And now that he's going to inherit all that money, eligible women will be coming out of the woodwork." She tried to stifle a sob. "He's already made comments about how old I'm getting."

Monica was glad Greg took her the way she was in her jeans and sweatshirts, her hair in a tangle and her face in need of a dusting of powder.

"And now this." Sherry put her hands over her face. "The police sniffing around asking questions, sticking their nose into my business. The past is ancient history. Can't they leave it alone?" She hiccupped.

Stevens must have done a bit of digging and come up with interesting information from Sherry's past. Did it implicate her in Violet's murder in some way?

Monica was dying to know.

• • •

Gina wasn't behind the counter of Making Scents when Monica got there. Penny, her occasional assistant, was manning the shop. She was a complete contrast to Gina with her short gray hair, flowered T-shirt and wraparound skirt.

"Is Gina out?" Monica said, one hand still on the doorknob.

"Yes. She ran down to the diner to get something to eat. She should be back soon."

"Thanks," Monica said as she closed the door.

She peeked in the window of Book 'Em and almost went in but decided she would do that after she'd talked with Gina. She didn't want to miss her. She hoped Gina wouldn't make a fuss when she gave her the news. Perhaps being in a public place would restrain her. Unfortunately, there wasn't much of anything that was capable of restraining Gina when she was on a roll.

The noon whistle blew as Monica walked into the diner. A line had already formed at the take-out counter and the booths were full.

Gus, who was flipping burgers and frying potatoes so fast his movements were a blur, nodded when he saw Monica and flapped a hand in her direction.

That was what passed for an effusive greeting as far as Gus was concerned — saved for residents of Cranberry Cove alone. Monica was highly honored to finally be included in that category. Tourists, on the other hand, got no acknowledgment whatsoever.

Monica scanned the dining room and finally spotted Gina in a booth at the back near the restrooms. Monica slipped into the seat opposite her.

"Penny told me you were here."

"I was going to call you when I got back to the shop." Gina nibbled a bit of her club sandwich. "We must be on the same wavelength or something."

Monica was hungry but she was almost too nervous to eat anything. It had taken her years to build her relationship with Gina and she didn't want to do anything to hurt it. She felt a stab of irritation. Weren't pregnant women supposed to be afforded peace and calm while they carried their baby?

"Did you want to see me about something?" Gina said.

Monica cleared her throat. "Actually, yes, I did. It's about the baby shower."

Gina put down her sandwich. "Yes, we have to plan that asap or you'll end up bringing the baby to the shower."

"That's what my mother said." Monica fiddled with the salt shaker. "She wants to be the one to throw me a baby shower."

Gina's eyes widened and her mouth formed an O. Then she took a breath that sounded like a bull about to charge, lowered her eyebrows and said, "Well!" She pushed her plate away. "Of all the . . . that woman has never forgiven me for taking your father away from her. She should thank me. I did her a favor—look how he turned out. A serial philanderer."

Gina was silent for a moment and then her face suddenly cleared.

"Well, she is your mother so there's that." She brightened. "We can hold the Christening party at my house! It will give me more time to plan."

Monica didn't realize she had been holding her breath until she let it out in a whoosh.

"Don't you want something to eat?"

Monica shook her head. "I'll get some takeout. I really should be getting back."

• • •

Now that that was over, Monica realized she was starving. She'd been too nervous before to even think about food. She decided she'd treat herself to one of the diner's Reuben sandwiches.

The line at the take-out counter had shortened a bit and she was grateful. She took her place and put a hand to her back. She really hoped it wasn't too much longer.

She felt someone get on line behind her and briefly turned around. It was a man with close-cropped hair, a grizzled face and a scar over one eyebrow. Monica realized it was the fellow who ran the ring toss booth at the carnival.

He obviously recognized Monica because he smiled. "Aren't you the gal who won the giraffe?" He glanced at her stomach. "For your baby?"

"Yes. I thought you looked familiar." Monica cocked her toward the menu hanging on the wall. "Don't you get something to eat at the carnival?" Monica said, thinking of the funnel cakes.

The man grimaced. "I'm sick of carnival food. There's only so many corn dogs you can eat."

"You should try the chili. It's the diner's specialty."

The man scanned the menu. "I don't see it listed."

"It isn't. Only Cranberry Cove natives know about it."

"It's that good, huh?"

"Yup." Monica nodded. "Not too spicy—just right."

"Sounds good." He glanced at his watch and then at the line ahead of him. "I'm going to be late. The boss isn't going to be happy."

"Is that the man I saw walking around the carnival? The one wearing the NY Yankees baseball cap?"

"Yeah, that's Chuck. Chuck Krauss. He manages the whole shebang—setup, running the carnival, breaking it down for the trip to the next location."

"I've seen him talking to Sherry. She's the woman with red hair. I know her." *Sort of,* Monica added to herself.

"Yeah, her. She's his wife. Or his ex-wife actually."

Grease was already leaking through the paper bag in Monica's hands as she left the diner, surrounded by the tantalizing aroma of the Reuben sandwich she'd ordered. She couldn't wait to bite into it. Gus had winked at her and had promised to add extra meat and cheese *for the growing baby,* as he put it.

But she had gotten more than just a Reuben sandwich, she thought—she'd learned that Sherry had an ex-husband. And it certainly looked as if he was blackmailing her. Why else would she have been handing over an envelope full of cash? And it wasn't the first time, either. She remembered their first visit to the carnival. She had seen Sherry giving her ex an envelope then as well. Was he blackmailing her about her affair with Aston or was it something else?

Monica had nearly reached her car when she heard someone call her name. She turned around to see Beatrice waving at her. She stopped and waited for her to catch up.

Her face was red and she had a shopping bag dangling from her arm.

"I can't believe I'm still here," she said, panting slightly. She swiped a hand across her forehead. "Is there any news? I got the impression you were friends with that detective. What was her name?"

"Stevens. And we're not friends. Our paths have crossed a couple of times, that's all."

"Has she told you anything? She won't tell us a thing."

"I think that's normal in most investigations."

"It's most infuriating. I can't imagine what's becoming of my poor garden in this heat. I don't have the luxury of a full-time gardener like Violet." Her chin quivered. "I do want to speak to Stevens though. I have something to tell her." Her face clouded. "Although maybe I shouldn't. Maybe it has nothing to do with Violet's murder. I don't want to get her in trouble."

"What is it?" Monica said. "I'm sure the police would want any information you can give them. They'll be able to decide if the information is relevant or not."

Beatrice took a deep breath. "It's something I saw." Her shopping bag rustled as she gestured with her arm. She lowered her voice, although they were alone on the sidewalk. "It was Edith. I saw Sherry giving her money."

Monica didn't know what she'd expected but it certainly wasn't that.

"Maybe Sherry was paying her back for something?"

Beatrice began to shake her head even before Monica finished talking.

"It was a wad of bills. I think Edith is blackmailing Sherry. If you'd seen the look on Sherry's face." She threw her hands in the air. "On the other hand, Edith was positively gloating."

Poor Sherry, Monica thought as she said goodbye to Beatrice and opened her car door. It looked as if she was being blackmailed by Edith as well and that Edith and her ex were bleeding her dry.

She remembered the incident at the Pepper Pot. Ray had wondered where the money he was giving her was going. If it wasn't for shopping—and he didn't seem to think it was—blackmail made the most sense.

And Ray was treading on thin ice financially. Sherry must have been desperate for Violet's inheritance to refill the family coffers.

• • •

Monica had just arrived back at the farm kitchen and was tying on her apron when Lauren opened the door. She brought with her the scent of warm summer air and sunshine.

"Hello," she called out in a cheerful voice. She had her usual battered tote bag hitched on her shoulder, which she put down on the table. She beckoned for Monica.

"I can't wait to show you these." Her face was glowing. She tucked her blond hair behind her ears. "I've taken some new pictures of the farm to put up on Instagram." She pulled out her phone. She tapped an icon and opened up a page of photographs. "What do you think?" she said breathlessly, holding the phone out to Monica.

Monica scrolled through the snaps. In one, Lauren had captured the sun breaking through the clouds and slanting across one of the bogs and in another, the sun was setting over one of the bogs making it look as if it was on fire. The newest photograph was a close-up of Mick's new invention—cranberry oatmeal sandwich cookies.

Lauren looked over Monica's shoulder and tapped the picture. "You're going to be swamped with orders for these."

"I hope we can keep up! But that's a good problem to have." Monica glanced at the phone again. "These are all wonderful," Monica said. "You're so talented."

Lauren's face turned a becoming pink. "Thank you. I got a cute selfie of me and Jeff that you have to see."

She searched through the pages of pictures then tapped one of them, enlarging it so it filled the screen. She gave the phone back to Monica.

"It's darling," Monica said. Jeff and Lauren were both smiling broadly, their faces relaxed, their eyes sparkling and on each other.

"We thought we'd use that for our save the date cards," Lauren said, tapping the screen with her index finger.

"It's perfect." Monica took a second look at the photograph. "Is this the bar at the Cranberry Cove Inn?"

"Yes. Jeff and I went for drinks a couple of nights ago. We spent time over cocktails nailing down some of the details for our wedding."

Monica looked at the photograph again. She put two fingers on the screen and spread them apart, enlarging the photo. There was someone in the background—a tall, blond-haired man in a polo shirt with a popped collar. It looked like Aston. It was definitely Aston, Monica decided when she looked again. He was sitting at the bar, his hand wrapped around a sweating glass of beer.

"Do you remember seeing this fellow?" Monica pointed to Aston.

Lauren rolled her eyes. "I certainly do. He created quite a scene. He was there with a friend. At least, I assume they were friends—they were sitting on bar stools next to each other and there were plenty of others that were empty." Lauren tucked her phone back in her tote bag. "They were talking when all of a sudden, the other fellow began yelling about something. I couldn't understand what he was saying at first. Something about his drink. The gist of it seemed to be that he thought the blond guy—"

"Aston. Aston Cargill. I recognized him. He's my friend Kelly's cousin."

"He seemed to think Aston had put something in his drink when he went to the men's room." Lauren frowned. "It's usually women who have to worry about that." She blew out a breath. "Aston denied it, but the other fellow said his beer had a funny taste to it. He said something about Aston wanting to keep him out of the race. The regatta, I guess he meant?" She picked up her tote bag. "One thing led to another and before we knew it, fists were flying. The bartender had to separate them." She shook her head. "It's not the sort of thing you expect to happen at the Cranberry Cove Inn. It's usually something of a snooze there. We wanted to go to the Pepper Pot but it was too crowded. People were three deep at the bar."

"What happened then? Did the bartender throw them out?"

Monica had an image of the bartender—a fellow whose muscles bulged through his shirt sleeves—picking them both up by the scruff and heaving them out the door.

"No. The fellow who claimed his drink had been tampered with stomped out. Aston stayed behind. To nurse his wounds, I guess. Literally and figuratively." She laughed.

The word *regatta* had stirred something in Monica's brain.

"When was this? Do you remember?"

"Sure. It was the night before the Fourth of July." Lauren gave a self-deprecating laugh. "That would make it the third of July, I guess. Duh."

Monica's breath quickened. LouAnn at the inn had said she thought someone had been in Sherry's room that night and that it had been around six o'clock.

"What time was this? Do you remember?"

Lauren raised an eyebrow but didn't ask why Monica wanted to know and Monica was grateful because she didn't know what she'd say.

"The two men — Aston and that fellow — were already there drinking when Jeff and I arrived. I had the impression those weren't their first beers either. Jeff had knocked off early that afternoon so we'd gotten there about four o'clock."

"What time did you leave?"

Lauren lowered her brows. "Around eight o'clock, I think? We got caught up in looking at wedding invitations and ended up ordering a couple of appetizers. The inn does great Buffalo wings and the nachos aren't bad either."

"So everything's on track for the wedding?"

Lauren gave her a quizzical look. "Sure."

"That's great." Obviously, Jeff hadn't said anything to Lauren about Mick. "Had Aston already left by then?"

"No. He was still there having another beer and nursing his knuckles while we paid the tab."

Well, that was that, Monica thought. It wasn't an iron-clad alibi — nothing that would necessarily convince the police of Aston's innocence or that would hold up in a court of law in front of a determined prosecutor — but it strongly suggested he was at the bar the entire evening that Sherry's medication went missing.

• • •

By the time Monica had finished at the farm kitchen and had said goodbye to Nancy, Janice and Mick, she was bushed. She couldn't wait to get back to her cottage, grab a cold drink and put up her feet, which had been swelling all afternoon.

Hercule greeted her with his usual enthusiasm. Mittens was relaxing in the sunbeam coming through the kitchen window and shining across the floor and merely swished her tail in acknowledgment.

"Come on, buddy." Monica leashed up Hercule and went out the door.

It was still hot but not oppressive and there was a cool breeze that made it very pleasant. Monica breathed in the sweet scent of the honeysuckle vines climbing up the trellis along the walkway to her back door.

Hercule was more interested in the scent of the small animals that scurried around the area and his nose was pressed firmly to the ground.

Even though she'd been on her feet most of the day, walking actually felt good and she let Hercule follow his nose down the path.

Her mind was whirling as she walked along. She told herself to relax and forget about Violet's murder for a while, but that was as successful as telling someone not to think about pink elephants.

She'd been going around and around in her head trying to figure out why Sherry was giving her ex-husband money. Did she owe it to him? It hadn't looked like someone simply paying a debt. It had looked . . . clandestine . . . which spoke to blackmail. But what did Chuck possibly have to hold over her?

Finally, she lured Hercule back inside with the promise of a treat. Mittens was still stretched out in the sun and barely looked up.

An idea came to her as she was retrieving the pitcher of lemonade from the refrigerator. She poured herself a glass and carried it and her laptop into the living room.

She sighed as she sank onto the sofa and put her feet up on the ottoman. Heaven. It was sheer heaven. She took a sip of her lemonade as she powered up her laptop.

First, she looked up Sherry's ex's name—Chuck Krauss. A long list of entries popped up and she began reading them one by one. Several were obituaries but Krauss was obviously still very much alive. There were links to profiles on LinkedIn, listings on company boards and websites listing cell phone numbers. There was even a Chuck Krauss running for county property appraiser.

She was about to give up when she came upon a link to the police blotter of a small town in Ohio. A Chuck Krauss had been arrested for drunk and disorderly conduct and that Chuck Krauss was the operator of a carnival. It had to be Sherry's ex. It was too much of a coincidence.

But that wasn't going to get her any nearer to the answer to the question she'd been repeatedly asking herself. She was about to shut down her computer when she had an idea.

It required a bit of searching, but she finally found a link to the correct site—the public divorce records. What if Sherry and Chuck had never formally divorced? That would invalidate Sherry's marriage to Ray. If that was the case, what was to stop Ray from ditching Sherry just when he was on the cusp of inheriting Violet's fortune? Surely it would invalidate any prenuptial agreement the two of them might have signed. Sherry would be left empty-handed. She'd have to fend for herself and it certainly looked as if she'd gotten used to the life of luxury that Ray provided.

Monica pulled up the records and begin searching through the alphabetized list. No Chuck Krausses were listed. Nor were there any Charles Krausses.

It wasn't definitive proof but it seemed quite likely that Chuck and Sherry had never dissolved their marriage. And that would certainly give Chuck ammunition for blackmail.

She refilled her glass of lemonade. Besides, she'd already suspected that Violet knew about Sherry's affair and had threatened to tell Ray about it.

If Ray threw Sherry out, and Monica suspected he would do exactly that—every time she saw them together, they were arguing or Ray was criticizing Sherry—her money would dry up and so would her payments to Chuck. Had she told Chuck about it and he'd been the one to switch the vials of medicine so that instead of being injected with insulin, Violet had been injected with the drug that had eventually killed her?

Chapter 15

Monica had stretched out on the sofa and was dozing when Greg arrived home half an hour later. She sensed his presence before she even opened her eyes.

"You looked so peaceful. I didn't mean to disturb you." Greg bent and kissed Monica's cheek.

Monica sat up and rubbed her eyes. "That's okay. I'm getting hungry actually. I should start dinner."

"I'll do it. What do you have in mind?"

"I've been craving pasta alfredo," Monica said sheepishly.

Greg smiled. "Pasta alfredo it is."

Monica struggled off the couch and took her empty glass of lemonade out to the kitchen.

"Did you ever find that missing book?" she said as she rinsed out the glass and put it in the dishwasher.

"The Margery Allingham? *Crime at Black Dudley*. It was the first in her Albert Campion series. I paid a pretty penny for it." He shook his head. "No, I haven't found it. Wilma combed the shelves and so did I. I've come to the conclusion someone stole it."

"How dreadful!"

Greg filled a pot with water and put it on the stove to boil. "I know I'm pretty lax with security but it's never happened before. I don't want customers to feel like their every move is being scrutinized. That's not the atmosphere I'm trying to create. I want customers to be able to relax and browse in peace. They're more likely to buy something that way."

Greg began grating Parmesan cheese for the sauce.

"I ran into Danielle Dubois, who owns that fancy boutique next to Tempest's shop, and she said she had caught someone trying to shoplift a sweater a couple of days ago. She also told me that the VanVelsens had noticed that a large tin of fancy chocolates had gone missing. This has never been a problem before in Cranberry Cove. At least not that I know of." He stroked his chin. "I guess I'd better be more vigilant in the future."

"Perhaps a glass case for your first editions?"

"That's not a bad idea." Greg slapped his thighs. "Now, how about that pasta?"

Monica tore lettuce for a salad while Greg prepared the pasta. He insisted she sit down while she was doing it and she wasn't about to argue.

"You look tired," Greg said as they were finishing up their meal. "Early bed?"

"I'm fine. I don't think I could fall asleep while it's still light out."

As soon as the dishes were done, they moved to the living room, where Monica stretched out on the sofa with the book she was reading. Suddenly she gave a little cry — more like a squeak.

Greg smiled. "Did the baby kick you?" He looked at Monica and his tone changed and became more serious. "Is something wrong?" He half rose from his chair.

"Not wrong. But I felt . . . something and it definitely wasn't the baby." Her eyes widened. "I think it was a contraction."

"Should we head to the hospital?" Greg sounded slightly panicked as he swung his legs off the ottoman and jumped up.

"Not yet. Remember in our birthing classes, the instructor said to wait until the contractions were coming at regular intervals."

"I'll get a pad and pencil so we can keep track."

"I don't think that's really necessary . . ." Monica began but Greg was already in the kitchen rummaging through the junk drawer.

He came back with a sheet of paper and a pencil, sat down, looked at his watch and immediately made a note.

Monica went back to her book and was turning the page when she felt a sharp pain.

"Was that another contraction?" Greg held his pencil poised above the piece of paper.

It took Monica a couple of seconds to catch her breath. "Yes. How long has it been?"

Greg glanced at his notes. "Twenty minutes."

Monica tried to concentrate on her book. She'd finished another chapter when she felt the same sharp pain in her abdomen.

"That was another one," she said to Greg when the contraction had passed.

"Maybe this is it," Greg said, his voice rising excitedly as he made a note tracking the time.

Hercule seemed to sense Greg's excitement and leapt to his feet, wagging his tail furiously.

"It's not a game, silly," Monica said, reaching out to pet him.

"Have you packed your bag?" Greg said. He frowned. "I suppose I can bring you whatever you need afterward."

"Not yet. But I think we should wait a bit longer. It could be false labor and the contractions might peter out if we give it some more time."

Greg's face fell.

Monica laughed. "Don't worry. The baby will be here eventually."

"I feel like it's taking forever." Greg leaned back in his armchair. "I can only imagine how it must be for you."

"I'm excited, yes. But I think we should also savor this time before our lives completely change."

"In other words, stay in the moment."

"That sounds a bit like a saying on a plaque in a yoga studio, but yes, that does describe it."

"We might not have a choice. Right now, it's in Mother Nature's hands."

Chapter 16

Janice pounced the minute Monica arrived at the farm kitchen the next morning.

"You look like you're about to burst." She pointed at Monica's stomach.

Monica rolled her eyes. "I certainly feel like it. I feel like a giant balloon. Someone pop me, please."

"I really thought by now . . ." Nancy's voice trailed off. "I'm anxious to meet my granddaughter or grandson."

"So am I. Believe me."

"Have you had any false labor?" Nancy's brow puckered. "That usually means real labor can't be far off."

"I did have some contractions last night," Monica said as she pulled out a chair and sank into it. "But they didn't last."

"I hope you have your bag packed," Janice said.

"Not yet. Maybe tonight."

"You'd better do it right away. There's a big storm predicted for later tonight. The barometer is falling and low barometric pressure is known to bring on labor."

Nancy shot Janice a look. "Did you make that up? Or is it one of your old wives' tales?"

Janice raised her chin. "I'll have you know, it's a proven scientific fact."

Nancy didn't look convinced. She shrugged. "For once, I hope you're right."

Monica decided the best thing to do was to get busy and stop thinking about it. The baby had its own timetable and she wasn't going to interfere with it.

Mick had already started on that morning's baking and Janice and Nancy had joined him.

Monica decided to take the time to straighten up the storeroom. It had been a while since she'd taken inventory of her supplies and she didn't want them to run out of something while she was on maternity leave.

She grabbed her checklist and began to go through it. When she was finished, she tidied the shelves—lining everything up in neat rows and dusting between them.

Nancy walked into the storeroom as Monica was finishing. She smiled.

"You're nesting," she said.

Monica turned around. She raised her eyebrows. "Nesting?"

"Yes. It's common for women who are about to begin labor to start getting their home ready for the baby. Preparing the nest, in other words."

"Is that another one of Janice's myths?"

"No, no. It's a well-known fact that women about to begin labor are suddenly motivated to nest."

"Does straightening the storeroom really count as nesting?"

Monica thought her mother was clutching at straws. She knew she was anxious for the birth of her grandchild but this sounded ridiculous.

"I think it might count."

"I guess between this and the falling barometric pressure from that predicted storm, I'd better get my bag ready," Monica said dryly.

It wasn't long before there were enough muffins, scones and other baked goods to take to the farm store. Mick loaded up the cart, and Monica offered to wheel it down.

The wind had picked up and it whipped Monica's hair across her face as she went out the door. She glanced at the sky. It had turned an ominous-looking gray with thick clouds blocking the sun. The air had an electric feel to it. She didn't doubt that the predicted storm was on its way.

A lone customer was in the store when Monica arrived. An umbrella was hooked over her arm and she had a number of jars of cranberry salsa and cranberry sauce on the counter in front of her. Nora was in the process of filling a bag with cranberry oatmeal sandwich cookies. She nodded at Monica.

Monica began transferring the items on her cart to the baskets and platters in the glass bakery case. Her back was to the door when she heard it open.

Two women entered and waited at the counter while Nora rang up the previous sale.

"What can I get for you?" Nora said when the other customer had left.

The woman in the pink and white gingham checked trousers and matching pink blouse ordered two coffees, a cranberry scone and a slice of cranberry walnut bread.

"Coming right up," Nora said.

The ladies were taking a seat at one of the tables when the door opened again.

"Monica!" Kelly exclaimed. "Edith told me I had to try your delicious cranberry muffins. I've always been a sucker for a good muffin." She looked at Edith, who walked in behind her.

Edith was carrying a canvas tote bag that had *Books and Stuff* printed on it in black script.

Kelly gave Monica a quick squeeze. "How are you feeling?"

"Perfectly fine." She was going to be glad when the baby was born so people would focus on it and not her, Monica thought. "What can I get for you?"

"I'll have a cranberry muffin, of course. Edith, how about you?"

"Just a coffee for me." She patted her stomach. "Must keep the weight in check or my doctor will be after me about it."

Kelly began to pull out her wallet but Monica stopped her. "Please. It's on the house."

Kelly and Edith took a seat while Monica picked out the plumpest cranberry muffin in the case and put it on a plate.

Kelly took a bite. "Edith's right. These are delicious." She pointed to the empty chair. "Can you join us for a few minutes?"

"Sure." Monica let out a sigh as she eased herself into the chair. She glanced at Kelly. There were dark shadows under her eyes. "How are you holding up? This must be so difficult for you."

Kelly made a face. "Okay, I guess. I'm still finding it hard to believe someone murdered Aunt Violet. Aunt Beatrice is beside herself."

Monica thought Beatrice was more upset about being detained in Cranberry Cove than over her sister's death, but she didn't say anything.

"I don't suppose you've heard anything new?" Kelly broke off a piece of her muffin.

"I haven't spoken to Detective Stevens recently so it's possible the case is moving forward and we just don't know it."

"I simply can't believe one of us murdered Violet." Edith crossed her arms over her chest. "It's unthinkable. I believe the police will find they've made a mistake and it was an accident."

Kelly frowned. "But how did Violet's insulin get replaced with the medication that supposedly caused her heart attack? I don't see how that could have been an accident."

Edith's face flushed. "I hope you're not blaming me for what happened. I was always very careful with Violet's insulin. I remember that morning clearly. There was nothing suspicious about it. How was I to know the vial had been tampered with?"

Kelly put her hand over Edith's. "No one's blaming you, Edith. You did a wonderful job of caring for Aunt Violet."

Edith's brow slowly cleared.

"Unfortunately, no one has an alibi for the time period when the medication went missing from Sherry's room."

Edith shot Kelly a look. "That's not true. I have an alibi."

"You do."

Both Monica and Kelly looked at Edith expectantly.

A flush of red crept up Edith's neck to her cheeks. "I do," she said emphatically. "I'll share it with the police if I'm asked to but that's it." She folded her arms across her chest.

What on earth was Edith's alibi? Monica wondered. Certainly, she couldn't imagine Edith doing anything inappropriate like visiting a strip club or partaking in an illegal poker game. The very thought nearly made her laugh.

There was an awkward silence and then Kelly pushed her empty plate away from her. "I suppose we should get going. I imagine you have things to do." She looked at Monica. "Are you ready for the baby?"

"I think so. Now it's a matter of waiting for the baby to decide to make its appearance."

Edith pushed her chair back and reached for her tote bag. She grabbed one strap but missed the other. The bag tilted and a book fell out.

Edith scrambled after it and quickly shoved it back in her tote.

But not before Monica saw the title of the book. It was Margery Allingham's *Crime at Black Dudley*. It was the book that had gone missing from Greg's shop.

It was always possible it was a different copy but that seemed like too much of a coincidence to be likely.

• • •

"Are you sure it was *Black Dudley*?" Greg said when Monica phoned him after returning to the farm kitchen.

"Yes. I'm sure."

Monica heard Greg breathing down the line.

"It has to be my missing first edition. It's too much of a coincidence otherwise."

"That's what I thought. I remember the day I ran into Edith in Book 'Em. She was carrying a large tote bag. It would have been easy for her to slip the book inside."

"And security at Book 'Em is hardly state-of-the-art," Greg said in a wry tone.

"What are you going to do?"

"Frankly, I don't know. I just want the book back. I'm not interested in seeing the poor woman prosecuted. Perhaps she has a mental illness."

"Kleptomania?"

"Could you have a word with Kelly and ask her to speak to Edith? I don't want to do anything drastic but that book cost me a decent amount of money and I already have an interested buyer."

Monica groaned. She hated confrontations or awkward conversations. "I suppose that's the best way to handle it. I'll give her a call as soon as I can."

Monica always found kneading dough to be soothing—like listening to soft music or taking a long hot soak in the tub. But today, her mind refused to settle down and jumped from one topic to another like a bird hopping around picking up crumbs off the ground.

Her thoughts flitted to Greg's missing book—she'd have to remember to call Kelly when she took a break—and then to Edith's shoplifting. She remembered Greg mentioning something about a rash of shoplifting in town—someone had tried to steal a sweater from Danielle's and the VanVelsens had also complained of missing items. All this was recent—shoplifting had never been a problem in Cranberry Cove before, despite the many tourists who flooded the town in the summer.

And it all seemed to have started when the Cargills came to town. Edith had stolen Greg's first edition—could she be the one responsible for the other thefts? If Edith had a real problem, it would make it more comfortable telling Kelly about it. It would feel less like she was tattling on the poor woman.

She finished kneading her dough, put it in a bowl to rise and wiped the flour off her hands with her apron. She needed to talk to Danielle before she called Kelly.

She looked around the kitchen. Mick, Janice and Nancy were working hard and the baked goods were piling up—enough to stock the store for the afternoon. She felt guilty leaving but she really wanted to talk to Danielle Dubois. And, frankly, her back was beginning to hurt.

"Are you leaving?" Nancy said as Monica took off her apron. "You look tired. I hope you're going home to get some rest. A cat nap at least."

"Yes."

Monica didn't like lying to her mother but surely a little white lie wouldn't hurt. Besides, she was going to rest . . . eventually.

It didn't take her long to get into town. The skies looked even more ominous now and she could feel the moisture in the atmosphere. It would be a relief when the storm started and cleared the air.

She parked the car and paused for a moment, taking in the display in Danielle's window. Danielle was already anticipating fall and cooler weather with mannequins dressed in jewel-toned sweaters and wool skirts and pants. In the corner of the window there was a small sign that said *Summer Sale*.

A bell tinkled as Monica pushed open the door. The interior of the shop was hushed and smelled faintly of expensive perfume. Monica spotted an essential oil diffuser behind the cashier's desk.

A tall woman with a long boney face was scrutinizing herself in the three-way mirror, turning this way and that. The price tag on the dress she was wearing fluttered in the air. Monica didn't even want to know how much it cost.

Another woman—she recognized her as Danielle Dubois, the owner, stood next to the woman, occasionally tweaking the dress and smoothing out the skirt.

Monica browsed the racks while she waited for Danielle to be free, fingering the luxurious cashmere sweaters and silky blouses.

Finally, the customer disappeared into the dressing room and

Danielle approached Monica.

"May I help you?" she said with a slight French accent. Her fragrance—it smelled complex and expensive—wafted toward Monica.

She was quite petite with pale skin and dark hair and was simply but elegantly dressed in a black linen sheath, which she somehow had managed to keep from wrinkling.

Monica bit her lip. How to begin the conversation?

"I'm Monica Albertson. My husband Greg owns Book 'Em down the street."

Danielle tilted her head and gave a cat-like smile.

"A rare book was recently shoplifted from his store."

Danielle's expression turned serious. "Ah, *oui?*"

Monica cleared her throat. "I understand you had a similar incident recently."

Danielle's face clouded. "Yes. It was most distressing. We've never had a problem before. Do you think it could be the same person?"

"It's possible. When did it happen?"

"It was July third. I remember because the next night we had the fireworks. It was almost time to close and I was counting out the cash register."

"You close at six o'clock?"

"*Oui.* It was a few minutes before six. The woman came in around five o'clock. She spent a lot of time looking through the racks and finally went into the dressing room to try on a sweater. It made me slightly suspicious so I made a point of watching her when she came out."

"What happened then?"

"It was so brazen!" Danielle's voice rose. "She was carrying the sweater she'd tried on and I expected her to approach the counter with it, but instead she slipped it into the tote bag she was carrying."

"Did you call the police?"

Danielle shook her head. "*Non.* She was an older woman and when I approached her about the theft, she began to cry hysterically and begged me not to call the police." She shrugged. "I felt sorry for her, you know? You never know about another person's background. Maybe she's never enjoyed any luxury in her life, although she was dressed quite decently and her hair was just so."

"Did you get her name?"

"Sadly, no. I decided to drop the matter if she promised not to come into my shop again."

It might have been Edith, Monica thought, or it might have been someone else entirely. She scrambled to think of something distinctive about Edith.

"Did you notice her tote bag? Was anything written on it? Was there a picture?"

Danielle pursed her lips. "There was something. It was on the front. It said *Books and Stuff* in fancy black lettering."

It was Edith. It had to be. And if it was, it looked as if she had an alibi for the time LouAnn suspected someone had gone into the Cargill's room.

Chapter 17

Monica had been handling the books for Sassamanash Farm since she arrived in Cranberry Cove. It had been in the nick of time, too. Jeff was being swindled and he didn't even know it. He'd been in danger of losing the farm.

Monica checked things regularly now and had set aside the late afternoon to go over the numbers and make sure they were running in the black.

By the time she'd finished, she realized the farm was barely breaking even. She didn't want to worry Jeff, but at the same time, as the owner of the farm, he needed to know. She quickly dialed his cell phone and waited for him to pick up.

"Hey, sis, what's up?"

His voice sounded strange — hollow. "Where are you?"

"I'm under my truck. A branch got caught up in the wheels and I'm trying to get it out. Hang on a sec."

Jeff came back on the line and this time his voice came through loud and clear.

"Did you want to talk to me about something?"

Monica cleared her throat. She didn't like being the bearer of bad news. Nobody did, she supposed, unless they were a sociopath.

"I've been going over the books . . ." She hesitated. "And" — she cleared her throat again — "the numbers aren't looking that great. I'm thinking we need another way to bring in more revenue but unfortunately, I don't know what that is."

"Relax. The crops are looking great this year so there will be a bump in the numbers this fall when we begin shipping orders."

Monica would have liked to see some money coming in sooner than that, but she felt buoyed by the confident tone in Jeff's voice.

She had just ended the call when her phone rang. She glanced at the number. It was Nora.

"You won't believe what happened." She sounded incredulous. "A tour bus stopped by the store and we're nearly cleaned out. The driver was standing outside having a smoke — nasty habit — so I asked him what brought them to the farm. He said the woman who was president of the club — the Avian Club or something like that — had seen your video on TikTok and decided to put us on the tour. Can you believe it?"

"That's wonderful," Monica said. She had to admit dollar signs were dancing in her head. "I must tell Lauren."

"The women also asked if we had any other cranberry-themed items — you know, like the aprons you ordered — and someone else asked about a cookbook. Maybe we should think about that?"

Monica felt her spirits rise. "We could do mugs and table linens, you know, place mats and matching napkins. Maybe even T-shirts. All sorts of things."

"What a great idea!" Nora said. "Maybe even gift boxes for holidays like Christmas or Valentine's Day or birthdays and anniversaries."

Monica almost felt Nora glowing over the phone.

After she'd hung up, she quickly phoned Lauren and gave her the good news.

"Let's set up a time to make some more TikToks," Lauren said. "Obviously, they're working."

"Just in the nick of time," Monica said. "The farm is skating on pretty thin ice."

Those words jogged something in Monica's mind. She thought about it after she'd hung up with Lauren.

She was filling Mittens's water bowl when it came to her. It was something about the pond near their soon-to-be home, where the VanVelsens said they used to skate when they were children. Dawn had also said she used to skate there along with the Cargills. Someone had mentioned some sort of tragedy taking place there. She thought it was the VanVelsens.

The library had an archive of past issues of the *Cranberry Chronicle*, the ones that hadn't been digitized yet. Maybe she could find that article the VanVelsens had talked about. It would be like looking for the proverbial needle in a haystack but perhaps the librarian, Phyllis Bouma, would be able to help. And whether or not it had anything to do with Violet's murder, she didn't know. She only knew her curiosity was aroused and she wouldn't rest until she found out.

• • •

The Cranberry Cove library had formerly been an old house off Beach Hollow Road near the Central Reformed Church. Gravel crunched under Monica's tires as she pulled into the parking lot. The front door of the library had been painted a cheerful red and still boasted the pineapple door knocker chosen by the original owner of the house.

The inside was charming, with a large fireplace surrounded by blue and white delft tiles depicting Dutch items like windmills and wooden shoes. It had been converted to gas and Monica loved sitting in front of it in the winter browsing through a stack of books.

Right now, though, the air conditioner was going full blast and the change from the temperature outside made her shiver.

The furniture was a mishmash of donated pieces with sagging seats and faded upholstery, but somehow it contributed just the right touch to the ambiance.

Phyllis Bouma was behind the desk, glasses dangling from a chain around her neck. She had a cardigan pulled tight around her. Winter or summer, Phyllis always had a sweater handy—in the winter the place was drafty and, in the summer, the frigid blasts from the ancient air conditioner dropped the temperature to Arctic lows.

She smiled as Monica approached.

"Any day now, I imagine," she said, nodding at Monica's protruding stomach.

Monica stifled the urge to sigh and smiled instead. "Yes."

"I'll bet you and Greg are on pins and needles waiting for that little one to arrive."

"We certainly are."

"Now, what can I do for you? I imagine you didn't come in just to chat." Phyllis fingered the gold buttons on her cardigan.

"I'm doing some research," Monica began.

"Ah, another investigation?" Phyllis raised her arched brows.

"Sort of. Greg and I are building a house—"

Phyllis nodded. "I went past it the other day. It looks like it won't be too much longer before you move in."

"I don't know if you noticed it, but there's a pond behind the house . . ."

"Yup. I used to skate there with my friends when I was in grade school."

Monica leaned on the counter. "I gather there was an accident on the pond? Something tragic?"

Phyllis closed her eyes and furrowed her brow. "I do remember hearing something about that. An accident of some sort. I'm afraid it was before my time. My older sister remembered it mainly because the accident happened on her birthday. What did you want to know?"

"I wanted to find out more about it. The VanVelsens said there'd been an article in the *Cranberry Cove Chronicle* at the time."

"I suppose it's natural to want to learn more given that you're building on that property." She tapped her chin with her index finger. "Let me see. I wish we had an exact year but I can tell you the month and day. It was on January sixth. My sister was around fourteen or fifteen at the time so at least that narrows it down a bit. I remember she had a cake with pink frosting that our mother had made and there was a small plastic figure of a ballerina on top. Barbara was nuts about ballet at the time. She wanted to become a prima ballerina. We all had our childhood dreams, didn't we? I wanted to be Nancy Drew when I grew up and have a snazzy little convertible. That didn't happen either."

Phyllis led Monica to a room at the back of the library where the microfiche was stored. Special archival boxes were lined up on shelves, each labeled with the contents.

Phyllis put on her glasses and ran her finger down one of the rows.

"It should be about here," she said, pulling out a box. She pulled out a second one and set them on the table next to the reader.

"You should be able to find something in here," she said, tapping the top of one of the boxes. "Assuming I'm remembering correctly." She sighed. "Unfortunately, I've reached that stage of life where I can't always rely on my memory being correct, so let's hope." She held up her crossed fingers. "I'll let you get to it."

She left the room, quietly closing the door behind her.

Monica hoped she was on the right track and wasn't just wasting her time. She inserted the first roll in the reader and began to scroll through it to the February issues of the *Cranberry Cove Chronicle* for the year Phyllis's sister would have turned fourteen. She was tempted to stop and read some of the articles but she forced herself to stay on task.

Finally, she reached the *Chronicles* that came out around the date Phyllis had mentioned. She scrolled through the issues published the weeks following the incident on the pond but there was no mention of the accident. Maybe it hadn't been deemed worthy of an article? She doubted that. Cranberry Cove was a small town and usually even the smallest event made it into the paper. After all, while skimming, she'd noticed articles with headlines like *Mrs. Perkins Adopts Stray Cat* and *Garden Club Meeting Canceled*.

She opened the second box, inserted the roll of microfiche into the reader and began to go through it. Her heart beat faster as she neared the date Phyllis had given her. Finally, two days after the accident on the pond, there was a write-up in the paper. As a matter of fact, the article was sprawled across an entire page, complete with pictures of the pond taken from every angle imaginable.

A chill went down Monica's spine as she began to read.

• • •

Greg was already home when Monica got there. He gave her a quick kiss.

"Where did you go? I was worried about you. I called the kitchen but they said you had left hours ago."

"I didn't mean to worry you. I went to the library."

Greg glanced at Monica's hands. "You didn't find anything?"

"That's not exactly why I went. How about we start dinner and then I'll tell you about it."

"I have a better idea," Greg said, grabbing both of Monica's hands. "Let's go out."

"But we just—"

"I know it's an indulgence but we don't have too many more days of freedom."

Monica's stomach knotted. "You're not sorry, are you? About the baby?"

"Good heavens, no." Greg squeezed Monica's hands. "I can't wait. But it's probably our last chance to go out as a couple—just us."

Monica's shoulders relaxed and she smiled. "I think it's a great idea. Where shall we go?"

"Given that Cranberry Cove doesn't offer an abundance of fine dining spots, how about the Pepper Pot?"

"I'll go freshen up."

• • •

Even though it was a weeknight, the Pepper Pot was bustling with diners, most of them tourists vacationing at the lake. They were easy to recognize with their dark tans and peeling, sunburned noses. A loud laugh rang out from one of the tables and Monica peered into the restaurant. A man in a colorful short-sleeved print shirt was telling an animated tale, his hands waving in the air expressively. Monica held her breath as he came close to knocking over his glass of wine.

Greg gave their name to the hostess and steered Monica toward a seat where several other couples were also waiting.

"I hope it won't be too long," she said.

Before Greg could answer, the hostess swooped down on them. "Come with me," she said, grabbing two menus off the hostess stand and tucking them under her arm.

Greg glanced at the other people waiting for a table. "But they're—"

Seeing the look of confusion on Greg's face, she said in a low voice, "Mickey always keeps one table free in case any of his friends show up."

They followed her as she led them to a table for two in the corner. Monica had to edge between the tables carefully and felt as if she ought to have a sign saying *Wide Load* pinned on her back. "Here you are," the hostess said, plunking the menus down. "Enjoy your dinner."

Greg chuckled. "I guess it pays to know someone."

After the waitress had taken their drink order, Greg leaned his elbows on the table. "So. Are you going to tell me what it was you were trying to track down at the library?"

"I wanted to find out more about the incident the VanVelsens mentioned that had happened on the pond behind our new house. I wondered if there was any connection between it and the bones we found."

Greg raised his eyebrows. "I have to admit, it would be interesting to know more about it. We're going to be living there, after all, and I don't want to feel like we're being haunted by something from the past. Did you find anything? Any links?"

Monica furrowed her brow. "I did get some information but I can't quite figure out how it's all related." She ran her finger around the rim of the glass of sparkling water the waitress had just handed her. "There was an accident on the pond. Two girls were ice skating and one of them fell through the ice. What's interesting is, the two girls involved in the incident were Violet and her sister Beatrice. Their last name was redacted at the request of the family for privacy purposes, but how many pairs of sisters are likely to be named Violet and Beatrice?"

Greg's eyebrows shot up again and he gave a low whistle. "Now that is a coincidence." He tapped his fingers on the table. "But I don't see any connection between that and the bones we found, do you?"

Monica made a face. "Not really. But I have a feeling there is a connection. I'm going to ask Kelly if she knows anything."

Chapter 18

Wednesday morning when Monica went down for breakfast, she found a gift box on her plate wrapped in gold paper and tied with a silver ribbon.

She swiveled around in her seat to look at Greg, who was at the counter filling his coffee cup. A lock of hair was falling over his forehead and despite approaching middle age, he had retained his boyish charm. Monica felt a rush of warmth flood her and her eyes filled with tears.

"What's this?" She waved the box at him.

He grinned sheepishly. "It's a little present. I thought you deserved it." He motioned with his hand. "Go on. Open it."

Monica undid the ribbon and put it aside. She slid her finger along the edge of the wrapping paper and under the tape, loosening it, then slid the paper off.

The box was also gold and written on top in fancy script was *Serenity Salon and Spa.* Now she was really curious. She opened the box to find an envelope inside. It was silver with *Serenity Salon and Spa* written on it in the same script.

Monica felt her heart speed up as she tore open the flap. What on earth had Greg gotten her?

She pulled out a gift certificate, elaborately decorated with swirls and stars. "What is this?"

She turned back to Greg, who was smiling broadly.

"It's a gift certificate for a hot stone massage. I thought you deserved some pampering. You've been keeping the baking going, overseeing the farm store and helping Jeff with the finances. It's time you had a chance to relax." He brushed his hair off his forehead. "As a matter of fact, you might want to think about taking it easy from now until the baby arrives. It's not going to be much longer."

He went over to Monica and put one arm around her shoulder and his hand on her stomach.

"I can't wait to see this little one. We'd better start thinking about a name."

At the start of Monica's pregnancy, they'd been so excited that they had started keeping a list but hadn't given it any more thought since then.

Greg took a last sip of his coffee, rinsed his mug and put it in the dishwasher. He kissed Monica on the cheek.

"I'm off then." He tapped the gift certificate on the table. "Why don't you see if they have any openings today? It's time you started your maternity leave. And tonight, we can work on that list of names."

That did sound tempting, Monica thought as she toasted some cranberry bread and got the butter out of the refrigerator. She'd call the spa as soon as she finished her breakfast to see if they had any openings. She ate one slice of her bread and half of the other before pushing her plate away. She'd been ravished throughout her whole pregnancy but suddenly she wasn't as hungry anymore.

• • •

"Well, it's about time," Nancy said when Monica announced she was beginning her maternity leave. "You should be resting. Rest is critically important for expectant mothers."

"And walking." Janice looked up from the muffin tin she was filling. "I walked five miles the day before my son was born." There was a look of smug satisfaction on her face.

Nancy rolled her eyes. "I'm sure walking is good." She shot a glance at Janice. "Be sure not to overdo it though. That's as bad as not getting any exercise at all."

Monica raised her right hand. "I solemnly swear not to overdo it."

"Pamper yourself. You'll be run off your feet soon enough," Nancy said and Janice nodded.

Monica pulled the Serenity Salon and Spa gift certificate out of her bag. "As a matter of fact, I'm making a reservation for a hot stone massage. Compliments of Greg."

"You certainly snagged a good one," Nancy said. "Your Greg is so thoughtful."

Monica felt a rush of pleasure. Her mother hadn't taken to Greg right away. She'd always envisioned Monica engaged to someone with money who had a high-powered career—a lawyer or investment banker—not someone who ran a bookstore in what she referred to as *that dinky town*. She'd slowly succumbed to Greg's charm though and now she was one of his greatest champions.

• • •

The Serenity Salon and Spa looked at odds with the more pedestrian buildings around it. The ends of the stucco building were rounded, like turrets on a medieval castle, and the tiled entrance looked as if it would have been more at home in the southwest.

Giant terra-cotta pots with colorful petunias spilling over the sides sat on either side of the entrance.

Monica pulled open the door and was immediately greeted by a gust of perfumed air that didn't completely mask the faint chemical scent of hair dyes and permanent solutions.

Chairs were gathered around a massive fake stone fireplace in the waiting area and the styling chairs were arranged around a rotunda, where the sun was shining brightly through the numerous windows and creating a dappled pattern on the floor.

Monica approached the reception desk with a certain amount of trepidation. Her own hairstylist worked at a place that was more old-fashioned beauty parlor than spa, where some of the styling chairs were mended with black electrical tape and the air smelled like hair spray, not perfume.

The woman at the desk peered at Monica over the rims of her cat-eye glasses.

"Can I help you?" She looked Monica up and down.

Two can play that game. Monica straightened her spine and looked the woman in the eye.

"I have an appointment for a hot stone massage. I called this morning. Monica Albertson."

The woman raised a carefully plucked eyebrow and ran her finger down the page of the appointment book in front of her.

"I see. Yes, a massage with Illiana. You're early," she said, making it sound more like an accusation than a statement. "You can wait over there." She swept an arm toward the chairs around the fireplace.

Monica headed toward the black leather armchairs in the waiting area and sat down. She hoped she would be able to get out of it without struggling. She was reaching for a magazine from the glass coffee table in front of her when she heard her name being called and Kelly Cargill slid into the seat next to her.

"This is a lovely place. I've never been here before."

"Neither have I," Monica admitted. "Greg gave me a gift certificate for a hot stone massage."

"Lucky you. I'm getting a haircut." She touched a hand to her blond bob.

This was the perfect time to ask her about the book Edith had taken from Book 'Em, Monica thought. She felt her muscles tense at the thought. She was definitely going to need that massage after this.

She cleared her throat. "I have to ask you something." *How to go about this diplomatically?*

Kelly raised her eyebrows. "Sure. What is it?"

"It's about Edith."

"Mmmhmm."

"That book she's reading—the Margery Allingham—well, she, um, borrowed it from Greg's bookstore Book 'Em." She'd decided not to use the words stole or shoplifted.

Kelly's mouth hung open. "What do you mean borrowed? Like from the library?"

"Not exactly. She took it without anyone knowing."

"In other words, she shoplifted it."

Monica searched Kelly's face, expecting to see her looking distressed. Instead, she appeared remarkably calm.

Kelly sighed. "Edith has a slight . . . problem. She's seeing a therapist about it but progress has been slow. I'll have a word with her."

"I don't want to upset her."

"Don't worry. I'll do it gently. I'm sure the book will be returned soon."

Monica felt a wash of gratitude. "Thank you." She ran her hands down the arms of the leather armchair. "I have another question for you. It's about Violet and Beatrice and something that happened a long time ago."

Kelly nodded, but before Monica could say anything else, Kelly's stylist swooped down and led her off for her haircut.

• • •

Monica's body felt totally relaxed as she walked to her car after her massage. Her limbs felt like liquid, as if they were melting. She had a sudden image of the wicked witch in the *Wizard of Oz* as she slowly turned to a puddle on the floor. Even the persistent pain in her neck was gone. *Why hadn't she gotten a massage sooner?*

Monica drove back to town and a feeling of lightness settled over her. It wasn't only the massage—it was the knowledge that from now on she could rest until the baby came. She hadn't wanted to admit it, even to herself, but she had been getting increasingly tired.

It also gives you time to investigate, a little voice in her head whispered.

She ran through the cast of characters in her mind as she drove. Edith and Aston had alibis. Kelly was out of the question. That left Sherry, Ray and Beatrice. And Sherry's husband Chuck. It was a long shot but he would benefit from Violet's death if that meant Sherry had money from the inheritance to continue meeting his blackmail demands. Perhaps he and Sherry had been in on it together. Monica hadn't liked the look of him one bit—his face was hard and there was something about his eyes, something slippery. Although she supposed that didn't necessarily make him a killer. He might simply be the sort who went through life conning people and taking advantage of them.

Ray was clearly in need of money and was sure to inherit the bulk of his mother's estate. And what about Beatrice? Was Violet leaving her money as well? She appeared to be living a comfortable enough life as it was, although it hardly compared to her sister's.

Monica suddenly wondered if all these thoughts of murder could harm the baby in any way. Janice would probably insist they could.

She was still enjoying the mellow feeling from her massage and was anxious to prolong the experience. She decided she would take a short walk along the lake. *Why not?* She was on maternity leave, after all.

She parked her car and headed toward the stairs leading to the beach. She paused at the top to remove her shoes, and as she descended, she relished the warmth of the wood and the graininess of the particles of sand against her bare skin.

Colorful umbrellas were staked in the sand nearly to the water's edge and children whooped and splashed in the shallow water near the shore.

Monica walked down to where the waves had wet the sand and began to walk. Occasionally the water reached her feet, foaming around her ankles before receding again. It felt heavenly to be outside and she breathed deeply of the fresh air, digging her toes into the moist sand.

The sun dipped behind a cloud, momentarily casting shadows on the ground but soon returned, sparkling off the tops of the waves and warming Monica's face.

She was careful not to walk too far, keeping in mind she'd have to make the return journey as well and it wouldn't do to use up all her energy.

She turned around when she reached the stone pier that stretched out into the lake, where the lighthouse at the end pointed toward the sky.

She was relieved when she reached her starting point—her legs were getting tired and she still had to struggle through the shifting sand to the stairs that would take her back to her car.

As she passed the Cranberry Cove Inn, she heard someone call her name. Shielding her eyes from the sun with her hand, she scanned the inn's patio and saw Beatrice sitting at one of the tables. Beatrice half stood and beckoned for Monica when she saw she had caught her attention.

Monica opened the gate to the stairs that led to the inn's patio. Beatrice was seated at the front, her umbrella tilted to shade her from the sun. She had a ball of yarn stuck through with knitting needles on the table beside her and a sweating glass of something cold at her elbow.

"Monica. Come sit." She patted the chair next to her. "Come get out of the sun and have something cold to drink."

That certainly sounded inviting, Monica thought. She was slightly out of breath as she climbed the last step and was grateful when she collapsed into the chair Beatrice had pulled out for her. She lifted her hair off her neck. She wished she'd thought to put it up.

"It is rather warm, isn't it?"

Monica nodded. "It was cooler down by the water." She fanned her face with her hand.

"What you need is a cold drink," Beatrice said and waved for the waiter, who was clearing a table that had just been vacated.

He bustled over and Monica ordered a tall lemonade with plenty of ice.

Beatrice twirled the straw in her drink around and around. "Do you have any idea if the police are any closer to solving Violet's murder?"

"I don't know. I haven't talked to Detective Stevens recently. I'm sure they're making progress."

"It's strange being back in Cranberry Cove," Beatrice said as the waiter slid Monica's lemonade in front of her. "We used to love it as children—the water, the beach, the chance to spend the day outdoors. It felt like freedom. We even liked it in the winter when we could skate and sled. We would stay out until our fingers were blue insisting that we weren't cold."

"That sounds idyllic." Monica took a sip of her lemonade.

Beatrice's face darkened. "It was. Until the accident happened."

Monica went very still. She didn't want to interrupt Beatrice's train of thought.

"Of course, I don't remember any of it—only flashes that come back to me from time to time, often when I least expect it."

Monica waited. Beatrice went on.

"I was told Violet and I had gone skating, although we'd been told not to. The previous few days had been unseasonably warm and sunny and it wasn't safe. But we didn't listen even though we were old enough to know better. I was eighteen and Violet was twenty. We'd only been skating for a few minutes when the ice cracked under me and a hole opened up. I guess I fell in."

Monica gasped. She could almost feel the icy cold water herself.

"That must have been so frightening."

Beatrice shrugged. "I imagine it was but fortunately I remember so very little. It's a blessing really. I was in a coma afterward, see, for three months. I lost my memory—not all of it, mind you. I knew my name, but at first I didn't recognize my own family or even my best friend. All the events of that day were gone forever. All I really remember is the feeling of terror. It haunts me still." Beatrice's hand trembled as she reached for her glass.

She took a sip and ran her tongue over her lips. "It was Violet who saved me. Somehow, she managed to grab my arm and pull me out of the water. She took a terrible risk. She could have fallen in herself. But she said there wasn't time to go for help. I can imagine her terror, standing on the ice and knowing it could crack under her at any minute and plunge her into the frigid water. Imagine. It would have been a double tragedy if we'd both gone under."

Beatrice pulled a tissue from her pocket and dabbed at her eyes. "Violet wasn't just my big sister, you know, she was my hero. She saved my life. I don't know what I'm going to do without her." She clenched the tissue in her hand. "We never went skating again. Mother wouldn't hear of it. She'd forbidden it. Besides, Violet had lost one of her skates and Mother had refused to buy her a new pair."

A gust of wind fluttered the edges of their umbrella. Monica took a deep breath. "What a frightening experience for you and your sister." She looked out toward the water, where a sailboat bobbed in the distance. "That pond is behind the house Greg and I are building."

Beatrice put a hand to her mouth. "I hope my story hasn't put you off. It was a long time ago."

Monica shook her head. "Don't worry. It hasn't. Like you said, it was a long time ago." She paused. "But something happened more recently. Bones were found at the site, in the woods near the pond."

"Bones?" Beatrice tilted her head. "Animal remains, you mean?"

"No. The police have identified them as human bones. They were in a shallow grave. Our dog dug them up."

Beatrice gasped. "How horrible. Two tragedies in the same place. But the two things can't be related, can they?"

Monica hesitated. "I don't know. Probably not. It's probably just a coincidence."

It probably was, Monica thought as she got up to leave. But it was still worth investigating, especially now that she had the time.

As Monica walked toward her car, her stomach grumbled. She mentally scanned the contents of her refrigerator at home but nothing appealed to her. The scent of sizzling hamburgers and frying potatoes drifted toward her on the breeze. Perhaps she'd go to the diner. Chili sounded really good, but she knew if she ate anything that heavy, she'd pay for it later with a killer case of heartburn. The doctor had recommended bland foods and eating smaller portions more frequently.

It was slightly past the lunch hour and the diner wasn't very crowded. As the waitress was leading Monica to an empty booth, she noticed someone waving at her. It was Edith. She was sitting alone, drinking a cup of coffee. A plate with crumbs scattered on it was pushed to the side.

"Why don't you join me," she pointed to the empty seat opposite her.

Monica sat down and reached for the menu, although she knew it by heart now. According to longtime Cranberry Cove residents, it hadn't changed in years.

She finally settled on a chicken salad sandwich, gave her order to the waitress, who was waiting impatiently by their table and slid the menu back between the napkin dispenser and the sugar shaker.

"I've had such a wonderful morning," Edith said, taking a sip of her coffee. "Sherry and Ray have been so kind. Ray may seem prickly at times but he's really quite nice. It's the stress of his job, you see. They took me to the carnival. I so enjoyed it—seeing the animals, eating funnel cakes and trying my hand at one of the games of chance." She gave a deprecating laugh. "Of course, I didn't go on any of the rides. Can you imagine me on the roller coaster? Those amusements are best left to the young people." She tilted her head. "Have you been?"

"Yes. Greg and I have been twice. I enjoyed the funnel cakes, too. And the churros."

Edith reached for a napkin and soaked up some of the coffee that had sloshed into her saucer. "It was strange seeing that man there. It's been such a long time."

"Oh? What man?"

"I recognized him right away. His name was Chuck or Charles or Carl something or other."

"Chuck Krauss?" Monica hazarded.

Edith wrinkled her forehead. "I think that's it. Yes, Chuck Krauss."

"How do you know him?" Monica leaned back as the waitress plunked down her sandwich and a piece of lemon meringue pie for Edith.

Edith gestured at the piece of pie. "One of my guilty pleasures, I'm afraid. I do have quite a sweet tooth." She scooped up some of the meringue with her fork.

"Chuck used to work for Violet as a gardener. It was a long time ago, and while I don't always remember names, I pride myself on never forgetting a face." She straightened up and pulled her shoulders back. "And now he's working for this carnival. I was quite surprised."

"Why did he quit working for Violet? Do you know?"

Edith leaned closer across the table, pushing her coffee cup out of the way. "She caught him stealing. Things were going missing and she thought it was the maid at first, but then she caught him red-handed. He begged her not to call the police and she didn't, but she fired him on the spot."

"Have you told the police this?" Monica took a bite of her sandwich.

Edith raised her chin. "I certainly have. I told that nice lady detective all about it. She seemed quite interested."

I'll bet she was, Monica thought.

So, Chuck had a bone to pick with Violet. Could he have still been carrying a grudge even though the incident was far in the past?

Who knows?

Chapter 19

Monica brushed the sand off the bottoms of her feet and slipped on her shoes. She'd decided that while she was in town she'd go to Bart's Butcher and get something for dinner. Now that she had the time, she wanted to make Greg a nice meal.

The shop was empty when she pushed open the door.

Bart looked up from the beef he was cutting into chunks for stew. He had a surprised look on his face.

"I didn't expect to see you still out and about. So, the baby still hasn't come."

"I'm sure you would have heard if it had," Monica said. "The grapevine in Cranberry Cove is very efficient."

Bart chuckled. "That it is." He put his hands down flat on the counter and leaned forward. "What can I get for you? I've just cut up some nice beef for stew if you're interested."

Monica fanned herself. "It's too hot for that, I'm afraid. Maybe something to put on the barbecue?" She peered into the display case.

"Those lamb chops would make a nice meal." Bart pointed at the display case looking as proud as a parent whose child had received a good report card.

"That does sound good." Monica continued to examine the contents of the case. "Okay," she finally said, "I'll take two lamb chops."

Bart selected two chops and laid them out on a piece of butcher paper.

"These would be really good marinated in some olive oil, garlic, rosemary and lemon," he said as he pulled some string from the roll.

"How is Dawn holding up?" Monica said.

"She's doing okay. She's feeling better now that she knows you are looking into things." Bart handed Monica the chops and moved to the cash register to ring them up.

Monica felt her stomach sink. She was no closer to solving Violet's murder than she had been while sitting on the terrace at the Cranberry Cove Inn on the Fourth of July.

• • •

Hercule was delighted to see Monica when she returned home. She bent down and he licked her face before poking at the package of lamb chops in her hand.

"Sorry, boy. These aren't for you," she said as she put the chops in the refrigerator. "But I'll give you a treat."

Monica stuck her hand in the dog-shaped cookie jar on the counter and pulled out a biscuit. Hercule devoured it in one bite.

She put on his leash and took him out for a walk. It was still fairly hot and they didn't have to walk far before Hercule's tongue was flopping out of his mouth. She made sure he had plenty of water before she left again to do some more shopping.

She thought she'd see what was on offer at the farm stand. Sweet corn for sure and maybe some tomatoes for a salad.

Monica's wheels kicked up dust as she drove into the makeshift parking lot next to the farm stand. She pulled into a space next to a pickup truck with bales of hay stacked in the back.

Baskets overflowed with a colorful array of fruits and vegetables — blueberries, cherries, leafy lettuce, squash, cucumbers, carrots and radishes with the dirt still clinging to them. Monica was picking through the cucumbers when she heard a familiar voice. Stevens was standing next to a basket of berries filling a bag with bright red cherries.

She and Monica looked at each other at the same time. Monica dropped a cucumber into her basket and walked over to where Stevens was standing.

"Those cherries look delicious," Monica said, eyeing the fruit. "Are you going to make a pie?"

Stevens laughed and rolled her eyes. "My culinary skills don't extend that far, I'm afraid."

"Is there anything new on the Cargill murder?" Monica said. "Anything you can tell me, that is."

"No, but I do have some information about the bones found on your property. It's quite sketchy though. The bones are believed to have been those of a man. According to the pathologist the male pelvis is narrower than the female's, and there were signs of his having broken his femur at some point. It's not much to go on. I've been combing through cold cases but since there's no rush to solve the case, it ends up on the back burner."

"Was there any clue as to how the man died? Was it natural causes?"

Stevens shook her head. "His skull was fractured." She frowned. "But the pathologist still hasn't come up with any ideas as to what the poor man might have been hit with."

"So not natural causes," Monica muttered, more to herself than to Stevens.

"Not unless you consider a fractured skull a natural cause."

• • •

A fractured skull, Monica thought as she drove back toward Sassamanash Farm. Someone had been murdered — or if not murdered then at least buried — on their property. She wondered if Tempest had a crystal for that, or at least a ritual to chase away any lingering bad karma. Maybe she'd have to visit Twilight at some point and ask her.

On an impulse, Monica decided to stop by their building site to look at the location where Hercule had found the bones again. She didn't know what she expected to find but maybe there would be something they'd missed. And she'd have a chance to check on the pump the foreman said had been installed in the pond.

She pulled into the driveway in back of a truck covered in dust. The air was filled with the sound of hammering and in the distance, the whine of a saw.

The house was slowly taking shape and she paused for a moment to admire it. She imagined rocking their baby in the nursery and eating dinner together as a family in the spacious kitchen. The thought gave her goose bumps.

She made her way around to the back of the house, skirting piles of lumber and bags of cement. One of the workmen gave her a friendly salute as she passed, and she smiled and waved hello.

She was surprised to see the foreman by the pond talking to another man who was wearing a pair of waders. He gestured when he saw her coming.

"The pump has been installed," the foreman said after greeting her, "and was working fine until this morning when I checked on it."

"It's probably clogged," the man in the waders said

authoritatively. "Most likely some debris from the pond is blocking the water intake pipe."

"Can it be fixed?" Monica had heard many stories about the horrors of home ownership and all the things that could go wrong, but she hadn't anticipated having a problem before she even moved in.

"Sure." The fellow tightened the strap on his waders. "That's why I'm here. I'm the man for the job." He smiled and stuck out his chest. He pointed at the pond. "I'll just get in there and see what's causing the problem."

"Okay," Monica said.

The fellow tugged on the straps of his waders one more time then made for the pond. He slithered down the bank and into the water with a splash. He took a few steps and the water was soon over his knees. He brushed aside some algae and stuck his hands in the water.

Several minutes went by before he called out, "I think I've identified the problem. Don't worry. It's an easy fix."

He felt around in the pond some more, plunging his arms deeper until the water was nearly up to the sleeves of his T-shirt. Algae clung to his arms as he pulled them out of the water. He had something in his hands—Monica couldn't tell what it was at first.

"Lookie here," the man said triumphantly as he held up an object. "This here's your problem. It was blocking the intake pipe."

He held the object higher and Monica finally saw what it was. And it wasn't what she'd expected—not a rock or a clump of weeds.

It was an ice skate.

Chapter 20

"Well, I'll be," the man in waders muttered as he held up the skate. "Who would have thought this is what we'd find blocking your water pump." He brandished the skate. "Let's hope there isn't a match for this still down there."

"It looks old," the foreman said, gesturing toward the skate.

"You would too if you'd been down in the pond for any length of time." The other man chuckled. "I guess it's yours now," he said, handing the skate to Monica. "You're the homeowner, right?"

Monica held the skate with two fingers. The exterior was slimy and several long, thin weeds trailed from the blade. She peered inside, where a rock was lodged in the toe of the boot. That must have been what had weighted the skate down and prevented it from rising to the surface. Had it been put there on purpose to sink the skate so it wouldn't be discovered?

She folded back the top of the boot. The size of the skate had rubbed off but the manufacturer's name was written in gold and still legible — J. S. Harrison Skates Inc. Monica made a mental note to look the company up. If the skate was old enough, it was possible it belonged to Violet Cargill.

• • •

Monica sat in her car, pulled her cell phone from her purse and dialed Stevens's number. She waited while it rang and ultimately went to voicemail. She left a message and ended the call. She didn't know whether the skate they'd found in the pond had anything to do with the bones that had been buried nearby, but it would be up to Stevens to figure that out.

As Monica started her car, she tried to imagine how the skate had ended up in the water in the first place. Had someone dropped it and when the ice melted, it had sunk to the bottom of the pond?

She carried the skate into the house when she got home and dropped it in the sink, wiping it off as best she could. The once white leather was discolored and the laces were stained. It had an old-fashioned look to it when compared to newer, sleeker models. Monica used to love to skate, although she hadn't been on the ice for years now. She'd have to get out her own skates when the baby was old enough to learn.

She peered inside the skate again and this time she noticed there were some initials stamped on the leather. They were wearing off but still readable — E.V.B.

Monica wanted to look up the skate's manufacturer, J. S. Harrison Inc., but first she whipped up the marinade for the lamb chops following Bart's recipe. She poured olive oil and lemon juice into a freezer bag, then added minced garlic and rosemary. It already smelled good, she thought, as she removed the lamb chops from their paper wrapping and placed them in the bag. She tilted the bag back and forth until she was sure the chops were both covered, then placed it in the refrigerator.

Her laptop was on the counter next to the coffee maker. She grabbed it and set it up on the kitchen table. She brought up her favorite search engine and typed in "J. S. Harrison Inc." More than one listing came up but only one of the three J. S. Harrisons sold ice skates. There wasn't a website for the company but there was an entry on Wikipedia.

Monica read through the information. The company was founded in 1867 but went out of business in 1968. Which meant the skate she'd found had to be at least fifty-five years old, maybe even older. Obviously, it had been in that pond for a long time.

Monica put the skate in an old grocery bag and tried to decide where to put it. It might turn out to be evidence, after all. She finally settled on a bench in the garage.

She returned to the house and reached for Hercule's leash. He danced around her, his nails clicking on the floor, making it sound as if he was wearing tap shoes.

Hercule was sniffing along the edge of the driveway and Monica was daydreaming when she had a thought. Was it possible Beatrice had lost a skate when she fell through the ice and into the pond? She hadn't mentioned it but she *had* told her that Violet had been missing a skate after the accident. Could that skate in the pond have been Violet's? She bit her lip. The initials were all wrong though, unless Violet had gotten the skates secondhand. But that didn't seem too likely given how well-off the family had been. Besides, did the skate even have anything to do with Violet's murder? She might be following on a wild-goose chase.

• • •

Monica was tossing a salad when Greg arrived home from work. The chops were on a platter and ready to go on the grill and she had a pan of potatoes roasting with garlic in the oven.

"It smells heavenly in here," Greg said, sniffing the air. He put his arm around Monica and kissed her cheek. "Any signs that the baby is ready to make its appearance?"

"No. Nothing yet. No more false alarms," Monica said as she added some dried cranberries to the salad.

"Still, it can't be much longer." He reached for a glass and took the pitcher of iced tea out of the refrigerator. "Is it time to preheat the grill?"

"It's already on." The timer on the oven dinged. "And the potatoes are done."

"I'll throw the chops on the grill then. They won't take long."

Hercule was at Monica's heels as she followed Greg out to the patio. Thanks to a cool breeze, the temperature had dropped and it was quite pleasant. She sat in one of the wrought iron chairs as Greg grilled the chops.

"I didn't tell you what happened," he said.

"Nothing bad, I hope."

"On the contrary. The Margery Allingham first edition has been returned."

Monica's eyes opened wide. "When? How?"

"It suddenly appeared on a shelf." Greg put air quotes around the word appeared. "Actually, it was Wilma who found it." Greg ran a hand through his hair. "I needed to do something to keep her away from me so I asked her to search the shelves again. An arduous task but I think the triumph she felt when she found the volume more than made up for the tediousness. A prospective buyer is coming by tomorrow morning to look at it. Fingers crossed. But if he's not interested, I do have someone else in mind who might be."

Kelly must have persuaded Edith to return the book, and by slipping the book onto one of the shelves, she was able to avoid embarrassment. Knowing Greg, he would have been embarrassed on Edith's behalf so it was the best solution all around. Greg got his book back and Edith was able to save face.

• • •

Nancy had managed to arrange a baby shower for Monica on Friday, late in the afternoon. She'd been afraid to wait any longer for fear the baby would have arrived before the party instead of after. Fortunately, the Cranberry Cove Inn had had a cancellation for their event room and Nancy was able to book it for the shower.

Monica stood in front of her closet feeling indecisive. She knew that Nancy and Gina would be taking a lot of pictures and she wanted to look good. It wasn't easy when your stomach was out to there, but pregnant women were supposed to have a special glow so she hoped she would have that going for her at least.

She hadn't bought too many maternity clothes. She'd relied on tricks and hacks to stretch her regular wardrobe as much as possible. But she did have a pretty maxi dress she'd splurged on because it had been on sale. She clicked through the hangers until she found it.

It was gauzy and light and perfect for warm summer days and festive enough for a party.

Monica put it on and stared with dismay at her swollen ankles as she slipped her feet into a pair of sandals. A final glance in the mirror and she deemed herself ready.

The air was cooling down and she drove along Beach Hollow Road with the windows open. The last few stragglers were packing up their things and leaving the beach while seagulls squawked and swooped down looking for any crumbs left behind.

Monica pulled into the Cranberry Cove Inn lot and parked. She was relieved Nancy hadn't decided to make the shower a surprise. She couldn't imagine that having friends jumping out at you suddenly was good for expectant mothers.

She decided to use the restroom first and was heading toward the back of the lobby when she heard a familiar voice. Nearly hidden in one of the secluded alcoves was Sherry Cargill. A man was with her and when Monica got a better look, she realized it was Chuck. She couldn't make out their words but the tone of their conversation was clear—they were arguing furiously.

She sank into the sofa positioned nearest to the alcove and prayed she'd be able to get up again, as it nearly swallowed her in its depths. She concentrated on listening but it was hard to hear. Occasional words drifted toward her but they were disjointed and she couldn't make any sense of them. She thought she heard the words *alibi* and *tell the detective* and *suspect*. Was Chuck now a suspect and had Stevens grilled him on his alibi?

By now, Sherry's neck and face were red and Chuck's fists were balled at his sides.

She finally gave up trying to hear anything more, eased herself out of the clutches of the sofa cushions and made her way toward the restroom.

Kelly was in there powdering her nose when Monica walked in.

"Don't you look lovely," she exclaimed when she saw Monica.

"I feel like I'm not walking anymore but rather steering myself." Monica gave a rueful smile.

"Don't be silly. You look perfectly graceful even if you do feel that way."

When Monica exited the cubicle, Kelly was waiting for her.

"Why don't we go in together?" she said, linking her arm through Monica's.

As they strolled through the lobby toward the Cove, the event room where the shower was being held, Monica looked around but both Sherry and Chuck were no longer huddled in the alcove and were actually nowhere to be seen.

When they reached the Cove, Monica paused at the door to take it all in. Her mother had chosen High Tea at Windsor Castle as the theme. A round table was set with a white cloth, gleaming silver, sparkling crystal and delicate china teacups. A three-tiered platter with crustless tea sandwiches, scones and sausage rolls sat in the middle. A Victoria sponge cake, a lemon drizzle cake and a Battenberg cake sat on the side board.

A chair covered in red velvet with ornate gold arms and legs had been placed at the table.

Monica was relieved. The décor was lovely and tasteful. She was glad her mother had given up on some of her earlier over-the-top ideas—like a safari theme or a Wonder Woman theme, an especially absurd idea since they didn't know if they were having a boy or girl.

Monica looked around the room. Kelly and Nancy, Nora, Janice, Gina, the VanVelsens, Tempest, and some of her friends from her days in Chicago were there. She felt tears spring to her eyes as Nancy led her to her chair.

"This is for you," Nancy said, handing Monica a plastic gold crown studded with glass "jewels." "We are at Windsor Castle, after all, and you are the queen."

Monica felt herself blush as she placed the crown on her head.

Gina was on Monica's right and Nancy on her left. Gina was wearing a hot pink off-the-shoulder blouse with matching palazzo pants. She leaned over toward Monica and whispered, "I have a surprise for you later—after dessert. You're going to love it."

Monica felt a rush of panic. She and Gina didn't always agree on what constituted something Monica was going to love.

A waiter came around with a pot and filled their teacups. "It's decaf," he whispered in Monica's ear.

Monica helped herself to some of the delicate sandwiches—cucumber, egg salad and coronation chicken. She was about to reach for a second helping when the cakes on the sideboard caught her eye. She took a small sausage roll but decided to save room for a slice of the Victoria sponge cake.

After dessert was served and more tea poured, Nancy herded the guests to the other side of the room, which was furnished with comfortable sofas and chairs.

She smoothed her sleeveless cream linen dress over her hips and clapped her hands.

"Time to open the gifts," she said with the enthusiasm of one of the carnival barkers.

Gina popped up from her seat. "But first a surprise."

Nancy looked doubtful. "What is the surprise?"

"You'll see," Gina said, wagging her finger at Nancy as she made her way to the door. "If I tell you, Monica won't be surprised."

That was certainly logical, Monica thought. She realized she was tensing her muscles in anticipation of what Gina was going to spring on them and she forced herself to relax.

Gina was gone for several minutes and the guests were becoming restless when she flung open the door.

"Ta da!" she announced. She had her phone in her hand. She fiddled with it for a few seconds and suddenly music boomed into the room.

A man burst through the door and began gyrating to the music.

He was wearing a tuxedo, and judging by the width of his shoulders, he was well-built.

Monica knew her mouth was hanging open but she couldn't help it. She watched as the fellow stripped off his jacket and tossed it aside. His white dress shirt was next. He lingered over each of the buttons, teasing the audience, before finally ripping it off and dropping it on the floor.

He was now wearing only a pair of absurdly tight-fitting black pants, a bow tie and a smirk on his face. He started to gyrate again as he slowly undid the bow tie, twirled it around in the air and finally tossed it to the audience.

That was when Nancy jumped to her feet shouting, "Enough!" She pointed at the performer. "Get that man out of here!"

She didn't have to say it twice. The stripper bolted from the room, dragging his shirt and jacket behind him.

Gina stood with her hands on her hips. "I thought it would be fun and now you've gone and ruined it."

"A stripper? At a baby shower?" Nancy said incredulously. Her face was bright red and her hands were clenched into fists and raised above her waist, as if she was preparing to land a punch.

Uh-oh, Monica thought. It looked as if an epic fight was about to break out. Relations between her mother and stepmother had always been slightly fragile but they'd both been dedicated to making it work.

She had to do something. She struggled to her feet, wishing she'd chosen a hard chair to sit in. It took her a few moments but finally she was standing, facing the guests. "Let's open presents, shall we?" She clapped her hands like an excited child on Christmas morning.

"Excellent idea," Nancy said through gritted teeth. "Tempest, would you mind passing them to Monica?"

"Not at all." Tempest stood up and walked over to the table where the presents were displayed. She was wearing black silk pants and a purple tunic that floated around her torso as she moved.

Janice's lips were set in a tight line and her hands were clenched in her lap. Monica knew she didn't approve of opening presents before the birth of the baby because she believed it to be bad luck. Fortunately, Monica didn't harbor any such superstitions.

"The gifts are all lovely," Monica said when she'd finished

unwrapping the last one.

Their baby was going to have a good start with some adorable onesies, sun bonnets and even tiny booties made to look like a pair of Converse sneakers.

Janice had reluctantly approached with a package wrapped in floral paper and tied with a white ribbon. She chewed her bottom lip as she handed it over.

"I know I've said it's bad luck," she admitted, "but you've already opened all these other presents so it can't really do any more harm."

Monica tore off the wrapping paper and opened the box to find a lovely blanket Janice had crocheted in both pink and blue yarn. Tears sprang to her eyes. She was really touched.

Finally, busboys appeared to clear away the dirty dishes and the guests got the hint and began to leave.

"Be sure to let us know when the baby arrives," Tempest said over her shoulder. "All of Cranberry Cove is waiting to hear."

Monica rolled her eyes and laughed. "I will. I'm sure it will be all over town in a matter of minutes."

Tempest shook her head. "In a matter of seconds is more like it!"

Kelly touched Monica's arm. "I wanted to show you something." She pulled a folded newspaper clipping from her pocket and held it out to Monica. "It's Aunt Violet's obituary. I think it's rather lovely. I thought you might like to see it."

Monica dropped into the nearest chair, eased off her sandals and began to read. The first thing she noticed was Violet's full name—she was born Elizabeth Violet Blakely.

"I didn't realize Violet wasn't your aunt's first name," Monica said, handing the clipping back to Kelly.

"Her parents couldn't decide on a nickname for Elizabeth. Her father wanted Betsy and her mother was insistent that she be called Beth. In the end they compromised and decided to call her by her middle name—Violet." Kelly put the clipping in her pocket. "It suited her. She loved flowers and had the most magnificent garden." She swiped a finger under her eyes where a tear was clinging to her lower eyelashes. "The house is called the Belvedere, which Violet said means something beautiful to look at. It's an Italian word. The house certainly is lovely—it's a brick Georgian set on really splendid grounds."

"Who will get the house now? Ray?"

"You'd think, wouldn't you? No, Violet is leaving it to Beatrice for her lifetime. After that it will go to Ray and his family."

"Does Ray know that? Is he upset?"

"Oh, no. It's been the plan all along. Besides, he and Sherry are quite happy where they are. Their home isn't as spectacular as the Belvedere but it's still quite lovely with plenty of room for the two of them and a lot closer to town."

The subject changed to other topics and eventually Monica said goodbye, thanked Nancy for arranging the party and headed to her car. She didn't realize how tired she was until she collapsed in the front seat. She paused for a moment to catch her breath and then started the car and pulled out of the parking lot.

Later, she blamed it on hormones and pregnancy fog but she was nearly halfway home before she realized the significance of Violet Cargill's full name and initials.

Chapter 21

Monica slept in on Saturday morning. It felt strange not to have anything she needed to do—no baking or delivering goods to the farm store—and it was slightly disconcerting. She felt at loose ends as she brushed her teeth and got dressed. The day stretched out ahead of her—she should make the best of it. She would be busy enough when the baby arrived.

She made herself a big breakfast of scrambled eggs, bacon and toast and sat down to eat. Both Hercule and Mittens hovered by her side staring balefully at her.

"This isn't good for you," she said to them, although she did sneak Hercule his bit of bacon.

She finished her breakfast, washed the dishes and tidied up. She walked Hercule and read a few chapters in her book. *Now what?* She decided she'd take a ride into town and surprise Greg and she'd pick out a new book to take to the hospital with her while she was there.

She checked Mittens's and Hercule's food and water bowls and gave them each a pat. It was hard to ignore Hercule's mournful look, but she assured him she would be back soon and went out the door.

The air was thick with humidity and the sky was overcast. Monica thought she heard the rumble of thunder in the distance, but it might have only been a truck jolting over a rough patch of road or a jet far off in the distance.

Despite the threatening clouds, a number of people were already at the beach, stretched out on towels or splashing in the water.

The carnival was just up ahead and the faint scent of hot oil hung in the heavy air. A large sign was hammered into the ground announcing the one-and-only Timmy Tucker's Carnival. A picture of a roller coaster snaked across the bottom. All the riders had their mouths open in a scream of either delight or abject fear—it was impossible to tell.

As Monica got closer, she noticed cars in the parking lot. The carnival didn't open till noon, which was still two hours away. She was about to drive past when she realized some of the cars were police cruisers, their red and blue beams sending flashes of light across the darkening sky. She quickly put on her blinker and pulled into the lot.

The metal gate at the entrance was closed but not locked. A patrolman was on guard but he had wandered off and was standing with his back to the gate and his phone pressed to his ear.

Monica decided to chance it. The gate squawked loudly as she opened it and the policeman spun around.

"Hey," he yelled.

"I'm with the *Chronicle*," Monica said. She hadn't planned on saying that. As a matter of fact, she had no idea where it had come from.

"Go on." The cop waved at her and went back to his phone call.

The carnival looked cheap and tawdry without the distraction of the flashing lights and the noise and excitement created by the enthusiastic barkers. The paint was peeling on the horses prancing around the carousel, the gold rubbed off their manes, and the sign announcing the Tilt-a-Whirl was fading. The lowering sky had darkened further, casting an eerie pall over the scene and Monica shivered.

She heard voices and followed the sound until she came to the Ferris wheel, where a number of people were clustered. A handful of carnival workers in jeans and T-shirts stood around, their hands stuck in their pockets, as well as several uniformed police. Detective Stevens was standing a foot or two away from the crowd wearing cotton pants and a short-sleeved blouse.

A body, covered with a sheet, lay at the foot of the Ferris wheel. It appeared to be a man, judging by the size and shape.

Stevens was talking to a man in a pair of overalls and work boots. Monica managed to sidle close enough to hear most of their conversation.

"I dunno," the man said. "I found him like that when I got here." There was grease on his hands and a dark line under his fingernails.

"Is it possible he fell from the Ferris wheel?" Stevens pointed toward the ride.

The man rubbed his chin. "Could be. He'd sometimes climb up there to do repairs."

"So perhaps it was an accident? He lost his grip and fell?"

The man looked up at the Ferris wheel. "It's possible. He was always careful though."

"When did he normally make repairs like these?" Stevens held her pencil poised above her notebook. "Morning? Night?"

Peg Cochran

"At night. After the carnival closed down. Said he wasn't a morning person." He chuckled, then, as if he suddenly realized the gravity of the situation, his expression turned suitably solemn.

"Would anyone have been around while he was working? Other staff?"

"Not usually. Most everyone bolts the minute they close the gates. Young people, you know? Always off to do something better. No sense of pride."

Stevens smiled. "I take it you have a sense of pride in the carnival."

The man pulled a plaid handkerchief from his pocket and blew his nose, making a noise like a trumpet.

"I don't know about that but I do have a sense of responsibility, if that's what you mean. If something needs doing, I'll stay until it's finished. Know what I mean?"

Stevens nodded. "Were you here late last night?"

"Nah. No need. Everything was done and I'd promised to take the missus shopping."

Monica was frustrated. Who was the man lying on the ground covered with the sheet? Stevens must have already gotten that information. If only she'd stopped by earlier.

"So, he most likely would have been up there doing repairs last night after the carnival closed and presumably, he slipped and fell but no one was around to call for help."

A shadow passed over the man's face. "I suppose you must be right. But he'd gone up there a million times before. Chuck knew what he was doing. And he didn't take chances."

Chuck! Was it Chuck Krauss? It's possible there was more than one Chuck working at the carnival. It was a fairly common name, not like Herman or Maynard.

Stevens's phone buzzed and she pulled it out and glanced at the screen. It must have been important because she walked away from the scene and appeared to be listening intently, the phone pressed firmly to her ear.

"Pssst." Monica beckoned to the man.

He frowned but made his way toward her.

"Do you need something, lady?"

"No, not really. But you said the dead man's name is Chuck."

"Yeah." His eyebrows rose. "You know him?"

148

"I might. But there are plenty of Chucks. What's his last name?"

The fellow scratched the stubble on his chin. "It's Krauss. He said his father was German or something."

Monica tried not to show any reaction but questions were swirling around in her head. What if Chuck's fall hadn't been an accident? What if it had been murder?

"Was there anything in particular that might have caused Chuck to fall? Something coming loose perhaps?"

Monica knew next to nothing about the operation of a Ferris wheel.

The fellow pursed his lips and furrowed this brow. "Something loose? I suppose that's possible but he'd have known better than to grab on to something that wasn't fastened real good." He inhaled sharply and shook a finger at Monica. "Unless . . . unless the wheel started somehow. I dunno how or why that would happen, but these rides are old and things go wrong, you know?"

"Could someone have started the Ferris wheel on purpose?"

"Why would anyone do that?"

"Maybe they didn't realize Chuck was doing repairs?"

"It'd be hard to miss. He always puts cones around the area to keep people away. What if he dropped a wrench or a hammer and it hit someone on the head?" He made a mournful face. "The carnival would get sued and it barely scrapes by as it is."

"But you said no one was likely to be here when Chuck was making the repairs."

He shrugged. "Yeah. Especially Friday nights. Everyone's off to grab a pizza or to the bars to get in a round or two before closing."

But what if someone had stayed behind? Monica thought. It would have been easy enough to stay hidden somewhere.

"Did anyone know that Chuck was planning to make repairs to the Ferris wheel last night?"

He flicked a fly off the front of his T-shirt. "Yeah. He'd been talking about it all day. Anyone could have heard him."

Accident or murder? Monica wondered. Did someone start the Ferris wheel knowing Chuck was up there and it was likely to cause an accident? Maybe even his death?

And if it was murder, was there any connection between it and Violet Cargill's murder? Or were there two separate murderers involved?

• • •

Monica ended up parking at the very end of Beach Hollow Road. The town was buzzing with tourists walking up and down, eating ice cream cones and peering into shop windows, leaving a trail of sand on the sidewalk.

The Purple Grape was busy with people browsing. A man in a plaid bathing suit and a baby blue golf shirt had a bottle of wine in each hand and one tucked under his arm. As Monica passed, another customer whipped out his reading glasses and began to examine the label on what was most likely a very expensive bottle of wine.

Bijoux was next door, where the salesman, who was in a black suit, stiffly starched shirt and rather colorful tie, was carefully displaying a diamond tennis bracelet on a black velvet pad. The stones were dazzling in the light from the chandelier, sending rainbows of color reflecting off the counter.

A woman examined the bracelet, reaching out a finger to touch it, then held out a slender wrist and with the help of the salesman tried it on. Monica realized with a shock that it was Sherry Cargill.

That was odd. Just recently Sherry had been crying in the ladies' room at the Pepper Pot and complaining that Ray wouldn't let her spend any more money. And now she was trying on diamond bracelets? It didn't make any sense. Had Ray come into some money?

Monica pushed open the door to Bijoux. Sherry looked startled when she saw her. Her face paled and her eyes darted from side to side, as if she was looking for an escape route.

It looked as if she was going to pretend she didn't know Monica but then she said, "Hello," her voice quavering ever so slightly.

"That's a lovely bracelet." Monica pointed to the piece of jewelry dangling from Sherry's wrist.

Sherry's frown faded and she began to smile. "Isn't it?" She turned her hand this way and that, admiring the sparkle of the diamonds.

"Ray said to treat myself to anything I wanted. He gave me his credit card." She waved it around.

"Carte blanche, huh?" Wouldn't that be nice, Monica thought. But then she realized she didn't want a diamond bracelet or a fancy car or anything like that — she was perfectly happy with her life the way it was right now. She already had all the riches anyone could want.

"Ray's newspapers must be doing very well."

Sherry flushed. "Well, now that Violet's dead, things are going to be much better. Ray is her executor, you know, and, well, when the will is read someone is going to be very disappointed."

Aston? Monica wondered. Or poor Edith?

"Did you hear about the accident at the carnival?" Monica said, watching Sherry closely. She knew that despite Cranberry Cove's extremely efficient grapevine, the news couldn't have possibly traveled that far already.

Sherry's hand jerked and the bracelet banged against the counter. The salesman ran a hand across his forehead. He looked slightly alarmed.

"Perhaps I should take that for you," he said, gesturing to Sherry's wrist.

Sherry ignored him. "No. What accident?" There was a wobble in her voice that hadn't been there before.

"Someone fell from the Ferris wheel. The police are there."

"The police?" Sherry's voice was a whisper.

Monica nodded. "It's standard operating procedure."

"Do you know who . . . who was killed?"

Monica tilted her head inquiringly.

"I . . . I assume the person died—falling from such a great height."

"I'm afraid I don't know who it was. The police aren't saying. But it was definitely a man and he was definitely dead. I'm sure we'll find out eventually."

Monica could have told Sherry it was Chuck but she didn't know whether or not the police wanted to keep the name under wraps until they'd made further investigations and notified next of kin.

Sherry swallowed hard and her face went whiter than it had when she'd first caught sight of Monica.

"I've changed my mind," she said to the salesman. She turned to Monica. "I forgot. I've got an appointment."

She barely nodded goodbye as she raced out the door.

Chapter 22

Book 'Em was busy when Monica got there. A line had formed at the counter, where Emily was dutifully, if slowly, ringing up sales and Greg was in the stacks discussing a book with a customer.

Monica climbed the stairs to the upper level. She had to pause at the top to catch her breath. The baby was now constricting her lungs as well as her stomach.

She was pleased to see that most of the tables were taken. Someone was sitting in the back typing furiously on a laptop and the other tables were mostly filled with women in bright summer frocks conversing with their friends.

Monica found the lone vacant table near the kitchen and sat down. It wasn't long before Kit plopped into the chair opposite her. He looked at Monica and frowned.

"You're looking positively peevish, my dear. I think some sustenance is in order," he said as he popped up again.

"I wouldn't say no."

"I'll brb, darling. Be right back."

"I'm not going anywhere."

Kit disappeared through the swinging doors into the kitchen and Monica stretched her aching legs out under the table. She sighed as she eased off her shoes.

She was nearly dozing when Kit reappeared with a tray. Ice cubes tinkled as he put a glass in front of Monica.

"Iced tea. Decaf, of course." He placed a plate on the table. "One of your very own delicious cranberry muffins for some sustenance."

Kit sat down again as Monica took a long drink of her tea. She hadn't realized how parched she was.

"I've had this idea," Kit said, folding his hands in his lap. He looked almost shy. "What if we expand the café menu? Everything cranberry, of course," he added hastily. "Nothing complicated."

Monica raised an eyebrow. She was intrigued. She hadn't thought of expanding beyond coffee and pastries.

Kit held up his hands and spread his fingers like a dancer performing jazz hands.

"We could do turkey sandwiches with cranberry sauce or turkey sandwiches with cranberry mayonnaise. And a Monte Cristo with turkey and cranberry and cheese. Something strong enough to stand up to those flavors." Kit put a finger on his chin. "Maybe an asiago or gruyere." He giggled. "It would add a gourmet touch to the menu."

Monica wasn't sure how the residents of Cranberry Cove would react to a gourmet menu — most of them thought that the diner's burger with Swiss cheese was the height of sophistication but it might appeal to the tourists.

"I've thought everything through." Kit ticked items off on his fingers. "We'll need to hire a cook and possibly another server."

"I'll think about it," Monica promised. "After the baby. Right now, my brain is so foggy I can barely focus on reading the newspaper."

Kit grinned and rubbed his hands together. "I can't wait. I know it's going to be a colossal success." He trotted off back to the kitchen.

Monica was picking up the last crumbs of her muffin when she sensed someone standing by her table. She looked up.

"Edith. How are you?"

"Well, you know. As good as could be expected." She sat in the chair opposite. Her mouth was pinched into a thin line.

Monica didn't know what to say. She scrambled to think of a topic.

"Ray has been busy with paperwork," Edith said, coming to Monica's rescue. Monica let out a sigh of relief. "He's Violet's executor. It's a big job."

Kit flew by their table and Edith ordered a cup of tea and a scone.

"Everyone is very curious to know what's in it. Beatrice certainly is."

"Oh?"

Edith leaned forward. "I think she was trying to get a peek at it," she said with satisfaction.

"Oh?" Monica was beginning to feel like an echo.

Edith gave a brisk nod. "Yes. I caught her sneaking out of Violet's study one day. You should have seen her face. She went all bright scarlet as if she'd been caught red-handed. Like a child with its hand in the cookie jar." She tapped the table with her index finger. "She said something about looking for a scarf she'd mislaid." Her lips tightened.

"Violet was very particular about who could or couldn't go in her room. I was allowed, of course, and so was the maid. But no one else.

Not even Ray. If the room needed something done like carpet cleaning or painting or a light fixture repaired, I had to stay and watch the entire time."

"So, Beatrice, her own sister, wasn't allowed in."

Edith gave a decisive nod. "That's right. So, if Beatrice had gone into Violet's study for something perfectly innocent—to fetch Violet a sweater or her glasses—why would she have reacted like that?"

Edith didn't appear to expect an answer and Monica was grateful because she didn't have one. What Edith had said made sense. Had Beatrice been snooping and had she hoped to find the copy of Violet's will?

"Do you think Beatrice found the will?"

"I can't say for sure but Violet's lawyer had recently visited so it's possible it was still out on her desk." She shook her head. "I don't think Beatrice was happy."

"Why do you say that?"

According to Kelly, Beatrice was due to inherit Violet's house. Wouldn't she have been pleased about that?

"The look on her face. She was obviously livid. And later I heard her and Violet arguing."

"Did you hear what they were saying."

"No, but I could tell by the tone of her voice that Beatrice was furious."

"And Violet?"

"It was hard to tell. She wasn't speaking very loudly but she didn't sound mad. As a matter of fact, she sounded quite smug."

• • •

Monica had just walked in the door when her cell phone rang. She quickly gave Hercule and Mittens a pat then reached into her purse. Mittens seemed perfectly satisfied with Monica's greeting, while Hercule continued to sit in front of her, a hopeful expression on his face and his head tilted to one side.

"Hello," Monica said, reaching down to pat Hercule again. He sighed and leaned against her legs.

"It's Detective Stevens. I got your voicemail. Sorry I didn't return your call earlier. You said it was something about finding a skate in that pond?"

"Yes. I'm wondering if the skate had belonged to Violet Cargill. Beatrice told me she'd lost one the day she fell in the pond."

Monica could almost hear Stevens shrugging over the phone. "It's possible."

"I thought you should know," Monica said, feeling rather foolish.

"I appreciate it. I have some information for you, too, that I thought you might be interested in."

Monica's ears perked up.

"It concerns those bones found on your property. We combed through some cold cases and miraculously got lucky."

Monica's heart rate picked up. "What did you find?"

"The bones are from a man who went missing many years ago. Nineteen sixty-two. He went out for a walk and never returned. According to the missus, they'd had a row. She'd discovered he'd been seeing someone else and when she accused him of it, he stomped out of the house."

"Do you know what date that happened?"

"Let me see. I have it here somewhere."

Monica heard papers rustling.

Stevens cleared her throat. "It was on January sixth."

January sixth! If Monica wasn't mistaken, that was the day Beatrice Cargill fell through the ice while skating. A coincidence or something more?"

"What was his name?" Perhaps the VanVelsens would know more about him.

There was a chuckle in Stevens's voice. "Aren't you too busy preparing for the baby to go snooping?" There was a pause. "I suppose it can't do any harm. His name was James Belinski."

"Do they have any idea yet what he was hit with?"

"The pathologist is working on it." There was a brief pause and Stevens's sigh was audible. "Just don't go getting in trouble, okay?"

Monica smiled. "Don't worry, I won't."

She said goodbye and clicked off the call. In truth, she realized she had no idea what she was going to do with the information Stevens had given her.

• • •

She was going to wear a rut in the road going back and forth to town at the rate she was going, Monica thought as she drove along Beach Hollow Road. She'd tried locating Mrs. Belinski's address and had failed. She yearned for the old days when they were still printing the White Pages and few people bothered to request an unlisted phone number. But if anyone knew where the woman lived, it would be the VanVelsens.

Hennie greeted her warmly when she walked into Gumdrops. As always, the smell inside the shop took her back to her childhood, when buying a bag of penny candy was a special treat when they were on vacation.

Gerda was behind the counter and quickly tucked the magazine she'd been reading away, but not before Monica saw the name of it. It was a tabloid magazine with lurid headlines that detailed all the comings and goings of various celebrities. She knew it was a secret passion of Gerda's, even though she no longer recognized the people who passed for stars and the ones she was really interested in were long gone.

"What can I get for you, dear?" Hennie touched a hand to her permed white hair.

"Actually, I have a question for you."

Hennie's eyes lit up. "Is it to do with the murder at the inn? Are you investigating it?"

"Yes and no. I'm just looking into a few things."

Hennie's expression clearly said she knew exactly what Monica was actually doing.

"How can we help?" Gerda had come out from behind the counter to join them. She put up a hand to smooth the Peter Pan collar on her white cotton blouse.

"I'm trying to find a Mrs. Belinski. She was married to James Belinski." Monica shrugged. "I don't even know if she's still alive."

"Oh, yes, dear," Hennie said. "She was in the other day to buy a tube of Salties. She said she had a yen for them. Her mother used to buy them salted licorice as a treat and it brought back memories."

Monica's hopes rose. "Do you know where she lives?"

Hennie and Gerda exchanged a glance.

"Isn't it that little house near where you're building yours? On the hill right before you go around the bend," Gerda said.

"Yes," Hennie agreed. "There are two or three houses there perched on that hill. It's an old farmhouse and she used to have a garden gnome by the front steps. I always thought it was a bit odd."

Gerda fingered the pearl buttons on her blouse. "It didn't seem like her at all but she said her husband liked it. As far as I know, she's never gotten rid of it."

"That surprises me," Hennie said dryly. "I heard from Betty at church that she threatened to throw all his belongings out onto the front lawn when she suspected he was having an affair."

"It was terribly mysterious the way he disappeared. He went out for a walk and poof! He was never seen again."

Monica debated telling them about the bones being found on her property but she decided against it. It would be in the *Cranberry Cove Chronicle* soon enough and she didn't want to jeopardize the ongoing investigation.

Gerda put a hand on Monica's arm. "You'll know the house when you see it, I'm sure. It's white with dark blue shutters. Her husband used to keep it real nice but since he's been gone, I don't know. We don't get out that way too often."

• • •

She might be close to getting to the bottom of things, Monica thought as she drove toward the Belinskis' house. At least, she hoped so. She didn't have much more time before the baby arrived.

As she approached the hill just past her property, she kept a close lookout for a house with a garden gnome out front. She spotted it immediately and was grateful that Mrs. Belinski hadn't removed it.

She pulled up a long, steep gravel driveway and parked in front of the Belinskis' garage.

The house still had the same dark blue shutters, although they looked as if they'd been touched up recently. Pink begonias bordered the front of the house, the grass was mowed and the slate walk had been swept clean.

Monica rang the bell and held her breath. Before long she heard footsteps approaching the door and it was swung open by a petite woman who looked to be in her eighties.

She was wearing jeans—the kind with an elastic waist, Monica suspected—a peach-colored T-shirt festooned with tiny bows and white sneakers. Her skin was surprisingly smooth and her white hair was becomingly styled.

She smiled at Monica. "Yes? Can I help you? Are you lost?"

Monica shook her head. "No. But I wondered if I could talk to you for a minute."

A shadow passed over the woman's face. "The police have already been here."

"I'm not with the police. I own the property where your husband's, er, remains were found."

"Oh. You must come in then."

She led Monica into a living room that was surprisingly uncluttered and furnished with mid-century modern furniture. Monica had expected an overstuffed sofa and chairs and a lot of fussy knickknacks. So much for stereotypes.

Monica sat on the sofa while Mrs. Belinski sat in a chair covered in beige fabric and with wooden arms and legs.

"Mrs. Belinski," Monica began.

"Please, call me Fran."

"Fran. I'm so sorry for your loss."

Fran waved a hand. "That wound scabbed over a long time ago. But I am grateful to have closure, although it's raised even more unanswered questions."

"Oh?"

"I told Detective Stevens about it." She gave a small smile. "I may occasionally forget someone's name or where I left my glasses but that day is still crystal clear in my mind." She knitted her hands in her lap. "I told the detective that Jimmy and I had a spat that morning. It wasn't anything serious." She smiled again. "I'm afraid I have a bit of a temper and can get pretty hotheaded at times." Her eyes twinkled and she laughed. "I actually threatened to throw all his belongings out on the front lawn. Can you believe it."

She ran her hands up and down the smooth wooden arms of the chair. "By lunchtime, we'd kissed and made up." She laughed. "We always did, you know. We didn't like being at odds with each other."

Monica could understand that. She and Greg rarely disagreed and she couldn't imagine staying mad at him for any length of time.

"Jim was a real creature of habit. Oatmeal for breakfast every morning since we'd been married. With five raisins on top." She laughed. "Never four or six but always five. He'd count them out one by one. Lunch was on the dot of noon — bologna and American cheese on white bread with mayonnaise." She sighed. "Fortunately, he was willing to switch up dinner or I'd have gone crazy."

With so many delicious foods to enjoy, Monica couldn't imagine having such a limited diet.

"Then there was his afternoon walk. He'd set off at one o'clock sharp every day, rain or shine." She crossed and uncrossed her legs. "I didn't think much of it at first but when he still wasn't back and it began to get dark, I started to worry. He was rarely gone for that long."

"Did you call the police?"

"I sure did. They said they couldn't do much since he hadn't been gone the required twenty-four hours. They suggested I call friends and family to see if he was with them. He only had the one friend — Ned Donohue, who lives over near the Cranberry Cove harbor — and his brother is in Wisconsin. I went out looking myself but it didn't do any good."

She gripped the arms of the chair. "It's not like today where you can ring someone on their cell phone." She looked off into the distance. "But knowing Jim, he would have refused to have had one of those anyway."

"Where did he walk? Did he take the same route every time?"

Fran snorted. "Of course he did." She pointed to the left. "Down the hill, past where the Fosters live, then up the road and over to the lake. He never varied it."

How did his remains end up on her property? Monica wondered.

"He must have gone in the opposite direction that day to have been found by that pond."

"That's what's so confusing." Fran tapped her fingers on the arm of the chair. "I don't have any answers. That would have been so unlike him."

"Do you remember anything else about that day? Anything unusual?"

Monica knew she was grasping at straws but she was desperate to uncover something, anything.

"Yes, and I told the detective about that, too. Jim hadn't been gone all that long—twenty minutes maybe, when there was frantic knocking on the door. I thought maybe it was Jim and he'd been injured or something, but when I opened the door there was a young girl standing on the mat." She took a deep breath. "She was terribly upset. She nearly fell into the room when I opened the door. At first, she could barely speak and then when she did, her words were all jumbled and made no sense."

Her eyes took on a faraway look. "She was distraught, and at first I couldn't understand what she was saying. I made her come in and get warm. The poor thing's teeth were chattering."

She fiddled with her earring. "She was gasping but I finally understood she wanted to use the telephone to call for help. She and her sister had been skating on that pond"—she pointed in the direction of Monica's property—"and her sister had fallen through the ice. She tried but couldn't pull her out." She shivered. "Can you imagine? How horrible." She gripped the arms of the chair again. "I read later they did get the poor girl out but she was in a coma for months afterward."

It must have been Violet who'd shown up at her door, Monica thought.

Fran put a hand to her throat. "Anyway, I tried to get the girl to stay here to wait until the police arrived—she was practically blue, the poor thing—but she insisted on leaving. I couldn't stop her." Her voice quivered. "I was so shaken up that it brought on one of my headaches. I had to lie down and rest. I must have fallen asleep because it was getting dark when I woke up and realized Jim still hadn't come home.

"Could your husband have been the one to rescue that girl?"

Fran knitted her brows. "I don't see how. He never walked in that direction. He wouldn't have passed the pond."

"Do you have any idea why someone would want to kill him?"

She held her hands out, palms up. "None. He didn't have any enemies that I know of. He wasn't one to stir up trouble."

Monica said goodbye to Fran and began the drive home. Even though Fran had insisted her husband would never have changed the direction of his walk, he obviously had. How else would he have turned up dead by the pond?

Chapter 23

Monica's stomach grumbled and she glanced at the clock—two o'clock already. The muffin she'd had at Book 'Em was now a distant memory. She needed to get some lunch asap.

The diner was on her way and the noon crowd would have finished their lunch by now. She ought to be able to get a booth easily enough.

She found a space in front of the drugstore and as soon as the traffic cleared, dashed across the street.

The aroma from the diner made her stomach grumble even louder. Gus was in his usual spot in front of the grill but he abandoned his position for a moment and leaned on the counter. He pointed at Monica. "Baby coming soon, no?"

Monica sighed. "Yes, hopefully."

Gus nodded solemnly. "I will pray for health of the baby and the mother."

"Thank you," Monica said. It was the longest conversation she'd ever had with Gus, who immediately went back to flipping burgers and frying eggs.

Monica had just ordered when someone tapped her on the shoulder. It was Detective Stevens. She must have already finished eating because she was holding the check in her hand.

"I thought you'd want to know," she began as she perched on the end of the booth, "we've had a more comprehensive report from the pathologist. It confirmed that Belinski's skull had been fractured so no surprises there. But what was surprising was that they discovered these odd ridges in his skull, and while some people do have dents in their head from previous injuries—falling out of a tree as a child or down the stairs, for instance—these weren't at all like that."

"Does he know what caused them?"

Stevens shook her head. "Not yet. No guesses either. But Dr. Rossi doesn't believe in making guesses—not even well-informed ones." Stevens glanced at her watch. "I've got to get going." She grinned. "Next time I see you, you'll probably be holding your baby."

She was about to sidle out of the booth when Monica put a hand on her arm to stop her. "Wait."

Stevens raised her eyebrows as she sat down again.

"Could a skate have caused those marks on Belinski's head? You know, the ridges by the toe."

Monica heard Stevens's indrawn breath. "That's perfectly possible. I'll run it by Dr. Rossi and see what he thinks. He'll probably need to examine the skate so I'll let you know what he says."

Monica was lost in thought as she left the diner and nearly ran straight into Beatrice.

"I'm sorry," they said in unison.

"My fault," Monica said. "I wasn't looking where I was going."

"Never mind, dear. I imagine your mind is on the baby." Beatrice shifted her purse to her other hand. "Any day now, right?" She frowned. "Shouldn't you be resting? You're looking rather peaked. Are you on your way home? I've just come from my hypnotist."

"Hypnotist?" Monica had heard of them and thought they mainly did what her grandmother would have called *parlor tricks*, like magicians or psychics or balloon artists.

She must have noticed the skeptical look on Monica's face. "It's all very aboveboard, dear. She's not trying to trick me into acting like a chimpanzee or something like that to amuse an audience. She's helping me deal with Violet's death and other things that have been bothering me. I've already had a number of visits with her and we've made great progress. It's been extremely illuminating."

"So it's really been helpful for you?"

"It most certainly has." Beatrice's lips tightened and her eyes narrowed.

• • •

On her way home, Monica passed the site of the carnival. The red and white WZZZ van with the huge antenna on top was parked in the lot. Reporters had obviously already gotten wind of the story. She'd have to turn on the news when she got home.

She breathed a sigh of relief as she opened the door to her cottage. She was more tired than she realized. She gave Hercule a brief walk and then stretched out on the couch. She had barely reached for the television remote before her eyes were closing.

The sound of the back door opening and closing woke her.

"Greg?" she mumbled sleepily as he came into the room trailed closely by Hercule, whose tail was wagging so furiously it was a blur. "I must have fallen asleep. The last thing I remember was reaching for the remote . . ."

"You need your rest." Greg smiled. He perched on the ottoman, took the remote and flipped on the news.

A chyron flashed across the bottom of the screen announcing breaking news.

A reporter was standing in front of the carnival's Ferris wheel, which was encircled with yellow crime scene tape. Her blond hair was blowing in the breeze coming off the lake.

"Thank you, Cynthia," she said, smiling before her expression turned serious.

"We are at the scene of an active police investigation at the Timmy Tucker Carnival here in Cranberry Cove. A man fell to his death from the top of the Ferris wheel." She looked up and pointed. "So far, the police are treating the death as suspicious. The name of the victim has not yet been released but it is believed he worked for the carnival and was in the process of repairing the ride.

She smiled broadly at the camera. "We'll bring you updates as soon as we have them. Stay tuned to WZZZ for more." She smiled again. "Back to you, Cynthia."

"Would you like to go for a ride after dinner?" Greg said as he poured dressing on his salad. "It turns out the customer who bought the Allingham first edition is a landscape artist. He sketched some ideas for our house." He pulled a folded piece of paper from his pocket and spread it open on the table.

"He's thinking bushes here—" He pointed to a spot on the sketch, with a flower bed in front. "I thought we'd drop by the house so we can visualize it better."

"Sure. I'd love to."

"You're not too tired?" Greg said, a wrinkle forming between his eyebrows.

"That nap has revived me," Monica assured him.

They cleaned up the dinner dishes—Monica had saved a bit of chicken for Hercule—started the dishwasher and left.

The clouds that had blanketed the sky earlier in the day had blown away and the air was no longer heavy with moisture.

Monica felt the same thrill she got every time they pulled up to their new home. The builders had made some progress and it was beginning to look more and more like a real house.

Greg took the sketch from his pocket and studied it. He pointed out various locations for bushes and flowers.

While they were circling the house, envisioning their new landscaping, a car pulled up in back of Greg's Volvo and an older woman got out. She was tall and solidly built although she limped slightly and leaned on a cane as she approached them.

"I noticed that someone was building a house here," she said when she reached them. "I had to stop." She held out her hand, which was rather large and mannish-looking. "I'm Sally VanVliet, by the way."

Monica and Greg introduced themselves. Monica wondered what the woman wanted.

"Lovely to meet you." Her blue eyes twinkled. "My grandparents used to live here." She waved a hand, encompassing the property. "The house was torn down years ago. Frankly, I was surprised it hadn't succumbed to gravity long before that. It listed terribly, and when my brother and I played marbles, they would slide across the room to the other side." She gave a huge laugh. "It was like living on a ship."

She thumped the ground with her cane. "I'm so glad to see some-one is finally building here and are going to raise a family here." She glanced at Monica's stomach. "But do be careful with that pond." She pointed toward the back of the house with her cane.

"Oh?" Monica said, suddenly picturing their baby as a toddler wandering off and falling into the water. Her heart began to race and she shook her head to dispel the vision.

"My brother and I used to skate on that pond when we came to visit our grandmother. We thought it was the height of luxury to have our own skating rink right outside the door. Other kids would join us, especially the Blakely girls. The one was quite serious about skating."

That must be Violet and Beatrice, Monica thought, curious now.

Sally twirled her cane between her hands. "But after that accident, I never went skating again."

"Accident?" Monica said.

She nodded. "I was quite young and it scared me half to death. I had nightmares for months."

"What happened?" Greg said.

Sally sighed. "I had laced up my skates, when I happened to look out the window. What I saw was chilling." She gave a wry smile. "No pun intended. One of the Blakely girls—I couldn't see which one but I later learned it was Beatrice—had fallen through a crack in the ice and was struggling to get out of the water. The worst part is that her sister Violet just stood there. She didn't make any move to help her sister."

"What did you do?" Monica said.

"My grandmother had gone shopping and my grandfather had dementia—such a sad thing—and I had never used the phone before or even knew who to call. I wanted to run and hide in the closet or under the bed but I couldn't stop watching." Her face clouded. "Poor Beatrice was struggling horribly and Violet was . . . just standing there doing nothing."

"I can imagine how traumatizing that must have been for you."

"It certainly was. The worst part was that I couldn't seem to tear myself away from the window. It was shock probably." She rubbed the handle of her cane as if looking for comfort. "But then this man came down the road. He must have seen them because he immediately hurried to help.

"My grandfather called for me then—he wanted a blanket for his lap. He was always cold, the poor dear. When I got back to the window, the man was gone and so was Violet. And poor Beatrice was left sprawled on the ice." She sighed. "A little while later I heard sirens coming in this direction."

Sally poked at the ground with her cane. "I assumed that man and Violet had gone for help together. I thought I saw some movement in those trees over there." She pointed at them with her cane. "Maybe they'd taken off in that direction to find somewhere to call for an ambulance? It's not like they had cell phones in those days," she said, echoing what Fran Belinski had said earlier. "There's a house on the other side of those trees. You can barely see it but perhaps he knew it was there."

Monica knew that the man hadn't gone for help. How could he have if he was already dead?

"Does anyone still live there?" Monica wondered if the house had changed hands or even if the old owner would remember the incident. There was always a chance that they had seen something.

"Yes. Mrs. Smit still lives there, although now she has an aide staying with her. She must be close to one hundred years old by now. She's not in the least bit dotty though, but she does need some help around the house no matter how vehemently she denies it. Mr. Smit is long gone and she's never remarried, although I heard William Armstrong had tried to court her for years. Poor thing never got anywhere, I'm afraid."

She glanced at her watch. "I'd better get going. It was lovely meeting you and I wish you all the best in your new home."

Monica took a last look at the pond in the distance and shivered. Would she ever feel the same way about it again?

"What did you make of that?" Greg said as they drove home.

"It sounds as if Violet wanted to kill her sister."

"Why would she want to do that?"

"I don't know," Monica said. She turned and looked out the window, watching the scenery go by.

She didn't tell Greg that she planned to find out, because if Beatrice was still carrying a grudge all these years later, it gave her a motive for murder.

Chapter 24

Rain pinged off the windows and rattled on the roof Sunday morning. Greg had headed off to Book 'Em right after breakfast. During tourist season, the store was usually busy on Sundays with customers looking for something new to read at the beach, or on a day like today, when the weather drove them inside their hotel rooms or rented cottages and they were in need of amusement.

Every day, Monica wondered if it was going to be *the day* – the day their baby finally made its appearance. The closer it got, the more nervous she became. Was everything ready for the baby? Did she have everything she needed? At least she'd finally packed her bag for the hospital.

She had to admit she was a bit nervous about the whole birthing process as well, in spite of the classes she and Greg had taken at the hospital.

It certainly wasn't the sort of day to take Hercule on a long walk either. She needed something to distract her. She decided to call Kelly and see if she was free.

Kelly enthusiastically accepted her invitation to have lunch. They decided to meet in an hour in the inn's dining room.

Monica glanced at her T-shirt and shorts. Her top was now stretched to capacity and she had a spot on the shorts that hadn't come out. And it wasn't as if going back to her regular wardrobe was going to be an improvement. It consisted mostly of jeans, sweatshirts and T-shirts.

She pulled out the pretty sundress she'd splurged on and decided to wear it again. She looked in the mirror. Much better. She ran a brush through her hair, slipped on some sandals and was ready to go.

She was pulling into the inn parking lot when the news came on. The radio announcer was talking about what they had taken to calling the *Timmy Tucker Carnival murder*. Monica stopped the car momentarily and was startled when the driver behind her blew his horn. She continued to listen as she absentmindedly pulled into an empty space. The radio announcer's voice rose to an animated pitch as he relayed the fact that the police had found a contact lens at the scene of Chuck's murder.

A green one.

Monica flashed back to the afternoon she'd pulled over to help Sherry. She had noticed that Sherry had one green eye and one brown. She'd looked up the condition, which turned out to be quite rare. Less than one percent of the population was afflicted with it.

She'd never noticed Sherry's eyes before that day. Was it because she hadn't looked or because they were perfectly normal? What if her eyes were actually brown and she wore green-tinted contact lenses to change the color?

If that was the case, there was every possibility that lens found by the Ferris wheel belonged to Sherry. Was she the one who had started the ride that led to Chuck's death?

She certainly had good reason to want Chuck dead.

Monica went inside and Kelly met her in the lobby. Her expression was grim.

"What's wrong?" Monica said after greeting her friend.

Kelly linked her arm through Monica's. "Let's get some lunch and I'll tell you about it."

The dining room was busy and they had to wait for a table of ladies in Lily Pulitzer dresses to finish their dessert and coffee and then for the table to be cleared.

Finally, a hostess led them to the table and handed them menus. Monica decided on the Cobb salad and put her menu down.

"So, what's been going on?"

Kelly looked around and leaned closer. "It's Sherry," she said quietly. "She's locked herself in her room and won't come out."

"Why not?"

"She's afraid she's going to be arrested."

Monica's eyebrows shot up. "Arrested? Why does she think that?" But even as she said it, she wondered if Stevens had made the connection between the contact lens found at the murder site or if there was something else altogether.

"The police came to see her. Or at least that detective did—Stevens. They were with her for quite a long time and when they left, she became hysterical. I don't know what to do. Aunt Beatrice is terribly upset and so is Edith."

"What about Ray?"

"He left early this morning to meet someone and hasn't been back yet. He's going to be furious."

Monica knew perfectly well why Sherry was in such a state but it wouldn't be right to give that information to Kelly. First, she would have to call Stevens and share what she suspected about the contact lens.

• • •

Kelly had suggested they talk about something else and they enjoyed their lunch while reminiscing about their college days. Monica devoured her salad and was beginning to feel like she needed a nap.

They were getting up from the table when Kelly suddenly snapped her fingers.

"Darn. I forgot something I wanted to give you. When I was moving, I came upon a box of old photographs I'd completely forgotten about. There was one of you and me and our whole gang. Remember? Arlene, Joanne and Carol were all in it. I had copies made for everyone." She motioned toward the lobby. "I can go up and get it if you don't mind waiting."

"I'll come with you," Monica said, scrunching up her napkin and putting it on the table. "It will save you a trip."

They took the elevator to the second floor and were approaching Kelly's room when the door to the stairs burst open and Dawn came out surrounded by a group of policemen.

Monica had a moment of panic. Were they arresting poor Dawn? But why bring her up here if that was the case? She wasn't in handcuffs so that was a good sign.

Both Monica and Kelly paused in the hall and watched as the group approached one of the rooms.

"That's Sherry's room," Dawn whispered.

One of the cops rapped sharply on the door then motioned to Dawn.

Dawn froze momentarily like a frightened rabbit, but then cleared her throat and yelled, "Management," in an unsteady voice.

No response. They waited several seconds and then one of the cops took the master key from Dawn, shooed her down the hall away from the room, and opened the door.

Kelly and Monica looked at each other, open-mouthed.

"What was that all about?" Kelly said.

Monica had a good idea of what was going on but she shrugged and said she didn't know.

Dawn scurried down the hall toward them. Her face was white and perspiration glistened on her forehead.

"This is so upsetting," she said when she reached them. "It's never happened before. I can't think what the manager is going to say."

"You don't have to worry," Monica said. "He can't blame you for this. It's not your fault."

"What's happening?" Kelly said.

"The police didn't say. They just came up to the front desk, demanded the master key and asked me to accompany them to the second floor."

They heard screams coming from the room the police had just entered and someone shouting "no, no." It sounded like Sherry.

Monica, Kelly and Dawn lingered in the hallway. "It's like something you'd see on television or in the movies," Dawn said in awe. She put a hand to her chest. "At first, I thought they were coming for me. I thought my heart was going to stop."

It wasn't long before the police exited the room with Sherry between two of them. She was handcuffed and her expression was a mixture of rage and panic. Her hair wasn't combed and it looked as if she hadn't completely finished her makeup. So far, Monica had never seen her without her full face on.

The police marched her down the hall to the elevator.

"They certainly brought the cavalry," Kelly said. "All those cops to arrest poor Sherry?"

"Must be a slow day in Cranberry Cove," Monica said.

They watched as the doors to the elevator opened and the police, with Sherry sandwiched between them, disappeared inside.

• • •

Monica was on her way home when she changed her mind. She thought about what Sally VanVliet had said about there being another house in the vicinity of their property. She didn't think it would be too hard to find. She only hoped that Mrs. Smit was as with-it as Sally had said.

She turned onto a little-used road, pulled over to the side and turned her flashers on. She had to dig through her purse to find her cell phone—why did it always end up at the bottom?—and brought up her GPS app. She plugged in the address of her new house, and she had to admit that gave her a bit of a thrill. She moved the map around until she found the street that was behind that small wooded area bordering her property.

It was called Briar Lane, and after a couple of wrong turns, she finally found it. It was also a dirt road and she cringed as her Focus jounced over the bumps and ruts created by decades of rain and snow.

The fields on either side of the road were barren with sparse patches of weeds here and there like tufts of hair on a bald head.

The house stood alone on a rise about a quarter of a mile down the lane. It was a modest home with a small lawn, a pot of bright red geraniums by the front door and yellowing lace curtains in the windows.

Monica didn't know what to expect when she knocked on the door. She noticed the curtain in what must be the living room twitch and then footsteps heading toward the door.

The woman that opened it clearly wasn't Mrs. Smit. She was middle-aged and wearing a shirt that had her name—*Susan Clark*—embroidered on it with *Heavenly Haven Homecare* beneath it.

"Is Mrs. Smit in?" Monica hesitated. "I don't want to disturb her but I wonder if I might talk to her for a minute?"

"Come in, come in, please." Susan held the door wider and motioned for Monica to enter. "Martha will be thrilled to have some company. She gets lonely, the poor dear, with no family nearby."

"If you're sure it's okay," Monica said, but Susan was already leading her into the living room.

Beams crossed the low ceiling in the living room and a huge stone fireplace dominated one wall. The furniture looked as old as Mrs. Smit herself but was in excellent condition. There were lacy antimacassars draped over the backs of the chairs, which were hardly necessary since men didn't oil their hair anymore, but she supposed they were the sort of thing someone Mrs. Smit's age was used to.

Mrs. Smit was sitting in one of the armchairs. Her age showed in the veins on the backs of her hands that were visible through her translucent skin, and the wrinkles crisscrossing her face, but her clear, bright blue eyes told a different story.

She lit up when she saw Monica and sat up straighter in her chair.

"Why hello, dear. Do we know each other? I'm afraid I sometimes do forget a face."

"We've never met," Monica said when Susan indicated she should take a seat. "I'm Monica Albertson."

"Should you be out and about in your condition?" Mrs. Smit said with a smile. "Of course, in our day, we were hidden away as soon as we began to show and we didn't emerge again until after we'd given birth like a butterfly from a chrysalis. So silly, really. It's a perfectly normal process." She cocked her head to one side. "When are you due? Soon, I should imagine."

"Any day now." Monica rubbed her stomach reflexively.

The aide bustled in balancing a tray of glasses and a pitcher of lemonade.

"I thought you might want a bit of refreshment." She looked at Mrs. Smit fondly.

"Will you pour, dear?" Mrs. Smit said to Monica as the aide left the room. "I'm afraid my hands have become a bit shaky."

Monica leaned forward, grunting as her stomach got in the way. She poured two glasses of lemonade and handed one to Mrs. Smit.

"It's so lovely having a visitor," Mrs. Smit said after she'd taken a sip of her drink, "but I imagine you came for a reason and not just to cheer up an old lady."

"I did." Monica nodded. "My husband and I are building a house on the land that used to be owned by the VanVliets. I wondered if you could see it from here."

"I can catch a glimpse of it through the trees now and then. I'm very fortunate to still have good eyesight."

"Can you see the pond behind the house?"

"Barely. Of course, it's different in the winter when the trees are bare."

"A long time ago there was a terrible accident on that pond. Two sisters were ice skating when the ice cracked and one of them fell in. Do you remember that?" Monica put down her glass of lemonade. "It happened on January sixth in nineteen fifty-eight."

Mrs. Smit's face paled and her hands began to shake.

Monica reached out for Mrs. Smit's hand, which was cold to the touch. "Are you okay? I didn't mean to upset you."

"I'm fine." She gave a tremulous smile. "It's the date, you see. That was the day after my dear husband Henry died. He passed away on the fifth of January."

"I don't suppose you happened to see the accident? When that girl fell through the ice?"

"No, I'm afraid I didn't. I was busy making arrangements. The minister came to discuss the service and my daughter took me to the funeral parlor. Henry had made provisions in advance. For both of us. Henry was very careful like that." The wrinkles on her brow deepened as she frowned. "I do remember hearing sirens though and wondering what had happened. I assumed it was another car accident. There are so many of them these days."

Monica thanked Mrs. Smit for her hospitality and said goodbye.

"Do come again," Mrs. Smit called after her as she walked toward her car.

She was disappointed not to have learned anything new, but regardless, a picture was finally forming in her mind and the pieces were beginning to fall into place.

• • •

Monica had just come back from taking Hercule on a walk when Greg arrived home carrying a grocery bag, which he set on the kitchen table.

"Your friend Kelly came into the bookstore today," Greg said, beginning to remove the contents of the bag. "We got into a lively discussion about unreliable narrators—everything from Amy Dunne in *Gone Girl* to Rachel in *Girl on a Train* to one of the original unreliable narrators, Christie's Roger Ackroyd. A customer came in and we weren't able to finish our discussion so I invited her for dinner tonight." He drew his eyebrows together. "I hope that's okay? I picked up a steak at Bart's to throw on the grill now that the weather's cleared, some salad fixings and corn on the cob."

"Of course it's okay. I don't think Kelly is going to be here much longer so we should take advantage of it."

Greg's shoulders relaxed. "You don't have to do a thing. I even bought some ice cream for dessert." He opened the freezer door.

Monica glanced at the container. "Sea salt caramel, my favorite flavor."

"I know." Greg kissed her on the cheek.

Monica sat down with the *Cranberry Cove Chronicle* while Greg began dinner preparations. There was an article on what the reporters had taken to calling the murder at the Cranberry Cove Inn and the arrest of Sherry Cargill.

Monica read a few more stories but her eyelids were growing heavy and she finally succumbed and fell into a light sleep.

The smell of charcoal burning drifted into the room and woke her up twenty minutes later.

She went into the bathroom, splashed some water on her face and ran a brush through her hair. She dug around in the vanity, found some clips and used them to secure her hair in a messy twist.

Greg had the salad made, the corn was in a pot on the stove and the steak was sitting on a platter on the counter, seasoned and ready for the grill. They went out to the patio to wait for Kelly.

Five minutes later, a car pulled into the driveway and Kelly got out.

After a quick greeting, Greg took their drink orders and disappeared into the kitchen, reappearing moments later juggling glasses on a tray.

For once, Monica didn't feel guilty about not helping. It was getting harder and harder to get to her feet after sitting for any length of time.

Greg soon had the steak grilled and the rest of the dinner on the table. After a lively discussion on books, Monica managed to turn the conversation around to the topic of Kelly's aunt's murder.

"That was such a shock seeing Sherry taken away by the police this afternoon," Monica said.

"I don't think I've gotten over it yet." Kelly cut a piece of steak.

"Do the police suspect her of murdering Violet?" Greg reached for the salad bowl.

"I don't know. I know they suspect her of murdering that man from the carnival. I still can't believe he was Sherry's ex-husband."

"Did Ray know that Sherry had been married before?" Monica said.

Kelly tilted her head to one side. "I'm not sure. Certainly, neither of them ever talked about it." She frowned. "Do you suppose Ray didn't know and that's why she killed Chuck? To keep him quiet?"

"That sounds like a good motive to me." Greg took a sip of his wine. "But why would Sherry kill Violet?"

"I don't know. To hasten the inheritance? But I know the police are still investigating. They were at the inn interviewing Ray when I left."

Monica decided to steer the conversation in a different direction. "I gather your Aunt Violet had a lovely home. Edith was telling me about the gardens."

"Oh, yes. Very lovely. Uncle Sebastian had inherited quite a lot of money. He had the gardens designed especially for my aunt."

Monica dabbed at her lips with her napkin. "How did they meet?"

Kelly furrowed her brow. "I don't know. I don't think anyone's ever said. I did hear that it was a whirlwind romance and everyone was quite surprised when the couple eloped."

"I'm surprised Violet didn't want a big wedding with her sister as her maid of honor."

Kelly shook her head. "Poor Aunt Beatrice was still in a coma, and by the time she came out of it, Violet and Sebastian were already married." Kelly finished the last of her steak and pushed the plate away. "Not long afterward, Aunt Beatrice met Uncle William. He was studying to be an engineer. They didn't have much money but she always said those were the best days."

"Did Beatrice and Violet get along?" Monica said to Kelly as Greg dished out ice cream.

Kelly frowned. "More or less. I don't think they fought—at least I never heard them rowing."

"How about when they were younger? Were they close growing up?"

Kelly spooned up some of her ice cream. "I think so. They often talked about the things they used to do together. I know they both loved ice skating until Aunt Beatrice had that accident. They'd both won awards in some local competitions."

"This is rather delicate and I don't want to upset you . . ."

Kelly titled her head. "What is that?"

"I met a woman who lived in the house that at the time was next to that pond where they used to skate. She had happened to look out her window just when Beatrice fell through the ice and she remembered that Violet did nothing to try to save her or even to go for help."

Kelly put a hand to her chest. "That's awful. I had no idea. I do know Aunt Beatrice was in a coma for several months afterward."

"Can you think of any reason why Violet might have wanted Beatrice dead?"

Kelly gasped. "No. Not at all."

Chapter 25

Monica was sitting on the patio with her feet up Monday afternoon when Gina pulled into the driveway.

"Is it hot enough for you?" she said as she approached. She fanned her face with her hand, her bright red nails flashing in the sun.

She was wearing a pair of short shorts more appropriate for a preteen, a halter top, and was balancing on wedge sandals with ribbons that wound around her legs like those on a ballet dancer's pointe shoes.

"I could do with a drink." She put out a hand. "No, no, don't get up. I can help myself. I assume the bottle of whiskey is still in the same cabinet?"

Monica laughed. "Yes. Be sure to blow the dust off it."

"Can I get you anything?"

"There's some orange juice in a pitcher in the refrigerator."

Gina headed inside and Monica closed her eyes, relishing the warmth of the sun on her face.

"Here we go." Gina returned several minutes later with a glass of juice for Monica and a rather full glass of whiskey on ice for herself.

Monica eyed it suspiciously. "You must be having a bad day."

Gina rolled her eyes and held up her glass. "It's medicinal. I cracked a tooth and I think it's becoming abscessed. And of course the dentist can't see me until tomorrow."

Monica knew how painful dental problems could be. "I hope it helps."

Gina leaned back in her chair and stretched out her legs. "I saw they arrested someone in the murder of that carnival worker. The carnival still hasn't moved on even though it's closed. Mickey heard they are waiting for the owner to send out a new manager to take care of things."

Gina took a gulp of her drink and began to sputter and cough.

"Take it easy."

"Is there anything new on that case involving your friend Kelly's aunt?" Gina said when she caught her breath.

"Not that I know of," Monica said vaguely.

Gina leveled a glance at her. "Come on. I know you've been up to your usual investigating."

Monica felt her face grow warm and it wasn't from the sun.

"I'm not investigating," she said, trying to sound as indignant as possible.

Gina raised an eyebrow. "Okay, fine. Let's say you have your ear to the ground. Have you heard any rumors? Do they know who poisoned that old lady?"

"Not yet. At least not that I know of. The case is becoming more complicated by the minute. It turns out that Violet—she's the woman who died—tried to kill her sister when they were younger. Or, at least it looks that way."

"Really? What did she do?" Gina sat up straighter and leaned closer. "This is getting really juicy."

"They were skating on that pond by our new house." Monica's voice caught in her throat. "Beatrice fell in and Violet did nothing to try to save her. She waited a long time before finally going for help." Monica ran her finger down the condensation on her glass. "They were both young, in their early twenties at the most. What on earth would make Violet want to kill her sister?"

Gina's eyes lit up. "There could be lots of reasons. Jealousy. Anger. Or perhaps her sister had something Violet wanted."

"I suppose any of those could have been the motive." Monica put her glass down. "A passerby pulled Beatrice from the pond and saved her life. But the odd thing is, his body—or his bones at any rate—were found hidden in the woods by the pond. There's no proof that he's the man who rescued Beatrice but it seems like too much of a coincidence that the day of Beatrice's accident was the day that man's wife said he went missing."

Gina's eyes widened. "This is better than *Law and Order*! Do they think the man was murdered?"

"It's a good guess. His skull was fractured."

"But that would mean that—"

"Violet killed him," Monica finished.

"But why?"

Monica bit her lip. "He was a witness perhaps. Maybe Violet shoved Beatrice toward the spot where the ice was cracking and he saw it. Or he saw Violet doing nothing to save her sister—she didn't try to pull her out of the water, nor did she immediately run to get help. She stood and watched as her sister struggled."

Gina yawned. She appeared to be getting bored with the conversation and began to tell Monica about her latest furniture purchase for her new house but Monica was only half listening.

She was quite sure she knew how Violet had killed James Belinski. But she still didn't know why Violet had wanted her sister dead in the first place.

Monica's cell phone buzzed as Gina was leaving and she retrieved it from the kitchen table, where it was vibrating furiously.

"Hello?"

"Detective Stevens," Stevens said economically. Monica thought she sounded weary. "I talked to the pathologist and asked him if those ridges in Belinski's skull could have been caused by the toe of an ice skate. He said it was quite possible but he'd like to take a look at the skate before coming to any firm conclusions. I swear that man wouldn't believe you if you said it was morning unless he looked out the window and saw the sun himself."

"So, Violet most likely did hit Belinski on the head with her ice skate. I think she stuffed it with a rock and then threw it in the pond. Afterward, she told her mother she'd lost it."

"Hold on," Stevens said. "Are you talking about Violet Cargill?"

"Yes. It happened in nineteen fifty-eight. Violet and her sister Beatrice were skating on that pond when the ice cracked and Beatrice fell in. Violet didn't try to save her. She must have been very disappointed when James Belinski happened to be out walking. He saw what had happened and pulled Beatrice out of the water. He must have noticed Violet standing there watching her sister struggle and yet not doing anything to help her. She must have decided she'd better make sure he wasn't going to tell anyone. Is there such a thing as murder by omission? Could Violet have been charged for not doing anything?"

"I don't know," Stevens said. "Either way, it wouldn't have looked good and would probably have caused a scandal at the very least."

"Poor Beatrice was in a coma for months afterward, and when she came out of it, she didn't remember a thing so Violet's secret was safe."

Stevens whistled. "That's some story. And now someone has killed Violet Cargill. I wonder if there's any connection?" She laughed. "Have you figured out that part as well?"

Monica sighed. "Not yet. But you'll be the first to know when I do."
"I'd better be." Stevens said goodbye and ended the call.

• • •

Monica was finishing lunch when her cell phone buzzed again.
The caller ID indicated it was Greg. She had a brief moment of panic.
What if something was wrong?

She was relieved when Greg said he'd forgotten his wallet at
home and could she possibly bring it to him.

Monica smiled and shook her head. Her doctor had reassured her
that her occasional absentmindedness was common during
pregnancy. Was poor Greg having sympathy symptoms?

She went upstairs with both Hercule and Mittens at her heels to
the bedroom, where she retrieved Greg's wallet from his bedside
table.

Beach Hollow Road was clogged with traffic. It was perfect beach
weather—the sun was bright in the cloudless sky and the lake was
relatively calm but with just enough surf to thrill the children jumping
the waves.

There were no available parking spots and Monica ended up
parking one street over and walking back.

The door to the Golden Scoops, the local ice cream parlor, opened
and the scents of vanilla and freshly made waffle cones drifted out.
Monica decided she would have to indulge herself with a salted
caramel cone on the way back to her car.

The first person she saw when she pushed open the door to Book
'Em was Edith. She greeted Monica with a smile. Monica noticed a
change in her—her frown lines had smoothed out and she looked
happier.

She wondered if the will had been read and that was what was
responsible for Edith's change in demeanor. Or, perhaps she was
simply more relaxed now that she was no longer at Violet's beck and
call.

"Lovely to see you," she said as she approached Monica.

Monica simply smiled.

Monica followed her as she walked over to the counter. Greg was
helping a customer and Wilma, for once, was nowhere to be seen.

Finally, Greg finished his conversation and walked over to the desk.

"Edith, hello."

Edith plunked the stack of books on the counter. She tapped the top book on the stack. "These are some of Violet's books she brought to read while on vacation. I must say she had rather eclectic taste — everything from cozy mysteries to the latest thriller."

"Do you want a store credit or — "

Edith waved Greg's words away. "There's no need. "I'm sure we will be leaving soon. No doubt the police must be close to solving Violet's murder."

She tilted her head to one side and looked at Monica as if the statement was actually a question.

"I shall miss Cranberry Cove," Edith went on when Monica didn't say anything. "It's a lovely place. As soon as Violet's will is read, I am making plans to do some traveling. I've always wanted to go to Ireland." She smiled at Greg then Monica. "I hope I will see you again before I leave, but if not, I wish you the best with the baby. Such an exciting time."

Edith left and Monica pulled Greg's wallet out of her purse. "Here you go."

"Thanks," Greg said with an abashed smile. "I'm sorry you had to come all this way. I don't know what's happened to my brain these days."

"It's no problem. I've already decided I'm going to pop into the Golden Scoop for an ice cream cone."

Greg began going through the books, holding them open and shaking them.

Monica raised her eyebrows.

"You wouldn't believe what people leave behind in books — things they've used as bookmarks like old grocery lists or receipts. Once a dead cicada fell out, pressed flat between the pages of the book."

He picked up the last volume and frowned. "This isn't the store's usual fodder." He showed it to Monica. It was a collection of daily devotionals and the book looked as if Violet had had it for a long time. The cover was worn and the pages were beginning to yellow.

"What's that?" Monica pointed to the tip of something peeking out from the top of the book.

Greg gave the book a shake and a folded piece of paper fell out. He handed it to Monica.

Monica opened it. It was so old, it was worn and nearly tearing at the creases, as if it had been unfolded and read many times.

"What is it?" Greg said as Monica scanned the letter.

Monica's mouth fell open. She was so astounded she couldn't speak.

Chapter 26

Monica couldn't believe her eyes. She nearly dropped the letter and had to read it twice before the contents registered. Certain words and phrases popped out at her. *Dear Violet,* it began. *I can't wait until we can be together! I've loved you and only you all along and I wish I had met you first. If your sister's condition is as dire as you say it is and there's no hope of her ever recovering from her coma, I don't think anyone could blame me for breaking my engagement with her. Then you and I can be together.*

Various terms of endearment were followed by *we should elope soon or there will be talk when our baby is born. It might create a scandal and I don't want that for you, darling.* It was signed *Yours forever, Sebastian.*

It took more than a few minutes before Monica was able to parse what the message meant. If she was reading it correctly, Violet's husband Sebastian had once been engaged to Beatrice but broke it off while Beatrice was in the coma. And from the sound of things, Violet had already been pregnant with Sebastian's baby.

Had they been lovers before Beatrice's accident? Had Beatrice's accident been planned? According to Kelly, Sebastian had been very wealthy. Did Violet want that lifestyle for herself? And her sister had somehow found out and decided to exact her revenge all these years later by killing Violet?

Monica began to put more and more of the pieces together. Edith had seen Beatrice coming out of Violet's room and thought it was possible that Beatrice had seen a copy of Violet's will. Was she disappointed in what was being left her? Maybe she felt she deserved more to compensate for what had happened to her.

She must have recovered her memory somehow. Monica suddenly snapped her fingers. Of course! Beatrice had said she had been going to a hypnotist. Had the hypnotist managed to bring her lost memories back?

Greg must have been watching the various expressions crossing Monica's face like clouds in the sky on a windy day.

"Is everything okay?" he said, his voice hoarse with concern.

Monica waved the letter in the air. "Yes, fine. But this letter changes everything."

"Oh?"

"I think Beatrice killed Violet to get revenge for Violet having stolen her fiancé while she was in a coma."

• • •

When Monica got home, Mittens was sleeping in a sunbeam and briefly lifted her head to say hello. Hercule was by the door waiting, as usual, to greet Monica, as if she'd been gone for days and not just over an hour.

She pulled her cell phone from her purse and tossed her purse on a chair.

Stevens picked up on the second ring. "Hello?"

"It's Monica. I've uncovered some information I think you should know."

She went on to explain about Greg finding that letter in Violet's book of devotions.

"So, you think Beatrice killed Violet out of revenge for something that happened so long ago?" There was a brief silence. "But didn't you say Beatrice didn't remember anything from that time period?"

"Yes. But she told me she's been going to a hypnotist. It's possible it brought some of her memories back."

"Hmmm. It certainly does sound like it's worth interviewing Beatrice again. If nothing else, it will close off that line of inquiry." She sighed. "It will be on the news tonight but Sherry Cargill is being charged with Chuck Krauss's murder. Edith Evans told us that he'd been fired from his job as Violet Cargill's gardener so we thought we should look into it. He got spooked when we questioned him. Apparently, Sherry was his alibi for the time period when her medication went missing, and when he told her he was going to tell us that, she decided she had to get rid of him.

"With her husband about to inherit a lot of money, she couldn't risk his finding out she'd been married before and had never actually gotten a divorce. It would nullify her marriage to Ray. She was already worried that she was getting too old for him and he was going to go out looking for some new eye candy."

"I imagine she didn't want to risk all that money slipping through her fingers."

"Yeah, she obviously likes the good life. Your telling us about the contact lens is what put us on to her. Otherwise, we'd still be chasing our tails." Stevens sighed. "With any luck, you're right about Beatrice as well. The chief wants this case wrapped up asap. He's afraid it will scare tourists away."

Monica lay down on the sofa with a groan of relief. She picked up her book but got no further than the first page when her eyes began to close. Twenty minutes later she felt something wet poking her arm. She opened her eyes to see Hercule standing next to the sofa gently bumping her with his big black nose.

"Okay, boy, I get the message. Let's go for a walk."

Hercule's tail wagged harder and he ran back and forth between Monica and the back door several times, as if urging her to hurry.

"Slow down, buddy." Monica grabbed his leash from the hook by the door. She bent down with a grunt and attached it to his collar. "Okay, let's go."

Monica felt revived by her nap and the fresh breeze blowing, and after Hercule had done his business, she continued to follow the dirt path that led to the bogs. It was slow going with Hercule stopping to sniff the ground every few feet, but that was fine with Monica because it gave her a chance to rest.

At one point she thought she heard someone behind her. Was that the snap of a twig? She turned around expecting to see Jeff or one of his workers but no one was there. It must have been her imagination. Hercule pulled her forward and she quickly forgot about it.

They hadn't walked far when once again she thought she heard a noise. She whirled around and gasped when she saw Beatrice standing behind her with a gun leveled at her.

Monica felt panic overtake her. Her baby! She had to protect it. She felt in her pocket for her cell phone, hoping she might be able to find the keys for 911 without looking.

Beatrice motioned with her gun. "Don't bother. The police aren't going to save you." She smirked. "I imagine you're surprised to see me with a gun. My late husband enjoyed target practice. He showed me how to shoot. He wasn't exactly thrilled when I became a better shot than he was. Suddenly, he didn't think it was such fun."

"You killed your sister," Monica said. It was a statement not a question.

"I knew you would figure it out. I'm not surprised. Asking all those questions. Yes, it wasn't until I went to that hypnotist that I discovered what Violet had done to me. Not only did she let me nearly drown, she stole Sebastian away from me while I was in a coma and helpless."

"I can imagine that made you mad."

"Mad?" Beatrice cackled. "I was furious. It was all I could do to not let on to her that I knew what she had done. It wasn't easy, acting all sisterly and loving when I was seething with hatred inside. After all these years, I'm sure she didn't expect me to remember. Or, maybe she thought I'd let bygones be bygones." She sniffed. "As if I could ever forget what she'd done."

Her face took on a dreamy look. "I had been so in love with Sebastian. He was handsome and dashing and very rich. I would have had such a wonderful life with him. Instead, Violet got everything that should have belonged to me."

"Do you think Violet ever felt guilty for doing that to you?"

The gun wobbled a bit and Beatrice steadied her arm. "I doubt she ever felt guilt. She never felt guilt about anything—taking the last piece of cake that Mother had been saving for me or stealing my favorite blouse and ruining it. Violet was the charmed one, the pretty one. She always got what she wanted. She felt it was her due."

"But didn't she leave you something in her will? Perhaps she felt she owed you something after all."

Monica looked around desperately for some means of escape. If only Jeff or one of his workers would come along. Would Beatrice dare shoot them? That made her panic even more.

Beatrice swung the gun in Hercule's direction. "And keep that mutt away from me."

"You're afraid of dogs?" Monica said, glancing at Hercule again, trying to telegraph to him that she was in trouble.

Hercule, meanwhile, couldn't have looked more innocent. He'd found a spot in the shade and was now stretched out, his head resting on his paws.

"I hate the darn things. I was bitten as a child and I've never forgotten it."

What would happen to Hercule if Beatrice shot her? Monica's heart was beating so hard she heard it pounding in her ears and felt sweat trickling down her sides.

Beatrice began to laugh — a sound that was closer to hysteria than humor.

"She was supposed to leave me that beautiful house and its magnificent gardens. She called it Belvedere because of the lovely view." Her voice caught on a sob. "She hated me. She'd always hated me from the moment I was born and took attention away from her." She snorted. "Very little attention, I might add. Violet knew how to get what she wanted no matter what. I was hardly competition, a colicky baby who spit up constantly."

While Beatrice was talking, Monica's mind was working. Surely someone would come along any minute now, one of the workers on their way home for the day perhaps.

"I caught a glimpse of Violet's will. She'd left it out on her desk after the lawyer had been. I think she wanted me to see it. I had to pretend I didn't know what she'd done."

Keep her talking, Monica thought. *Stall for time.*

"What had she done?"

"She'd cut me out of her will!" Two indignant red patches appeared on Beatrice's cheeks. "Not completely. She left me some absurdly small amount. It was more insulting than if she'd left me nothing." She glared at Monica. "Knowing Violet, it was meant to be."

"You took the migraine medicine from Sherry's room, didn't you?"

Beatrice raised her chin. "I thought it was quite clever of me." She tapped her head. "I've always had a good brain. I waited until we were all here together on vacation. One big happy family." She gave that maniacal laugh again. "That way there'd be enough suspects to muddy the waters." She waved a hand in the air. "They all had motives. Ray couldn't wait for Violet's money to expand his newspaper business. Violet knew Sherry was having an affair with Aston. If she'd told Ray, that would have been the end of their marriage. And she might have decided to disinherit Aston, even though he was the golden boy."

"What about Edith?" Monica said.

"Oh, Edith. Such a timid little titmouse, isn't she? But I'm sure she has it in her to kill. Especially since Violet treated her like a serf. She barely paid her anything, hardly more than a teenager's allowance these days, insisting that she ought to be grateful enough for room and board."

"Why didn't Edith leave if things were that bad?"

Beatrice shook her head. "She couldn't afford to. She barely had a dime to her name. And who is going to hire a companion these days? The one time she made noises that she was going to quit, Violet threatened to withhold a reference."

Goodness! That sounded like something out of *Downton Abbey*, Monica thought.

Beatrice wiped a hand across her forehead, which was glistening with sweat.

"I substituted Sherry's migraine medication for Violet's insulin. Edith was the one who gave her the shots. I figured that would make Edith the first person suspected."

"How did you know the medication would kill Violet?"

"I did my homework. Sumatriptan can cause a heart attack in people with a weak heart. Violet was suffering from congestive heart failure. Quite clever of me, don't you think? The death could have occurred at any time and would have looked as if she'd simply had a heart attack. It was my bad luck that they decided to do an autopsy."

She smiled. "But it was an incredible bonus that the woman at the front reception desk at the inn also had a motive for wanting Violet dead, although no one took her that seriously as a suspect, but it did add to the confusion. And then Sherry's not-so-ex-husband appeared. Another suspect!"

"You really think you'll get away with it?"

Beatrice shrugged. "I don't care. I have nothing to lose." She hung her head. "I've been diagnosed with cancer. It's terminal. According to the doctor, I only have a few weeks, maybe a couple of months if I'm lucky. I don't want to die like that—incapacitated, in pain. I plan to die on my own terms."

She leveled the gun at Monica. "And I'm taking you with me."

Chapter 27

A mist swam in front of Monica's eyes and she felt as if the world was spinning. She knew she had to do something, but what? She looked around wildly but the scenery hadn't changed. No one was coming down the path. If only she could sic Hercule on Beatrice, but Hercule had never shown any inclination to attack anyone.

Monica glanced at him. He had gotten to his feet and the fur on his back was standing up. He obviously sensed something was wrong.

Monica took a deep breath to clear her head. She noticed a tree branch barely within reach. It was large enough for her purposes but still young enough to be flexible. Before she could get cold feet, she grabbed the branch, pulled it toward her and let it go.

It swung forward with sufficient momentum to smack Beatrice in the face. She wasn't hurt but it stunned her enough that she dropped the gun.

Monica went to lunge for it, but before she could reach it, Hercule had obviously picked up on the fact that Monica was in grave danger and that Beatrice was foe, not friend. He gave a low growl and launched himself at Beatrice, knocking her to the ground.

Beatrice stretched her arm out, trying to reach the gun, but Monica kicked it out of the way and into the underbrush. Beatrice attempted to get up but Hercule bared his teeth and stood with his paws on her shoulders, his strong jaw inches from her exposed throat.

Monica said a prayer of thanks that she'd remembered to stick her cell phone in her pocket, pulled it out and dialed 911.

It seemed an eternity before she heard sirens in the distance. She was dying to sit down. Her feet were swollen and her back hurt but she didn't dare take her eyes off Beatrice.

Every time Beatrice made a move to get up, Hercule growled until she shrank back and lay still. Her face, which was an unhealthy, pasty white, was a mask of fear and loathing. Finally, there was a distant rumble and two police cars came into view, kicking up dust as they sped down the dirt path toward Monica.

The cars had barely come to a stop when the doors were flung open and several policemen jumped out, their guns drawn and at the ready. Hercule still had Beatrice pinned to the ground and it wasn't long before she was in handcuffs and being led to the waiting patrol car.

They had just driven away and Monica and Hercule were walking back home, her legs feeling a bit wobbly, when Greg came running toward her.

"Thank goodness you're all right. I saw the police cars and I panicked. I didn't know what was going on."

He put his arm around Monica and Monica sagged against him as they headed home, Hercule happily trotting ahead of them.

• • •

When they reached the cottage, Greg insisted Monica lie down on the couch while he made dinner. Monica couldn't help but smile as he fussed over her.

"I think Hercule deserves a big treat, don't you? He saved my life."

"He certainly does." Greg bent to pet Hercule. "I'll cook a piece of chicken just for him."

Monica had to admit, she was more than happy to rest after her harrowing ordeal. It wasn't the first time that she'd faced someone threatening to kill her, but she certainly hoped it would be the last.

Greg set up trays in the living room and they ate in front of the television. The news was on and Beatrice's arrest was, of course, the main story. A dark-haired woman interviewed Stevens, whose answers were terse and didn't give much away. The camera then switched to some footage of the front of the Cranberry Cove Inn, before focusing on a reporter who was standing on the inn terrace saying breathlessly, "this is where the victim, Violet Cargill, died from poison administered by the suspect."

Greg switched the television off and he and Monica picked up their books. Monica was engrossed in hers, when her cell phone rang.

She looked at the caller ID and groaned. It was her mother.

Nancy didn't bother with the formalities. "When is that baby coming? Has anything happened?" she asked as soon as Monica answered.

Monica groaned again, only silently this time. She felt as if she'd answered that question a million times already.

"Nothing yet," she said.

"Does the doctor have a plan if it doesn't come soon?"

"We haven't discussed anything yet. But I'm sure he will have something in mind if I go too far past my due date."

"Hmph. You wouldn't think he'd wait that long." Her tone brightened. "Remember Janice said that eating spicy food can bring on labor. I could make you a curry if you'd like. If that doesn't work, there's always castor oil."

"Mother, those are old wives' tales. I'm certainly not taking castor oil, but if it makes you feel any better, I'll put some pepper on my dinner tomorrow night."

"There's no need to snap at me," Nancy said. "Call me the minute anything happens."

"I will, don't worry."

Monica hung up and went back to her book, doing her best to engross herself in the relative calm of Miss Marple's St. Mary Mead, but her mother's call had unsettled her. When *was* this baby coming? She was now officially six days overdue. Surely it would be soon. The doctor had told her not to worry, that first babies were often reluctant to arrive on time.

She settled back down but hadn't read more than a few pages when a strange sensation had her sitting up, startled.

"What's wrong? Is it time?" Greg said, starting to get up from his chair.

Monica motioned for him to sit down. "I don't know. Anyway, the doctor said not to go to the hospital until the contractions were five minutes apart. He said I would be a lot more comfortable at home."

"Oh." Greg leaned back in his chair, looking slightly disappointed.

Monica smiled at him. "Go back to your book. It could be hours yet."

Contractions continued to be mild and sporadic. Monica was beginning to wonder if she was having false labor again.

Things still hadn't progressed by bedtime. Monica put on her nightgown and got into bed. Greg fell asleep almost immediately and Monica smiled at him. Anticipation had clearly worn him out.

Hercule seemed to sense that something was afoot, and instead of settling down in his bed curled up on the rug beside theirs. Mittens was unperturbed by the evening's events and was already asleep.

Monica finally fell into a restless sleep herself and had been dozing for about an hour when the contractions suddenly became sharp enough to wake her up. Another one arrived almost on the heels of the previous one and Monica was now quite sure this was the real thing.

She reached out and shook Greg's shoulder.

"Whaat?" he murmured sleepily.

"I think this is it," Monica said, wincing as another contraction started.

"What?" Greg sat bolt upright in bed. "Aren't you going to get dressed?" he said to Monica.

The contraction ended and Monica began to pull on the clothes she'd left out just in case. Greg was already dressed except for his shoes, which, in his excitement, he kept trying to put on the wrong foot.

Finally, they were both ready and Greg had Monica's suitcase in hand.

Hercule escorted them down the stairs. "Jeff will come and walk Hercule in the morning," Monica said. "Assuming the hospital doesn't say it's too early and we're sent home."

"I'm more afraid we're going to be too late," Greg said. "I'd have no idea what to do."

"I think the whole process happens quite naturally. You won't have to do much of anything, so don't worry."

Greg bundled Monica into the car as carefully as if he was packing a fine piece of china that was to be sent halfway around the world.

They headed down the dirt road that led to the main one. It was eerily quiet with a shaft of moonlight illuminating the way. As soon as he pulled out onto the main road, Greg stepped on the gas and the car shot forward.

"Whoa." Monica put a hand on his arm. "You don't want to get pulled over."

"There's no one around. Besides, perhaps they'd give us an escort."

Monica could picture arriving at the hospital led by several police cars, sirens blaring and lights swirling red and blue against the front of the building. She would die of embarrassment.

But no one stopped them and they pulled into the emergency room parking lot without incident.

Greg helped Monica out of the car and through the automatic doors. They both blinked at the sudden bright lights. The nurse behind the desk took one look at Monica and immediately got on the phone to summon a wheelchair.

Moments later they were whisked to the third floor and led into a labor and delivery room. The wallpaper had tiny flowers on it and there was an old-fashioned rocking chair in one corner and a bassinette in the other ready and waiting. Monica couldn't believe that in a short period of time, their baby would be in it.

• • •

The sun was well over the horizon by the time Monica was finally in her room, settled in bed with her baby safe in her arms. She was wearing the lacy bed jacket her mother had given her and the baby was swaddled in the blanket Janice had knitted. Greg couldn't stop beaming at the two of them. He'd already taken several dozen pictures of her and the baby.

It was almost lunchtime when there was a knock on the door and Nancy swept in. Moments later, Gina arrived, a stack of boxes in her arms nearly up to her chin. She dropped them on the chair and scurried over to Monica's bed.

She and Nancy gazed at the baby with rapturous expressions and both had to reach for a tissue from the box by the bed to dry their eyes.

"Perfect," Gina declared, clapping her hands together.

"I love that little tuft of reddish-brown hair," Nancy said. "Although babies often lose the hair they were born with and sometimes their new hair comes in a completely different color."

There was another tentative knock on the door and Kelly walked in, her face all but obscured by a huge flower arrangement. "Where shall I put this?"

"I'll take it." She handed it to Greg and he placed it on the dresser. "They're beautiful, Kelly. Thank you."

Kelly leaned over the bed and gazed at the baby. "What an adorable little peanut."

Monica laughed. "While I was pregnant, it felt more like a watermelon."

"I'm glad I got to meet the new member of the family," Kelly said. "We're all leaving for home this afternoon."

"I imagine you must be anxious to get back to your normal routine," Greg said.

Kelly rolled her eyes. "You bet. I can't wait. This has been quite a trip." She sighed. "Certainly not what anyone expected." She glanced at the baby again and smiled. "Ray shared the contents of the will. Aunt Violet left Edith enough to enjoy a comfortable life and Ray inherits the rest except for a small trust set up for Aston." She laughed. "He's not going to be too happy about that since his father is the trustee. Ray has been after him to get serious about a career. So far, he's had one job after another—none of them particularly demanding. Ray offered him a position at his company but Aston wasn't interested. I fear he's in for a shock when he tries to wheedle more money out of his father.

"I'm getting a modest sum myself that won't make me rich but will certainly make life easier."

"Did she leave Dawn anything? I know she was hoping there'd be a little something."

"She did," Kelly said. "I'm sure Dawn will be very pleased." She glanced at her watch. "I'd best be going. Congratulations again on your little bundle of joy!"

"Well," Gina said, "shall we open the gifts?"

"Yes, of course."

"I'll hold the baby," Nancy said, reaching toward it.

Gina placed the pile of boxes on the bedside table and Monica reached for the first one.

Monica read the card. "It's from Tempest. How nice." She opened the box and nestled inside was a deep purple crystal along with a note.

Monica read the note out loud. *"I hope this amethyst brings you and the baby better sleep and calm."*

"Better sleep," Nancy said. "What every new mother needs."

Monica opened the card on the second gift. "It's from the VanVelsens." She felt tears forming in her eyes and dashed them away with her sleeve. She tore off the wrapping paper and lifted the lid on the box. Inside were several pairs of hand-knitted booties in white, yellow and green.

"Here's the next one." Gina handed her another box. The card said it was from Dawn and Bart. Inside was an adorable mobile with horses dancing around a carousel.

"It looks like it plays music." Greg pushed a button and it began playing a lullaby.

The final gift was from Edith. Monica moved several layers of tissue paper to reveal a silver rattle.

"How lovely," Monica exclaimed. "Everyone has been so kind." She dashed a hand across her eyes again. "I can't believe my good fortune. A beautiful baby, loving husband and family and the best friends anyone could ask for."

Nancy scowled at Monica. "You're looking tired. I think we should go and let you get some rest." She began to shoo everyone out and Gina glanced at the baby one more time and then reluctantly picked up her purse.

Nancy handed the baby to Greg, kissed Monica on the cheek and said goodbye.

She was tired, Monica realized. The baby was still sleeping so she let her eyes slowly drift closed.

"We're so very lucky," she mumbled sleepily to Greg.

He kissed her on the forehead. "We certainly are."

Recipe

Sassamanash Farm Cranberry Oatmeal Sandwich Cookies

Cookies:

½ cup plus 5 tablespoons softened butter
½ cup brown sugar
¾ cup granulated sugar
2 eggs
1 teaspoon vanilla
1½ cups flour
1 teaspoon baking soda
1 teaspoon cinnamon
½ teaspoon salt
3 cups of quick or old-fashioned oats
1 cup dried cranberries

Heat oven to 350 degrees.

Cream softened butter and sugars. Add eggs and vanilla and beat.

In a separate bowl, combine dry ingredients: flour, baking soda, cinnamon, and salt. Add to butter/sugar/egg mixture and combine.

Add in oats and cranberries and mix well.

Drop tablespoons of dough on an ungreased cookie sheet.

Bake 8–15 minutes, depending on your oven. Let cool on baking sheet for one minute, transfer to cooling rack to cool completely.

Filling:

½ cup softened unsalted butter
1⅔ cups powdered sugar
½ teaspoon vanilla extract
zest of 1 orange
1 orange juice (or more as needed)

Beat all the filling ingredients until smooth and spreadable. Add more orange juice or powdered sugar as needed to achieve desired consistency.

Choose cookies of comparable sizes. Spread filling on flat side of one cookie, top with second cookie and press together.

About the Author

Peg grew up in a New Jersey suburb about twenty-five miles outside of New York City. After college, she moved to the City, where she managed an art gallery owned by the son of the artist Henri Matisse.

After her husband died, Peg remarried and her new husband took a job in Grand Rapids, Michigan, where they now live (on exile from New Jersey, as she likes to joke). Somehow Peg managed to segue from the art world to marketing and is now the manager of marketing communications for a company that provides services to seniors.

She is the author of the Cranberry Cove Mysteries, the Lucille Mysteries, the Farmer's Daughter Mysteries, the Gourmet De-Lite Mysteries, and also, writing as Meg London, the Sweet Nothings Vintage Lingerie series, and as Margaret Loudon, the Open Book series.

Peg has two daughters, a stepdaughter and stepson, and two beautiful granddaughters. You can read more at pegcochran.com and meglondon.com.

Made in United States
Orlando, FL
06 November 2024

53516202R00125